The Coves

T0166718

David Whish-Wilson was born in Newcastle, NSW, but grew up in Singapore, Victoria and WA. He left Australia aged eighteen to live for a decade in Europe, Africa and Asia, where he worked as a barman, actor, street seller, petty criminal, labourer, exterminator, factory worker, gardener, clerk, travel agent, teacher and drug-trial guinea pig. He is the author of three crime novels in the Frank Swann series, the most recent being *Old Scores*, with Fremantle Press in 2016. His non-fiction book, *Perth*, part of the NewSouth Books city series, was shortlisted for a WA Premier's Book Award. He lives in Fremantle and coordinates the creative writing program at Curtin University.

The Coves

DAVID WHISH-WILSON

FOR MY FAVOURITE STORYTELLERS—MAX, FAIRLIE AND LUKA

Murmurs of Leviathan he spoke,
and rum was Plato in our heads …
—Hart Crane, *Cutty Sark*

It was a common saying in early San Francisco, whenever a particularly atrocious crime was committed, that 'the Sydney Ducks are cackling in their pond'. They were pioneers in the viciousness and depravity for which the Barbary Coast became famous, and the echo of their unholy cackling was not stilled for more than half a century…The Sydney Ducks opened lodging houses, dance-halls, groggeries and taverns… all were described by a contemporary journalist as 'hives of dronish criminals, shabby little dens with rough, hangdog fellows hanging about the doorways'.
—Herbert Asbury, *The Barbary Coast: An Informal History of the San Franciscan Underworld*, 1933.

August 1849

1

The bones of the whaler groaned as they rode a swell so hump-backed that the bunkhouse angled for long seconds while they waited for Sam Bellamy to continue. All eyes on him—heart a-gallop, face hot. Twelve years old and putting himself forward.

Sam pressed the dog against his ribs and tried to ignore Dempsey; tamping his pipe with a cracked thumb, eyes full of black light.

The sneer Dempsey gave him on boarding in Sydney—Sam was waiting for it. Didn't want to see the yellow teeth in the cankerous hole again. Had thought to make comment to the towering stranger but was glad he hadn't.

Sam made his voice hard as he could. 'Oh, that black Chief was a savage and no mistake.' Sam looked to the faces of the men in the lamplight and saw his voice could be harder; the gentleman's accent got to be gone. Once again he cursed Magistrate George Moore, who'd trained him to speak like his betters. Saw a mockery in Dempsey's eye that hadn't made it to the murderer's face. 'A savage who speared my father through the guts. Da was a limeburner and covered in a mad white dust and the blackfellows stood off for a moment and we thought him saved. But then the fish spear shot out. My father not wailing but a red spittle on his lips; horrible red against his white-powdered face. Watched us hidden under the bed. My brothers, and me just a wean. That warrior putting the spear in his groin, his guts, his throat. Then over the top comes the woman, the Chief's wife, with a hatchet. Goes a-hackin on my Pa till his head is cleave straight off his shoulder. My brothers all hushed, Jemmy the eldest pinchin my mouth an' nose.'

The words had done work. Even Dempsey was nodding, looking into his pipe, scratching at the eagle tattoo on his neck. Darky Malone saw his chance and spat on the boards. 'What happened to ye then? The savages come back onye?'

Sam nodded, grateful for the enquiry. He had seen Malone skulking at the edges of the murders, more bark than bite, some human feeling left in him. Just like Sam Bellamy, Malone was now putting himself forward to remind them, of his being there, before they finished the work. The piracy hours old, and the blood still up. More killing to get clear of, once the drinking was done. The second mate, still lashed to the gunwale, with his head down the privy-hole. Sam thinking again, I got to make my mark with these men. He didn't want to go the way of Sarah Proctor, sitting behind Dempsey, where he had dragged her. Come onto the ship a single woman although her trade no secret. Handsome proudful woman. She got herself alongside the Captain as soon as they set sail, looked into his eyes, saw what she needed. Went straight to his cabin, didn't come out till Dempsey fetched her this very morning, six weeks out from port. Held her by the scruff while the Captain watched, hand on his knife. Dempsey ripped off her calico garments till she hung white and twisted as a wrung sheet. Shook her while she gagged and hissed, emptied a tankard over her head, kicked her in the slappy-arse. She said nothing. Knew what was happening, as did they all.

Dempsey had spat from the side of his mouth, eyes never leaving the Captain. The American, all vainglorious until then. Not saying nothing now. Knew he was beat. Took his hand off the knife, let them rush him.

Dempsey got the Captain tied to the mainmast. The American must've thought he was in for a flogging, but Dempsey got under him with a cruelly hooked flensing knife and opened his guts, pulled them tumbling onto the deck. Pitiful wailing then, till the shock took him, eyes paling like a dead fish.

The blood was up and they cut some throats and threw a couple over; some kind of blackfellow and a cannibal. They stood watching them ride the fluming wash—carolling voices like a false rope thrown to the drowning: *she's a long swim back to New South Wales.* Sam Bellamy hid under the netting lashed over the trunks on the foredeck, the dog under his armpit. Tried to make his face clear although his heart sickened and his hands trembled. He'd learned in the Boys Home to shut his mouth and see nothing when the older boys turned spiteful on the weaker boys, but this was a new kind of horror. He watched the naked Sarah Proctor on her hands and knees go down to the bunkroom, to find a bed and wait for Dempsey.

Sam wanted to console her, or reveal his hiding places, but like the others he said nothing and looked away.

Sarah Proctor was looking at Sam now, both of them marked. He knew that look, and knew her for an enemy. Only way she could improve her position was to put someone else beneath their feet. None more likely than Samuel Bellamy, twelve years old and concealing the child's comfort of his mangy pet. Sam's thin arms and small hands. Cast seed of freckles over his gaunt face. Twelve years old but no man's hair on him, only ginger curls. Had the look of a waif in his work-rubbed clothes and bare feet. They were looking for it, and none more than Sarah Proctor. The mark they might have left; those hands of older men, the filthy bruising of his soul. The common tale of the boy alone. Had Sam become tempered hard like Dempsey, or was he gone blowsy like spoiled fruit? So they could do to him what they done to Sarah Proctor.

So he had to keep talking. His tale of woe. But no pity in it—no signal that he come out of it a weepy plaything for the stronger hand. In his own words, not theirs. Because Sam Bellamy didn't speak the Flash. The Cant. Didn't grow up with it. So he had to speak it hard, and harrowing, though it hurt him to say it. 'My Jemmy, he saw to the warrior in court. They had him in chains. My Jemmy pointed his finger like an arrow. The blackfellow knew it then. They dragged him out howlin. Didn't know what he'd done wrong, see. Like spearin an unarmed man in the groin and cutting off his head was all in a day's work. They tied him to the guardhouse door, shot him down. Hung 'im from the nearest tree, slung in chains—'

'The gibbet. Took my Da like that.'

A spasm in Sam's guts. It was Malone again, but did he pity the blackfellow? Had Sam gone too far in the telling?

'My brother Michael, he went and cut Da down,' Malone continued. 'Capital offence in them days. Had to leave Ireland, over in Boston now. Where I'm headed, boys.'

A slosh of porter round the circle, nods and grunts. 'Let 'im finish,' growled Dempsey. 'The story of the boy and his puppy ain't finished.'

Sam leaned forward to begin, but Dempsey laughed. 'Haven't got to the part about the *silver focken spoon* yet.'

Laughs formed and bust, and Sam had to go along. He'd survived the Boys Home, and the mutiny thus far, when Dempsey and some of the men had gone crazed with the murderousness, even laughing while they killed, but now Sam felt like a rat flushed from a pile of straw. And there was something in Dempsey's eyes that was even more worrying—a quiet burning curiosity like he might prefer Sam in his bunk, over Sarah Proctor.

'My Ma was a broke woman. She got to sellin herself to the soldiers, for our food. Word got around. No room in a village of married men for the likes of my Ma—'

Dempsey laughed, the brute. 'Let me hazard. Put in by the womenfolk. Pitchforks in one hand an' Bible in the other.'

A look from Sarah Proctor, who'd been leaning forward, waiting to get in.

'The Magistrate's wife—'

'Barren, I wager.'

Sam nodded, because he wanted to finish. 'Ma was flogged, then transported to Van Diemen's Land. We never saw her again. We were put on the street, middle of winter. Everybody in that Perth village was hungry. The colony was broke. They'd sent for supplies, see, but the storehouse was empty. We were beggin. The church fed us for a bit. Jemmy took us seaweed and samphire from the river. He ate an orange nut from a palm tree, and died. Robert, only six, wandered into the bush, lookin for native victuals, never came back. They found him later—he died of cold, they say. That left me.'

'The silver spoon. The barren sow, the Magistrate's wife. Took you for her own.'

'She *did*.'

Said too loud; a foolish challenge. Sam's story, his only property, something foul in Dempsey's mouth. Sam took a sip of the rum that had burned his throat this morning, but now tasted like water.

'Don't pine, *silver spoon*, my Ma was a slag too. They give her the hearty-choke with caper sauce at Newgate, for beatin a Jew...'

Dempsey was inclined to continue, so Sam kept his head down. There was no drunkenness in the ringleader's voice, just the taking of voice from the others. They'd heard these stories in the weeks before the mutiny. To listen to Dempsey's stories you would think him an idiot but he was cracking dumb. All the while Dempsey had droned he was fiercely watching them, and the question in his eyes was always the same. Who was on his side? Who had the temper? He was looking for followers, not fellow leaders. Made that clear when he took a sealer's club to the sleeping form of a Scotsman called Dundas who showed some mettle in an argument about rum. Dempsey had described the plan for them—take the ship and make for the Caribbean islands—sell off the New Zealand sealskins and fill the hold with barrels of rum. They would arrive in California rich men, a share for each. There were guns enough; old breech-load carbines under lock and key, plenty of powder and shot. He'd seen them himself. They wouldn't turn up empty-handed in San Francisco town, no, they'd be welcomed like lords. Sell the ship. Sell the lot. Dempsey described them in new clothes, even Sarah Proctor, up there in the Captain's bed. Made a picture of her in a gingham skirt with lacy petticoats and silken knickers. New set of teeth.

'Away to shite, yer feckin blowhard!' Dundas had shouted from behind them. 'I know you was a peeler in Sydney. I seen you meself.'

But Dempsey had just laughed. Looked around the bunkhouse, little nods, racking the numbers. 'Man's gotta eat. No peeler's uniform gonna hide my junked back. I won't never forget what I am.'

With that he lifted off his sweat-soaked cotton smock, the tropical heat in the bunkhouse and their smell the one vile thing. Dempsey's back was like a vast snowfield ploughed by a demented hand. Junked all right. White skin ripped by long ridges of proudflesh; red straps of dried meat, cauterised by the branding-iron. Put his shirt back on and sang. 'For the smell of the sea is like vittles to me, and I'd trade in my bed for a new wooden leg, and my head is as bald as a newly laid egg, for the life of a sailor is all of my joy.'

'You ain't no sailor,' Dundas had said. 'You's a ignorant bog Irish arse-licker. If you wasn't, you'd ken there's no rum this side of the Americas. Less you can make your ship fly, you won't be dockin no ship in the Caribbean islands. This coast just Induns, vermin and sickness, all the way up till you hit California. It's gold we're goin for lads. Save your strength, for diggin's hard work.'

'Pay him no mind, boys. Tis the pox talkin.'

The Scotsman grunted, turned in his bunk, which is where they found him the next morning, head caved in. Dempsey and another carried him onto the deck and tipped him into the Pacific.

There was no more talk of trading for rum, but no chance either that Dempsey would be faulted in his plans for San Francisco. He took their silence for consent, described them going from the boat mob-handed, his very own hand-forged tribe. The Californian colonials wouldn't know what hit them. Appealing to a native Australian pride that was alien, after all they'd suffered. And weren't they leaving their home, to follow the gold?

It was late when Sam curled into his hessian rags. He didn't have a bed, but slept on the bunkroom floor. He was hungry, and the rum he'd drunk on an empty stomach made him feel poorly. The silver timepiece he'd stolen from the Boys Home master in Van Diemen's Land had paid for his ticket, but no more. He'd heard that a man could live weeks without rations, not that he wanted to test the theory. In his leather pouch he had one hundred yards of catgut and a can of different size hooks. It was fish that he'd contributed to the communal feed. Fish that he plied his dog with, who ate them whole, no mind for the bones. The dog nuzzled into his armpit, drank up his smell. He'd taken it off the Sydney Rocks, barely weaned. Sam had no picture of what the dog'd grow into, much like himself, when he finally started growing. In the meantime, the dog stuck by him, never more than a foot away—its first time on the waves. Sam'd been transported from Perth to Hobart when he was eleven, but spent the weeks below deck and saw nothing. Had gone under one side of the world and come out the other—just the abiding fever-dreams and swell-sickness.

Tonight he would not sleep. It might be Dempsey come for

him, but it could be any of them, emboldened by the casks of rum, ale and porter plundered from the foredeck hold.

The little knife waited in his pocket. He imagined where he would sink it, but didn't believe the pictures he made. The dog would be no help, beyond yapping, a danger to itself. So that he would not sleep, Sam retrieved two of the largest hooks from the can and pierced his thumb, licked away the blood, closed his fists around the barbed hooks. It stung something terrible, but Sam looked out into the eerie shadows, beyond the drunken babble and creaking timbers and groaning ropes, saw himself sinking into the dark waters like the silent Scotsman, and there was a strange comfort to that.

2

The sun was a yellow glaze behind the clouds. A storm was coming, and the swell pitched the whaler down into black valleys until jagged black hills rose impossibly sheer and they were dragged upwards with bile in their throats. Sam peered into the flume behind the ship and watched his silver lure jerking free. He'd fashioned the lure using scavenged taffeta and silver foil. The flying fish were attracted to the skipping lure and there were five in a wooden slops bucket that the dog circled and sniffed. Their necks were broken as Sam had been taught by the Swan River blacks, and their little dragonfly wings curled in the dull heat.

If Sam concentrated on the sight of the shimmering lure and the sparkling wash then it was almost like he was back on the Swan River, staring into the tea-coloured shallows and feeling himself absorbed and ghostly. Last night he'd sat in the bunkhouse, and to will himself from sleeping had imagined himself invisible, and watched the picture of the empty space he occupied in the dusty corner until the dog stirred in his lap. But he hadn't been able to make the dog disappear. He kept returning to the picture of Dempsey tossing the dog overboard, and the panic in its golden eyes as it stared up at him. Sam imagined himself the dog in the ocean, and he endured the dog's terrible loneliness, watching the ship sail to the horizon, and then he jerked awake and knew he'd been swimming the surface between wakefulness and dream.

Sam stared at the lure and stroked the dog's ears. Most of the others were asleep in the weak sunlight, snoring out the rum in a sprawl of legs and tilted cabbage-tree hats. The murdered Captain had been felled off the mast and dragged to the edge and flipped over, minus his fancy leather boots. The rats had been at him during the night, but no one had dared cut the Captain down until Dempsey roused from his sleep in the bunkhouse. He stood now over the third mate, another American, lashed to the steering. The American had steered the course all night, by the stars, pissing in his breeches, for the promise of his freedom. Sam didn't believe that Dempsey would free the man. Piracy of an American ship, and they were headed for America. The second mate would go the way of his Captain, and the rest of the crew.

There were few places to hide on the ship but Sam knew them all—the nook beneath the heaped sealskins in the hold where several had slipped from the pile and formed a darkened fly. The locker in the Captain's cabin that Sam had emptied of old newspapers and some molasses tins and which could be locked from inside.

Sam heard a creak behind him and it was Sarah Proctor, waylaid by the staggers. Dempsey hadn't taken to her last night, although she shared his bunk. At some point, while Sam watched, Dempsey had pushed her off the shelf onto the floor, where she slept until dawn. Since then she'd wandered the deck, trying not to look at the slaughtered Captain, expression of a caged cat on her face.

She sat behind Sam and he sensed her watching him regard the skipping lure that followed the ship. He saw her tented shadow pick up the dog, which keened like it did sometimes. Dempsey was fifty feet toward the foredeck but you could hear his forceful brogue. Sam turned to the woman only when he remembered the knife in the bucket, his prize possession. She was smiling at him strangely, although he expected this. She wanted to use her molly's charm to get him to confess something she could parlay to the mutineers. Sam felt his age and size beside the woman, but her eyes were kindly, and he figured her for two score years, although it was hard to tell. Her teeth were crooked and chipped like his own, although his hadn't yellowed so.

'My bones is achin,' she whispered, as though that was a secret worth sharing.

'It's the scurvy. I have it.'

She didn't respond for a long while, then whispered, so quiet, 'I was locked up these past months, before I came aboard in Sydney. Bread and water rations.'

Sam stared into her lap, at the dog, but her breasts dragged his eye. He hadn't sat with woman or girl for two years. 'The American, he must've fed you. You was in his bunk for six weeks. We hardly saw you.'

She laughed, but her voice was sour. 'He fed me enough to stop me strayin, like every man I've known. Mutton and biscuit, mostly.'

'You got to eat them turnip greens in the store,' Sam said. 'Nobody but me eatin them.'

'Never been one for the rabbit food. And you just complained of the scurvy too.'

'Sure I did. Why I'm eatin them greens. I'll get better. You won't.'

'Aren't you the wee sawbones...'

Her tone was gentle, which kept Sam on his guard. 'No I ain't. But I had a master once, who put me to schooling.'

'And where's that master now?'

'Where he lives, on the Swan River, I expect.'

'Long way from here. And your head was shorn when you got on. You're on the break. Just like me.'

'I ain't like you. And I ain't on the break.'

That look in her eye, like she was playing a game, finding him out, although they both knew the truth—you don't ever confide about such things.

'Sure you are,' she said. 'I know it. You got passage on this ship, same as me, with a shiny thieved thing. Nowhere else to run. And neither of us is goin to America for the gold.'

Sam didn't reply. He wasn't sure how Sarah Proctor had got him so quickly to the truth of it.

He thought of his mother then, just a thought with no memory, because he had no memory.

Just what every child has—a mother—although Sam hadn't spoken of her to another aboard the whaler. A secret he owned. He listened to them nightly voice their dreams of gold and riches in California, product of the posters nailed down the main streets of Sydney harbour. 'Gold! Gold! Gold in California!' With the names of the shipping companies and freight carriers listed in small print. A race to get there first, and away from the hardship at home.

But Sam's purpose was different. He'd tracked his mother to a brothel in the Rocks. Heard she'd gone out on the first ships, along with a madam and her complement of mollies. At least that's what the proprietor of the now lodging house said. He didn't know Sam's mother, but he'd carried all their trunks down to the docks, just to get rid of 'em. Sam didn't have a description beyond her long red hair and stooped shoulders and so he'd hoped and followed, as he'd been hoping and following all these years.

Sarah Proctor leaned toward him, put the dog back to the bucket, where it began to sniff and dance around the fish. Her eyes grew larger, drawing him in. He decided to get her back then. He wouldn't have her make love to him, for plot or diversion. 'You've left children behind.'

Her eyes became pinched. Her brow notched in bitterness and confusion. 'You stupid boy. I want only to be your friend.'

'Dempsey wouldn't have you befriend me. Me or no other.'

Sam hoisted a thumb down the deck, where Dempsey was still lording it over the lashed steersman, unfurling a length of hide. Their eyes met and the Irishman stamped toward them.

No new outrage for a few hours. Days from the foreign shore, if they made it. The second mate with his head down the privy, arse reared in the air inviting Dempsey's savage boot. Whatever Dempsey planned for the second mate would suffice to keep the mutineers in awe of his violent hand. There was no other reason for stringing it out.

Sarah Proctor whispered from the side of her mouth. 'You're right that I've left children behind, but ain't none of them still alive. My only boy would be your age now. I bore him when I wasn't no older than you. Me and you and some of the others, we got to make an alliance...'

Sam let the dog wriggle under his shirt, feeling the clumping boots approach. He glanced at Sarah Proctor and saw that she was just as fearful, shrunk now into the bulwark. The sun behind Dempsey's great shaggy head, a sulphurous halo. Dempsey looked into the bucket and grunted. Sarah Proctor angled her head to take in the span of his majesty, widening her eyes and opening her mouth, reading for the invitation or curse.

The change that came over Sarah Proctor shocked Sam, and he waited for her lies. To put him in, or slight him with a manufactured story, but there was nothing, only the empty eyes and slack jaw.

'You seen a cat?' Dempsey asked of him, ignoring Sarah Proctor.

Sam couldn't hide his panic. Nor could he reply. But the woman took Sam's side, and spoke his words. 'A cat with nine tails?'

'Lift up your shirt, boy.'

Sam turned before he knew he was moving. He put aside the dog and hoisted up his cotton shirt, showed Dempsey the stripes. He'd been whipped many times at the Boys Home, as had every other boy, excepting the most expert liar and seasoned betrayer.

'That's not cat-claws. That's a bamboo switch. Nothin more than scratches. I'm talkin about the cat. I seen you makin things and I asked if you seen one.'

'I have.'

Sam dropped his shirttail and turned. Dempsey was now holding a pistol under his nose, smelling it like a fine cigar. The breech-loaded pistol had a walnut handle and a single percussion cap. Snub-barrel fixed with a polished brass ring.

'That's a navy model deringer,' Sam said.

Dempsey looked thwarted in some way, and Sam saw him glance at the letters on the rifled barrel, understood that the Irishman could not read. 'Philadelphia,' Sam blurted, as though the word would redeem him. 'I seen it in a catalogue I got to studyin back in Van Diemen's Land. It had every gun in it, American or British. Drawins, an' all. Every brand an' every model.'

But Dempsey just grinned. 'Well, I never seen the like of it. *American*. No craftsmen of such fine things in the blighted land we just departed. They must be real savvy to the crafts of war in this new colony. Home to half of Ireland.'

'The cat. Yes, I seen one.'

A lie, beyond the toy-model cats the boys'd made in their games from torn cotton slops, knotted over pebbles. 'You desire me to fashion one.'

'To put your pretty little fingers to use boy, yes.'

Dempsey tipped the rawhide sheet off his shoulder. Under it was a leather jerkin that he likewise tipped at Sam's feet. From his waistcoat he produced a handful of lead fishing weights, fashioned into dough-balls and speared with a hot pin. 'Found these in the hold. Not to be used for fishin.'

Dempsey nodded to Sam's knife in the bucket. 'Best get to work. This storm-cloud clears, the moon's face will be showin tonight. The Tawny Prince will have his honour.'

Sarah Proctor waited until Dempsey was shy of her voice. Hissed, 'I knew him for a tinker.'

Sam Bellamy found a whetstone in the Captain's cabin, used it to put an edge on the deadman's sword. The sword was hung off a nail and he wanted to have it. Knew it to be ex-army, and reckoned it to be his now. Sam held up the weapon and imagined himself in the corner locker, the sword pointed toward anyone who dared break the lock and drag him out, that eerie light in their eyes. But soon as he saw himself thrusting the sword it became heavy in his hands. The image shrank from his sight.

The rawhide cut easy but the jerkin was tough. Sam knew he was doing wrong, which made it harder to cut. Dempsey would want the cattails to be rawhide, so they soaked up blood and got heavier, but it was the jerkin Sam cut into nine long strips, and the rawhide he pleated into a single rope. After that he bound the lead balls into the tails and fixed the rope and nine tails with some twine.

Dempsey would certainly be angry. There he was outside the cabin, capering around the mutineers like a priest at his liturgy, assailing them with couplets taken from some gypsy song. Whatever Dempsey planned would have the way of unholy ritual about it, and Sam making the whip arse-around would worry Dempsey's superstition in whatever happened next. But Sam had done it anyway, the way he was used to doing. Small acts of defiance done inside a thing, like the boys in the Home sewing the shape of guns and knives inside the sleeves of their shirts, no way for the master to see them but their satisfaction in the knowing.

Sam didn't present Dempsey the whip but left it draped over the netting by the mainmast. The storm had passed and the swell returned to its long slack hooping. Sam knew nothing about boats and wanted nothing to know. Still couldn't look at the liquid horizon without a tightening in his bowels. Couldn't believe some men found comfort in the absence of land. The sun was falling to the invisible seam between water and sky, and it felt like they were sideways on the world. There were monsters beneath them, too, of that he was sure, waiting in the depths. He feared night on the ocean but he feared tonight even more.

All day he hadn't been able to think straight. Not one moment when he looked at something and knew it to be an aspect of the true nature of things. No birds in the sky or flowers on trees. No dirt-smell or dew-glistening animal hide. No laughter but the cruel laughter of the men. Even the dog, his familiar, was distant from his heart.

Sam Bellamy took up the dog and sat in the last sunshine, the light coming apart into golden pieces. He nuzzled the dog's whiskered face, wondering if his distance from the feeling of things was a portent of death coming. The body knowing all. The eyes blind. Sam had no prayer but the words of the poet-seer that the Magistrate had schooled into him. '*Thou still unravish'd bride of quietness... Thou foster-child of silence and slow time...*'

He stared into the dog's eyes and recited the words, but saw nothing of the mystery that had sustained him until now, those rare moments when there was something uncanny about an ordinary thing: a finger of light on a patched blanket, or a mote of dust in a darkened room. Steam rising off a bowl of porridge and shrouding the face of a boy in a wooden hut. The blue crayfish in the tannic creeks near the Boys Home. And his earliest memory, which still had a hold of him: the vision of a black boy with a raised spear on the Swan River flats near the Magistrate's estate, upriver from Guildford. Early morning sunlight playing across the skin of the black boy and the brown river, so placid that the water looked an aspic, and the boy not moving either, but poised eternally. Smoke from their campfire rising in a perfect grey column into the sky. A troop of *koolbardi* carolling in the flooded gums, and the air so warm on the skin it was possible for the five-year-old Sam Bellamy to imagine himself indivisible, part of the quiet stillness, and just the feeling of watching himself being watched by the whole living thing. Then a quick action, and the thin spear was gone from the boy's arm, only the surface slicing as the spear jiggered and danced and the silver flank of the mullet bowed and straightened then floated to the surface. The black boy's smile. '*Djildjit ngaarniny*!'—and the voice not the boy's, but Sam's own.

A cloud crossed the sun and the ocean turned grey. A rope creaked and the dog whimpered in his arms. Smoke from the cooking brazier at the foredeck drifted down. Sarah Proctor's cackle from below deck. Sam turned his back and cradled the dog like a baby, as he'd seen mothers do. The dog lay there in his arms, watchful and still, aware that the cradling was a human language for something that it understood, and was grateful for. Sam's heart finally swelling with tender feeling, the dog's heart throbbing on his ribcage, its belly-skin slack and rubbery. Sam Bellamy drew upon the tenderness and let it guide him, and it was with his eyes closed, and his mind on the remnant feeling of loving communion that Sam smelled the fire on the wind to starboard. He opened his eyes as the sun sank into the horizon. He knew the smell. Not the fumes from the rough brown coke used in the iron brazier, but the angry smoke of a bushfire. Invisible to the eye, but there on the low wind that walked the ocean from the lands to the east.

The dog scampered around his feet as he carried the bucket of fish to the cook-pot. He returned to the lashed steersman with a ladle of water. The third mate was an American, wore moleskin breeches and a natty blue coat. Had brass rings that hung from his ears, sunburned like the rest of his face. Eyes the colour of Spanish beans. Long hair and black beard tied with leather braiding. Wrists lashed to the iron spokes inside the ship's wheel. Lips cracked and scabbed. Sam lifted the ladle and the American buried his face, reclined his neck as Sam lifted higher.

'You smell it, I hazard,' Sam stated in a whisper. The American closed his eyes and nodded amid his supping. When he had drank off the ladle he tried to speak but his doused tongue made a strangled hiss. The man retched and coughed, wiped his mouth on his shoulder.

'That's the smoke of the mountain forests. No the desert. No far to go now. And we're in the trade lanes, boy. Tis but a matter of time before we have company. My countrymen. You want to be on the right side of this traitorousness, you loosen my bonds and get me a knife. I gut that Irish savage, the rest will fall away.'

Sam kept his eyes on his feet, tried to measure the heat of the American's voice. Found it wanting. More desperation than rage.

Given a knife, this man would not gut Dempsey. Sam wanted to help, but within the sadness of his feelings was a cold fear, and a picture of what that meant. He'd learned all his life how the strong bettered the weak. And it was only his own weakness that made him reply, in whisper, the lie, 'I shall return during the night.'

The American spat, knowing.

8

The ocean had chilled to a temperature barely above ice. For a moment Sam panicked, thought maybe the American had sailed them back to Van Diemen's Land, where the water was always cold and blue-black. The night was perfect stillness but for the cold rising off the water and the cold falling from the stars. The whaler's try-pot sat awkwardly on the brazier, too large, sparks from the coke giving off into the mist.

There was no sight of land but Sam could smell the smoke in the air from the eastern continent. Dempsey called down the watchman in the rigging and greeted the shivering Cornishman with a mug of rum. The twenty mutineers gathered on deck, at Dempsey's bidding. The try-pot bubbled, a poker in the flames glowed red iron. All the Irishman's doing. No questions had been asked. The lashed steersman couldn't see them, slumped and facing into the dark, awake or unconscious, it was hard to tell.

The mutineers had been drinking heavily, and Sam could guess why. None of them knew what barbarity Dempsey had planned, beyond the cat-o'-nine-tails that Sam had fashioned, there on the webbing. Only the Irishman's proclamations throughout the day about family and blood and loyalty, amid the indecipherable Cant lingo that Dempsey preferred: snatches of phrases such as *Snichel the Bear-garden Discourser*, ordering Malone to go around *nigging the nappers*, and pointing directly to Sam, to make sure *the nose-gent* don't try to shirk, neither.

Sam had his own mug of rum, the wooden handle stained with blood, the dog sniffing and worrying Sam's lap to get it.

He'd attempted to hide in the Captain's locker but the door was barred with a whaler's spear lashed across the entrance. To get to the sealskins in the hold Sam would have to pass through the bunkroom that Dempsey was guarding. Sam looked around the gathered faces. Malone and some others nodded with their chins, indicating for him to drink, their eyes bright in the firelight, and worry there too. Sam pretended to drink, faked the sour burn, feared the loss of his faculties, although he feared too the men's determination that he drink; what visions it might protect him from, like ether-fumes before the surgeon's knife.

Sarah Proctor took a seat beside him, gave a little nudge whose meaning Sam couldn't decipher. He didn't look at her, but noticed her new-fashioned hessian moccasins, tied around her ankles with a leather band—offcuts from the cat makings. She said nothing, but gulped at her rum, and he watched the faces of the men opposite, regarding her. Something about their eyes. Each of them looking around the firelight, reading for a sign. A leader among them. The waiting, abrading their nerves. Worried about Dempsey's absence. Worried about America. Starting at every sound, a possible American ship, the fate of pirates known to all.

Sam looked into their eyes and saw that they would follow Dempsey unless the Irishman was dead. Their discomfort, like his own, the product of not knowing what came next. The nakedness of a face between masks. This recognition was Sam's first feeling of kinship with the men he'd feared, but who were now his equals in cowardice. He could see the patience in the faces of the old convict lags, the enduring spirit behind their survival, their months on prison hulks, the transportations, the hunger and cold in the new country. The patience of the beast in the field, and that second thing the Magistrate had described to Sam, important above all others, the day Samuel Bellamy was himself transported from the Swan River colony to Van Diemen's Land—the endurance of suffering. Not waiting it out, or desiring for it to end, but understanding that to suffer is to survive, and to survive is to suffer. The Magistrate's hands warm on Sam's shoulders, tears in his eyes, a great man reduced to hardship and misery. Sam Bellamy must accept his due suffering, as punishment for his sins, as Christ had accepted his suffering. Sam wanting to reply, Jesus-like, with a question. Hadn't Christ suffered so that we might be forgiven our sins? Was Sam's crime so terrible that he deserved exile, slavery and orphanhood? But the sadness in the old man's eyes was bitter to Sam, who was one more failure the Magistrate had to endure. A gentleman defined by his distance from suffering, so to develop the refinements of the higher faculties, but the Magistrate brought low so many times, all his teeth fallen out, sunken eyes and jaundiced skin, that he was no longer a gentleman on his own terms.

There was no moon, and when Dempsey appeared in the firelight the men flinched. The giant Irishman made of noise and bluster gone eerily silent, a pious cast on his face. Eyes pecked clean by the fierceness of his observing. In his hand a rope leash, and out of the darkness behind him, a crawling thing, hessian sack over his head, the second mate, shirtless and mute.

The men shifted on their haunches to give Dempsey access to the circle, but he ignored them, led the American with a tight rein to the mainmast, where yesterday he'd gutted the Captain. It was here they observed that Dempsey's leash ended in a noose-knot, resting behind the sailor's ear. The man was groaning in pain, although there were no visible wounds. Two days with his head down in a wooden hole, his knees trussed to his chest, had crippled him of easy movement.

There was pity in the eyes of the men. No reason for the second mate to suffer like this. An American whaler, not a hated redcoat, or a peeler. Gone to savage, perhaps, judging by his tattoos and earrings, clothes fashioned from the cured pelts of seal, possum, kangaroo. Leather moccasins rubbed with animal fat. But no different to any of the men. And they understood, with a wrench, that this was no punishment, but a sacrifice, and the uneasiness became open fear. The Irishman taking them back beyond the pale, behind the centuries. Darky Malone so struck that he crossed himself, an involuntary action that wasn't lost on Dempsey. He kicked out, took Malone by his orange beard, dragged him up. Looked into his eyes, and finding what he was looking for, passed the leash, indicated that Malone should cast it over the aft boom, which he did, nobody watching lest they catch Dempsey's eye.

Malone stood aft of the boom and reined in the leash while Dempsey stalked the edge of the circle, gesturing to Malone that he should hoist the American onto his feet. The sailor groaned as his back straightened. The noose came tight and Malone reached for a higher grip and was lifted on his toes, the heavier American not rising but choking.

'Wait!'

Dempsey emptied his tankard of rum. Kicked a hand-tied wooden stool toward the sailor. Signalled to the two nearest, a pale longhair the name of Starr and a stout old lag the name of Sweeney, to hoist the American onto the stool. When the two men took the American's legs and hefted him, faces averted to hide their revulsion, Malone took the slack and wound the rope around the horned cleat on the mainmast. Stepped away and scampered back to the anonymity of the circle.

Each of them had been through a court. They could hear the prosecutor's voice. 'And who lashed the rope that hung the man? And who lifted the man from the deck? And who turned the man off when the order was given?'

Dempsey just laughed, but you could hear it—the worry that he'd lost them. Would he next howl at the moon? Get down on all fours and rip at the legs of the condemned man? He began to mutter, an incantation of some sort, punctuated by hard laughter. He'd told them the story of his grandfather, fighting under Wellington for the British at Waterloo. How before the battle Wellington selected five squaddies at random from the front line of his own troops; had them tied to a frame and flogged—'to get the scent of blood in the air, to rouse the bloodlust of his men', a strategy he'd learnt in India. So it was no surprise when Dempsey took from his belt the flensing knife and tossed it to Starr, the longhair northerner. With his other hand drew out the deringer pistol and pointed it at Starr.

'On yer feet, allerya. We're in this together, and spilt blood is our bond. You will recite, as I recite, and you will draw blood when I mark the signal, or I'll blow out your belly with this primed shot. Mark my words, for this bloodletting marks the conception of the Dempsey Gang, united by common purpose and the bloodseal of our order, sanctified and watched over by our Lord the Tawny Prince.'

The men and Sarah Proctor rose from the firelight shadows into the hard light cast by Dempsey's stare. You could see in the shoulders of some men that their minds were on charging Dempsey, bringing him down, now that he'd forsaken his cruel-hooked knife. One went, the others would follow, but Dempsey was watching too and waving the deringer across the herd. Sam Bellamy, carrying the dog, whose ears were flattened, worked his way to the back of the rows, for there wasn't space to form a line. His hands shaking. Knees too. Felt the strength leaving his body, or was it the goodness of his soul?

'You boy, no. You be our Jack Ketch. Take your place behind the dangler, for it's you who'll turn him off, on my order.'

Sam had expected some kind of cruelty, but not to be made a murderer. He glanced into the darkness, as though it might reveal a saviour, but nobody was coming to help him. Sam skirted the rows with his eyes on the hanging man, whose toes gripped the edge of the stool, dirty feet straining white, not a sound from his sacked head.

Dempsey nodded to Starr, who approached the sailor. Reached up with the flensing knife, made a clean cut across his breast, drawing a red ribbon, then a prickling of red teardrops, as Dempsey began to intone, quietly at first but building in volume. 'I am the roguish strowler. The principal Maunder. I mourn not my mother who died a rope-dancing for your honour. My brother morts, repeat after me. I do swear to be a True Brother...'

Waving the deringer, eyes afire with righteous possession, smiling to hear the men and Sarah Proctor recite his proclamation.

'...and in all Things, obey the commands of the great Tawny Prince, and keep his counsel, and not divulge the secrets of my brethren.'

As a second, then a third man drew a stripe of blood across the condemned man's torso. '...I will not forsake this company, but obey the instruction of Anderson Dempsey, who is the roguish Strowler, the Principal Maunder, whose mother died a-dancin on the rope in your honour. I will not teach anyone to Cant, nor betray my fellow morts to the Peeler or Outlyer, although they flog me to death. To die on the rope is to die in your name, and I swear to take your bloody part against all who oppose you, or any of us. We are bonded forth as only brothers-in-arms may be bonded, against every Ruffler, Peeler, Abram, Hooker, Swaddler, Irish-toyl, Swig-man, Whip-Jack, Kark-man, Bawdy-basket, Clapperdogeons or Curtals...'

Some enthusiasm now, as the line diminished, and those who'd drawn blood took their places in the shadows, a lilt in the voices. '...I will share my every winning with my fellow Ruffman, and for the company of us. I will cleave to my Brethren stiffly, and will bring them peckables and spirits, goblets and Praters, or anything else I can come at. In your name, Tawny Prince, we give you this our Jack Ketch and this dangling man. Reward us in this new country, and abide with our depradations, us fellows of the Dempsey Gang.'

The American had long ceased his moaning. Sam Bellamy

had not seen, but one among the men had showed the kindness of severing the artery inside the thigh of the sailor, whose leg now pulsed blood over his feet and toes, down the verticals of the stool, to sluice across the boards.

The moaning was now from the lashed steersman, thrashing at his bonds in the darkness.

Dempsey inspected the flayed body of the sailor, peered at the death-wound administered to the inner thigh, and nodded to Sam. 'Boy, we shall dispense with the floggin. Turn him off. Out of this world and into the next, where he will join the Tawny Prince, and look down approvingly upon the exploits of the Dempsey Gang. Turn him off!'

But Sam couldn't move. He had only to kick the blood-slippery stool. It would slide as soon as topple. Sam's eyes were on the stool, paralysed as the rest of him. He felt it draining: the soul that animated him, replaced by a terrible weight; the fear that was too familiar. Dempsey took his fear for bloody-minded sabotage and roared. 'The ritual. The dangling man. Turn him off!' But saw, and hissed, 'You focken coward! I honoured you thus!'

With a stride he was at the mast and booted the stool, smashing it with the blow. The rope groaned on the cleat and over the boom; Sam felt every inch of the straining hemp as the man began to dangle and twitch, silent but for the trickle of blood from his toes, painting the bare patch of board beneath the stool.

The deringer was at Sam's ear and Dempsey had his hair in a rough grip but Sam couldn't move. It was ever thus. He was there but not there. In a way, he was free, had slipped behind the curtain of hateful air like a conjuror's apparition; couldn't feel Dempsey's fingers gouging his scalp or the cold eye of the pistol now pressing his throat. He was free, in his cowardice, absent of human feeling, and of consequence. Could float away or sink through the boards. Walk through walls, or gallop across the waves. A living ghost, which is what Dempsey saw now and laughed, and cast him aside. The dog growled, and Dempsey aimed the deringer but the dog scuttled into the darkness, a ratter who knew when to be a rat.

Not a word from the others, who'd turned their backs on the dangling man, rejoined the firelight and their mugs of rum. Dempsey kicked at Sam and returned to them, the Principal Maunder. He began to sing as the lashed steersman groaned and the dew-wet sails riffled and the dog whimpered and gathered Sam's sleeve in its mouth to tug him.

4

Sam lay paralysed on the creaking deck until the cold formed a blue shellac on his skin. The only warmth the dog's nose thrust into his armpit, its tremors against his ribs. He wished the cold to take him, could feel the weight of air pressing down from the frozen stars in the black sky. Rising too from the great black depths, a force that would grind him in its icy teeth and turn his bones to dust.

He dragged himself into the webbing cast over the plundered stores. His length gave him away, but the cold at least abated as his shivering diminished to a tremble. The stars above him burned cold and the hissing of waves on the ship-flanks sounded like flames on wet wood. The smell of smoke on the wind was gone as the whaler sailed north into the icy climes. A hoarse whispering came to him on the wind, and he thought it the spirits of drowned sailors, until the whisper was punctuated by coughing, and he remembered the steersman. Sam had taken the American some water as the only consolation left to give, but the sailor had slept on the wooden wheel pinioned like a staked hide. Now the steersman was calling him. *Boy. Boy.*

Sam left the sleeping dog and went to the man. 'Curse you, boy. Were it not for you, I'd have turned us onto rocks. We are there. We are arrived in San Francisco.'

To the starboard side of the foredeck Sam made out sulphur-coloured lights in the distance. 'Set the lamp aglow, boy. Load the brazier with coke. And loosen my bonds. I will speak well of you, should I survive.'

The sailor cracked his ankles, warming his legs with movement, rolling his neck.

Sam did as he was told. He lit the wick of the whale-oil lantern that hung on the boom of the foremast. Quietly placed chunks of coke in the coals of the fire. Blew on them. Returned to the sailor, who was shifting his weight from one hip to the next.

'Do not cut the rope, for they'll know you a traitor. Unhitch that shank from the spoke-handle.'

Sam unhitched the rope, and the American worked his hands loose, but didn't remove them. 'Can you swim, boy?'

Sam nodded.

'The water will shock your heart to stillness, but I plan to run us into the shallow muds before Sydney-cove. You can swim or wade to your countrymen. I will not speak against you to my chums, or to Tom Miller, the owner of this venture, and his men. They will break the bones of the pirates. They will have their vengeance. They are a fierce company.'

Below deck, the sound of chain on boards. Links clashing.

The sailor pulled free his hands. 'Boy, give me a minute to swim free of musket range. Then sound the alarm. Keep the course and it will take you to mud, rather than rock, or the great timber jetty.

Sam felt a pang of fear. 'Take the longboat. Take me with you.'

The American shook his head. 'The longboat was ruined in New Zealand, chasing the whale. We lacked the pitch to fix it. It will surely sink.'

With that, the American padded to the edge of darkness, placed a bare foot on the timber rail and dived into the night. No sound of a splash. No more sounds from below deck. Only the lights ashore and the smell of wood smoke; the tinkling of a piano across the water, like the speech of metal birds. A fiddle note curling around itself. The wheeze of an accordion.

Sam did not do as instructed. He would no sooner rouse Dempsey from his slumbers than enter a bearpit. The numbing fear came upon him again, his feet rooted to the cold boards. The wind had dropped in the lee of the hills whose grey sides he observed curving around a broad bay. The moon heading to the western horizon, not far to dawn. Ropes creaking as the sails emptied of wind.

The sound of oars in the crisp dark. Now Sam left his station by the wheel. Peered across the black waters and watched a longboat materialise out of the blackness. No distinction between water and air but for the silver flecks of moonlight on the ribbed flanks of the boat. A musket raised and aimed at Sam, who ducked into the webbing by the mainmast, drew the dog into his arms.

The American had dived toward land. The longboat appeared out of the sky, floating in the gloom like a ghost-ship. No chance the sailor had raised an alarm. Sam thought to join the sailor in the waters but his heart was beating weakly. He instead burrowed into the hemp webbing, listening to the clambering of soft boots onto the rear deck, the splash of rope, the drawing of a cutlass from a scabbard. More boot-steps, more scraping steel. From his position he watched the raiders pass. One man took the steering, began to shank the wheel to port, toward the great wooden jetty the American had warned about. Three men with muskets knelt around the opening on the waist deck that led to the bunkroom. The men were dressed in blue trousers and calfskin boots. Wore pelts across their shoulders. The woollen skullcap of sailors.

A tall man appeared with a dragoon pistol, the beast cradled across his forearm. He wore a suit of dark wool, a waistcoat and top hat, his face in shadow. At his signal, another began to ring the brass bell that hung from the foremast. Rang it loud and clear and didn't stop. Shouts from below. Dempsey's rough cursing clear through the pealing. Sound of boots on boards and the dropping of dull and heavy things. The raiders tensed as the Dempsey gang rose to the deck, the Irishman foremost. The look of violence on his face at the sight of the sailors crouched with muskets and cutlasses in the shadows.

Dempsey threw back an arm and held the others behind. A smirk broke the rictus of his war-face. 'Our saviours!' he proclaimed into the silence that rang with the absence of bell-pealing. The tall man cradled the dragoon and indicated for Dempsey to lay down the deringer, which he did like a man accustomed to surrender.

The tall man nodded. 'Lay them down, and come into the lamplight. Let us see what manner of vermin the tides have brought us.'

Dempsey's surprise. The tall man's Australian voice.

'Sit in three lines. Expose your heads.'

The sailors armed with cutlasses formed around the seated men and Sarah Proctor, keeping her head low. She caught Sam's eye, and nodded.

'Where is the crew? The Captain and mates? The harpooners and cook?'

'Our saviours.'

Dempsey had continued his intoning, ever weaker. The tall man took the oil lamp off its hook and held it to the Irishman's face. 'Speak.'

Dempsey swallowed the harsh light with mournful eyes. 'We hit a storm a few days back. I heard the Captain cry, "All is lost", before they took to a longboat, left us, and now you have saved us.'

The tall man grunted. 'The longboat is cradled still. You lying scum. And what of this blood?'

Dempsey looked at the crust of blood at the base of the mast, ruby-red in the dawn. 'A curiosity captured by the Captain in Van Diemen's Land, for what purpose I cannot say. A boomer. A great grey kangaroo. We butchered it, and it sustained us. As for the longboat, that is needing of repair. The other was taken, as I have truthfully related, by those who left us to our pitiful fate. We are not sailors. Where are we? Which coast have we reached? Are we back in our beloved homeland?'

The tall man turned the lamplight onto the others, spoke to his men. 'As you can see, most of these men are the convict wretches of my native land. Their heads are shorn but weeks ago. The Irishman and a few longhairs aside—'

'I was a police constable in New South Wales, a servant of Her Majesty—'

The butt of the dragoon crunched the back of Dempsey's head, knocking him out for a moment. He awoke like a drowning man and clutched the shoulders of those around.

The first rays of sunlight broke upon the rim of hills to the west. Denuded slopes and green gullies running down through sandhills to a large town of wood and white stone, wattled huts and canvas shacks, wraithed in smoke. And from the shabby streets nearest the foreshore, a sound that made those aboard cock their heads.

'*Coooooiiiieeee!*'

A lone voice, and then another. Another. And then a chorus, in joyful unison, the call of their native land. Darky Malone broke his smile to put his hands to his mouth. Returned the call until the flat blade of a cutlass caught his skull. The Dempsey men arose as one mass of flailing arms and hard-charging heads into the bellies of the sailors who fired and slashed at the wall of men exploding outwards. So far from home and so near their destination. The calls from shore sailing over their heads. Dempsey and the tall man wrestling by the mast, the dragoon braced crossways at Dempsey's throat and the Irishman's flensing knife slicing at the Australian's face. The brazier had tipped and thrown coals across the webbing and hessian that concealed Sam. He scrambled ahead of the flames to the deck's edge and cradled the dog, made ready to jump. On the muddy flats by the shoreline a line of men were waving hats and pistols and raucous-calling. The Dempsey men that survived the cutlass and ball emptied into the black waters, Darky Malone among them, splashing at the water like he was trying to climb. Sam turned and saw a musket aimed at his head and he jumped and sank and hit the muddy bottom, feet driving him up toward the light. He surfaced with the dog under one arm biting him and ducked as a musket was fired, before surfacing closer to shore. The water was colder even than the icy waters of Van Diemen's Land, knocking the breath out of him, and he gasped too soon, sucking in water, his lungs burning as he touched ground and bobbed his head, coughing and spitting, the dog biting his bicep until he held it aloft. The sight of the sodden dog brought a great cheer from the drunks at the shore, waving him ever closer. Sam leaned into the water and fell and floated toward land, emerging on his knees. Rough hands grasped him and drew him upright, cheering and clapping his head and back. He turned to the waters and saw the others wading fearfully from the musket-fire that rang out from the bows of the grounded whaler. Some men beside Sam began returning fire, but the gesture was mocking, accompanied by full-throated imprecations punctuated by laughter. Three eager men waded to their chests to drag Sarah Proctor, floating on her circle of skirts, into the mud, where she retched to their lewd cheers.

A strong hand grasped Sam's neck, drew him close, the dog scratching at his ribs. 'Welcome to Sydney-town, California, son. This place will dirty your mind and sully your virtue. She'll teach you things you wished you didn't know. She'll steal your maidenhood. My name is Patrick. Let me stand you a drink.'

5

Sam watched the steam rise off his trousers and sleeves. His feet were cut and stank of the sewage slime in the embayment shallows, but at least they were warm beside the pot-belly stove that pulsed heat into the crowded groghouse. Patrick—the man who had brought him to the tavern, his great hot hand never leaving the back of Sam's neck—left and returned with others from the whaler, easily noticed in the dawn streets on account of being sodden. One by one the number increased and the space around them grew larger as the drinkers who plied them with rum and porter stood back and tossed them questions from behind crossed arms, thick beards and sceptical eyes, as though the whaler refugees carried the plague.

Perhaps it was the shock of the icy water, or the new world of the San Francisco shore, but the numbness that blighted Sam's feelings was gone and now he was alert to every sight and sound. He couldn't put a name to it, but felt like he was being watched. Once or twice he glanced over his shoulder at the screen of hung carpet, which trembled as he did. He stared at his bony fingers coming out of blue, avoiding the eyes of the Dempsey gang who spoke furtively behind their hands. At Sam's feet, the dog looked warily to the growing crowd of men and women who caroused in the cinder-coloured shadows. The low roof of the tavern and the roughly milled pine-plank walls made him feel like he was inside a coffin. Rain started to fall outside, and the man Patrick returned a final time with Dempsey in a jolly embrace. The two men were of equal stature and the easy look on the Irishman's face disappeared at the sight of his gang crowded into a corner of the tavern like they were returned to the chain. He looked at the man Patrick for an explanation and reached instinctively for his cruel-hooked knife, but was greeted instead with a broad grin and mug of rum, and the offer of a chair dragged from under an old man with a tattered cabbage-tree hat who fell onto his arse. The ensuing laughter seemed to put Dempsey at his ease, and he turned to his men and toasted them, and the new country, and all his new friends. As he spoke, he ran a hand through his sodden hair and opened the pale slice on his forehead that began to bleed into his eyebrows, down his nose and into his beard.

Sam had the feeling of being watched again and bent into himself, having caught the sneer from Dempsey, who leaned toward him and hissed, loud enough for the mutineers to hear. 'I know it was you that betrayed us. Let the raiders aboard. Freed the American. I advise against breaking your fast, for shortly I'll be opening your guts.'

Dempsey dragged the stool into the middle of his people who looked unkindly at his profile, remembering his snaky protestations to the tall man on the whaler, avowing himself a peeler and them just lags. He sat there like a king, his legs stretched out, steam rising off his back. He drank the rum in a gulp and stood and strode toward the low bar made of roughly hewn boards, behind which stood a whiskered ancient in a tattered redcoat and black tricorne hat. When Dempsey placed his tankard on the wood, the tavern fell silent.

The old man shook his head and indicated with his chin that Dempsey should return to his seat. Dempsey nodded in assent, before snatching at the old man's jacket, taking for himself the small revolver at the ancient's belt. This was an opportunity for Sam to escape. Dempsey was occupied and Sam made to stand, but Dempsey turned and smiled. He thrust the old man away, and took the bottle of rum back to his party, holding it aloft before filling their wooden mugs and pewter tankards, placing himself back on his throne, reading the tense silence and staring faces of the natives for threat. Satisfied, he threw back his head and emptied his rum, poured himself another.

The crowd was stood back for a reason, but that only became clear when the old man in the tattered redcoat came round the bar with a bucket made of shiny pressed tin, shuffled into the space and waited with his face down until the giant Patrick claimed from behind the bar a double-barrelled fowling piece that he cocked twice and pointed at them all.

'Lady and gents. This is a civic ordinance required by the owners of this here groghouse we call The Stuck Pig. For your benefit as well as our own. If you'd be mannered enough to sit there quietly until the gunpowder burns and the cleansing is done.'

They all looked to Dempsey, who stared into the octagonal eyes of the shotgun like he was newly sighted. Shrugged as he watched the old man circle them while pouring a line of gunpowder until they were all contained. Patrick laughed.

'No, lads, we're not setting you aflame. Some recent boats have brought the fever and the white-curded shits. Take a deep breath of air while we purge the miasma.'

At this the old man struck a match on the floorboards and tossed it to the line of powder, which fizzed and burst into a shearing orange flame that billowed around them an acrid black smoke. The flame died down and the stench of gunsmoke settled, and only then did Patrick lay down the mighty fowling piece whose stock was newly varnished and barrels tended with oil. Dempsey cleared his throat and spat, eyes watering with the effort of staring at Patrick amid the vapours of war.

'I take it that we freemen now have your permission to avail ourselves of the hospitality of our own kind, and the unearned riches of those parasitical upon the poor white man. For I have heard this town is rife with Indian, Spaniard, Russian and German, Jew and nigger.' The small revolver was in Dempsey's hand, and the smile on his face was cruel.

'You have heard right.'

The Australian voice came from the edge of the room, where the rug-curtain dropped. Into the booming voice walked a man whose giant oiled boots made the nails in the floorboards complain. He stood at six feet, without a hat. A longhair with a black beard and blue eyes in a pale and unweathered face. Pinstriped blue suit and waistcoat with fob watch. A revolver in a holster both thickly belted at his narrow waist and strapped above his knee. On his fingers jewelled silver rings, moving to his grim mouth.

Dempsey laughed, but there was nerves in it. 'I was waiting on a rooster, so I didn't expect a maiden-hair. Imagine my surprise.'

The man nodded in mock-admiration at Dempsey's wit, his eyes alive with the same dark humour. 'I see there are some among you who, like myself, having been prison-barbered, have vowed never to suffer the shears.'

'Then you have been free long enough, I can see from the length of your flower-scented locks, to have forgotten the temper of men such as my band, newly free, and it would seem constrained here at your orders.'

The tall man nodded. 'Your freedom is of no interest, and you are not constrained. But a pirated ship aflame mere yards off Sydney-town? That is a matter of regret. That is the kind of trouble that brings neither wealth nor opportunity. Explain yourself and you may leave unmolested. You and your *band*.'

It was the hint of mockery that set Dempsey's shoulders tighter in the wet shirt, some weight now on his planted feet. The revolver still pointed at the stranger's belly, who appeared unconcerned, looking out over the gathered heads and reading their faces, and understanding. Turning again to Dempsey.

Dempsey chuckled. 'I won't be stood-over in a bowsing-ken by a pretty mort such as yourself, or be shifted into the darkmans—'

'Don't indulge your Egyptian Cant with me, Tinker. For I see that you have fashioned yourself into a leader, and that you fear me. Why do you fear? The only gun drawn is in your shaking hand.'

And it was true. The faces of the others in the shadows. The red-glimmer off the iron stove. The stink of the foul-water on them. And Dempsey's hand, shaking. 'But we are both sons of Cu Chulainn are we not?' the Irishman said.

'I'm Parramatta born.'

'Then our language remains brotherly.'

The tall man put his hand on his holster-belt. 'It's true that in the Old Country there was nothing beyond the liturgy of the Crows. And that your kind have survived by casting dark spells, inverting. But that is also a failure to see outside their circle of darkness. This is a new country, and we have no need of arcane wordplay. Or the performance of ghoulish mask-wearing. Speak plainly, or I'll take your head off your shoulders.'

With that the tall man drew out the giant revolver that had weighted his leg. It was like nothing Sam had ever seen. A six-shot chamber whose mouths were sealed with lard. Walnut handle visible even in the giant hand of the gunman. Its weight not a burden on the wrist that held the gun steady.

Dempsey whistled. 'Cometh the hour; cometh the gun. What kind of country is this, that such a killing beauty might be conceived in evolution of the humble duties of the pistol? Are the men here giants or are there fabled beasts afoot?'

Dempsey's verbosity an obvious prelude to a sneak attack, and the tall man cocked his fearsome revolver.

'It is the Colt Walker, sired out of a cannon and a lance. Born for the cavalry charges of the Indian frontier. Can kill a horse at a hundred yards, as I can attest. Of you, it will leave nothing but a red mist cast upon this company.'

The men behind Dempsey began to edge away, and wisely so. Sam's book-learned knowledge of firearms told him that the ball of such a weapon must pass through many bodies before it came to rest.

Like the others, he stared at the mighty weapon and in doing so caught the eye of its owner, who held his stare. 'Boy, you may stay around. There are few boys in this town and you'll be useful, unless you have other designs. You, *woman*. The same invitation I extend to you. There are few women here and if it's money and advancement you desire then you shall have both. You men, those not heading to the goldfields, must make your way in the streets of Sydney-town, as we call it here, although Patrick Ryan over there will school you as to the conventions of our society. In short, if you're wise in your schemes then you'll return a pinch of everything to my pocket. For I own the peelers of this town, and if you're caught and working for me, I will protect you. If you aren't, I'll advise them to hang you as the kind of example that cheers the hearts of the local citizenry, and puffs the chests of the peelers. But you ... your name.'

'That was a fine leaders' speech sir. A fine speech for a lag's son born in Parramatta.'

'I advise your return to my question.'

'My name is Anderson Dempsey. And these here are my kinfolk brothermen, sworn in blood.'

'And yet, I see you for what you truly are, Anderson Dempsey.'

Dempsey smiled, scratching at his neck. 'Many have made that claim, too late. But do you see me, for what I shall become?'

A look of exhaustion passed across the gunman's face. He said, 'Alas, I do.'

Pulled the trigger, levering into the room a spear of muzzle-flame and a brute roar whose shockwaves belted the organs in Sam's belly and chest, filled his ears with a ringing silence. He sat stunned and looked at the place where Dempsey's head used to be. Just the stump now of his neck and twin geysers of blood and two smaller vents spurting through. The corpse sitting straight up. Pistol leaking from slackened fingers.

The gunman looked across them all, seated docile like the pious in chapel and he the minister, opening the chamber of the revolver like a priest checking a songbook, thumbing it closed and placing it gently into its holster. No pleasure or light in his eyes. A man who had killed many. Distant enough from Dempsey to have avoided the curtain of gore thrown upon them all. Looking again at Sam, and Sarah Proctor, and calling them out of the assembled felons with the barest cock of his head.

6

It was the shaking that awoke him amid squalls of lashing rain. Sam riding the crests and troughs of the vast ocean with the wood-bones groaning and his cot tossing and the dog jumping like it was ant-bitten. He saw his slops in the corner wet the edges of the earthenware jug and knew himself on land, and jumped to his feet, and ran for the door. The two-storey lodging-house jounced on its stumps, but fared better than the stone building alongside, that shucked nails from its shingled roof and sent them into the lane. Cracks appeared in the lime-wash render, and the mud-bricks jumped and spat dust. Out in the deep-water harbour, the dozens of ships and lighters sloshed about like leaves in a bucket. The denizens of the groghouses and brothels flooded into the street, leaning into the rain and making shelters of their jackets, keeping clear of the horses kicking at their tether-posts.

Then it stopped—the deluge and groundswell. The horses were first to settle, but glared at the people who wrung out their hats and stamped muddy boots on the plank thresholds and laughed in excitement and relief. A piano started to play scales, and a bugler began a morose parody of a battlefield rally, but Sam's heart beat faster as he scanned the street. He thought it the confusion of his awakening, until he saw the picture of his mother clear in his mind, based on the Magistrate's description of her—tall and thin with stooped shoulders. A milky face with pale lips and green eyes and dark red hair. An oddly high voice like that of a child. A voice suited more to singing than speech. The Magistrate bringing his description to an end because of a quiet shame in his eyes, as though his memory of her was somehow indecent.

Now Sam looked for her in the street, as if it was the most natural thing in the world that the people around her would keep moving while she stood quiet and still as a daguerreotype image, staring back at him. But there was nothing of her there, and he turned away, the better to drive the picture from his mind.

The sun was low, and Sam couldn't gauge whether it was mid-morning or mid-afternoon because he didn't have bearings. He had no idea how long he'd slept, except that nobody had disturbed him. Looking down the landing of the lodging house balcony, he could see the doors to the other rooms cast open and knew himself to be alone. The dog emerged from its hide under his cot and leant into his leg, shivering with fear. The building was unfinished, and in the muddy court were piled sawhorses and scaffolding boards and hand-fashioned ladders of unstripped pine and a sign painted crudely with the words 'MRS Hogans Lodging'. There were many buildings the same nearby, and now that the rain had stopped the smell that arose from the damp streets was wood smoke and the blood-resin of unseasoned timber. To his right, a path led to the peak of a great bald hill upon which snapped a flag that he didn't recognise.

The lower hills were trodden bare with muddy tracks that became narrow streets cut through sandhills. In the interstices between the streets and the dunes were gathered great muddy puddles laid over with planking. Eager to take his bearings, Sam walked the length of the balcony, looking for the row of brothels he'd seen last night on an adjacent block. One of them now housed Sarah Proctor, and possibly his mother. He shielded his eyes from the weak sunlight, but he couldn't tell at this quiet hour which of the timber shacks were the molly-houses. He'd seen no map of San Francisco because none existed in the Australia. He didn't know east or west but only left and right, and beyond the first dozen blocks to his left the streets ran according to no plan, massing in canvas slum-shanties flattened by the quake that steamed as ant-men crawled over them. Some grander houses lined a track that rose to a terrace cut onto a great craggy hill covered by heath and saltbush.

By Sam's reckoning, San Francisco was near the same size as Sydney, with a similar harbour of bays and peninsulas and small islands, but in the brightening light reminded him more of the Swan River port of Fremantle.

Down on the mudstone flats stalked the gulls he knew from home, and cormorants drying their wings on guano-basted rocks. Three pelicans sat on the deck of an unmanned lighter, although they were brown and not white. Some mallard-ducks slept beside, heads buried beneath their wings. Egrets and small brown grebes picked in the mud. The familiar raven sat newly returned on rooves down the shoreline street. And now, putting a lyric to the sunshine that bathed Sam's face—the birdsong that had inhabited his sleep. He looked under the open eaves for the source of the warbling, and had to walk several rooms along the balcony before he saw the flitting form of what sounded like a finch but looked more like a robin, with a bronze breastplate and yellow beak and yellow-and-blue underside tail-feathers. There was a pair of them and they were building a nest, the dun-coloured partner returning from the yard with sawdust strings while the other sang and looked at Sam.

'Not a good place to nest, mother,' he said, and the robin twitched its head and was silent. 'This building's so new that the wharf rats haven't come. But they will come and eat your young.'

She ducked back under the eaves and stayed quiet, and Sam grew uneasy because the picture of rats consuming the nestlings recalled last night's dream of the black snake, its glowing red eyes watching from its corner. He tried to shrug off the dream but fear began pooling in his belly.

Sam hadn't slept deeply for many months, and had thereby

eluded the snake dream that waited for him when he was most deeply asleep, and most alone. The weeks of pursuing his mother, sleeping rough and being woken by hunger and cold or the rough boot of a landowner or policeman, then the horrors of Dempsey's reign on the whaler and his bloody end had doubtless roused the serpent that was more real than any waking vision.

Sam unclenched his fists and turned to the weak sunlight and drove the dream from his eyes with a focus on the horizon of hills and the wood smoke haze over the townsite. The needs of his body were always a balm against the dream, and he peered into the court looking for the privy. He could smell the slops in his room from outside and didn't want to anger the owner of the lodgings.

After the longhair gunman took Sarah Proctor to the rear of a brothel, he had delivered Sam to the unlit and empty lodging-house at the end of the street. The gunman didn't speak, and Sam's ears were still deafened with the discharge of the Colt. The tall killer climbed the internal steps of freshly hewn boards and led Sam onto the rear balcony. He pointed to a bunk in a dark empty room and then was gone.

That departure, and Sam's collapse into an exhausted sleep, might have been this morning or it might have been days ago. The only gauge of time passed was the queasy hunger in Sam's belly. He was used to days without food, and the nausea he now felt was the intermediate period between a bladed intestinal gnawing and the outright staggers. If he returned to his cot and slept through the discomfort, he couldn't be sure of getting to his feet again.

There were no workers in the building, although the street along the shore was bustling with horse and wagon and clots of drunken men. In case he discovered his mother this day, Sam wanted to make himself presentable, and so he combed his hair with his fingers and picked the sleep from his eyes and wiped his face on his sleeve. He didn't want to appear before her an urchin and a likely burden. Sam patted his arms and legs looking for wounds but it was only his bare feet that were tender. His ribs ached from the sleeping and his skin was filthy despite the dunking in the harbour. He walked to the end of the balcony and looked across a plank fence to see a man fell a steer with an axe. The steer fell silently into red mud and the man set about taking off its head with slopping blows. In an open stable, closed off with hessian sheets, hung the carcasses of sheep and pigs. Joints of bone and assorted hooves boiled in a glue-pot, the grey scum roiling off the surface into the hissing fire. Sam thought to trade the man some labour for meat, and once again drew his fingers through his hair and hoisted his trousers. His stomach convulsed at the thought of food, but his parched mouth and cracked lips needed water. He could drink from the puddles in the court below and wash in the same. But first he needed to make his bed. Ignoring the slops, he straightened the kapok-stuffed mattress and three woollen blankets. He didn't know how long it would take to find his mother, or if he would return to the room, or what awaited downstairs, only that his immediate survival depended upon the encouragement of strangers. The only man who'd shown him recent kindness was a killer who felt nothing when he killed, and only because Sam might be useful.

Downstairs was the smell of fresh sawdust and cigar-smoke. Sam followed the dog's footprints in the sawdust as it tracked to the door. The guard outside the door was asleep at his post, face hidden beneath a green felt slouch hat. Sam watched his slumbers and thought about waking him, but the oriental kris at the man's belt and six-foot musket with bayonet attached laid across his chest dissuaded him from the idea. The wind was cold and briny, and there were dozens of people further along by the groghouses. He thought it best to retrace his path to the tavern from last night. The tall man who'd murdered Dempsey had not been summoned there, but hid behind a rug curtain, the probable owner of the place. It didn't seem an idle boast when he spoke of his influence. His dress and manner were leader-like. He had the knowledge that Sam required.

The groghouse called The Stuck Pig was near empty of patrons and what humanity was there looked like they'd slept where they passed out. Sam recognised the longhair Starr from his tattooed hands. His face was bloodied and he looked dead, or dead drunk. No steam on his breath like the steam that Sam exhaled as he made his way to the plank-bar. The ancient in the tattered redcoat was emptying spittoons into a wooden tub. He nodded at Sam and indicated for him to follow.

They went through the drape-wall and upstairs into a room illuminated by a paneless four-square window where four men were seated around a sawhorse table. The room was an armoury, with hardwood stands holding muskets and Hawken rifles and shotguns along one wall. The men didn't look at Sam, busy with their bomb-making. On the table was a pile of carpentry nails and halved copper piping and lead shot. A jar of coal-oil that smelt sulphurous. Cotton wicks soaking in kerosene. A ceramic bowl piled with gunpowder and a wooden spoon perched in it. Empty tin cans with the lids peeled back in rough serration.

Sam waited, but when he wasn't acknowledged, sidled to a table covered with slate tiles. The dog looked to the men and was reluctant to enter the room, and only came when Sam tapped his hip. On the table were different bullet moulds, and pigs of lead, and iron melting pots. Lead-shot of different sizes in bowls and smaller buckshot and tamps made of wax paper and rawhide. Paper cartridges for the buckshot. Balls of a kind he'd never seen before. Not round but conical, with a skirt at the bottom. And four homemade pig-iron flechettes, sand embedded in the pitted cast. He picked one and weighed it in his hand, looked around for the weapon that would deliver such a heavy dart, but couldn't decide its owner.

The men hunkered down, muttering, the stack of grenades growing on the table. The door behind Sam creaked on its hinges but none of the men looked up. It was the tall killer, dressed now in white canvas trousers and knee-boots that looked military issue. A leather coat lined with tartan. He looked at Sam and nodded.

'We don't oil the hinges round here. You can guess why.' Indicating the rack of weapons, his gaze hawkish on the men, his long hair fixed with a buckle, eyes not on Sam but on the dog cowering at his feet; a picture that appeared to sadden the man.

'You ever been around guns?'

Sam shook his head. 'Only in books. But I have an interest, and I can learn.'

The tall man appraising him, matching words with his reading of Sam's face. 'You're lettered eh?'

'Somewhat, sir. I am.'

'Then you'll be wasted in here. I was thinking your young eyes and steady hands. We've had accidents in this room, the result of shakes, and haste. Follow.'

The door creaked shut and they entered a hallway with all the doors closed except for one room with a low bunk and a white table. In a bucket by the door were bloody bandages, and the room stank of gunpowder.

'Infirmary,' said the tall man. 'Where you get your teeth pulled and musket-ball removed and knife-holes sewed up again.'

To a big room at the end of the hall. The door creaked so loudly that it made the dog back away. Another sawhorse table but covered in maps. Roughly made bookshelf, empty. Books piled on the floor beside. A wooden trolley with bottles and glass. The tall man waved at a stool beside the table, and put up his booted feet and inclined his head into a box of sunlight, dust swimming in the eddies caused by his breath.

'Show me on the globe where you think we are.'

The globe was eggshell cool beneath Sam's fingers. The master in the Boys Home had a globe too, but it was decades old. The Swan River colony Sam'd recently arrived from had not been on the master's globe—just Van Diemen's Land and New South Wales and a great swathe of brown island whose northern borders looked drawn by a child. Sam now spun the globe until he found the Old Country and worked west with his fingertips, across the Atlantic until he hit Newfoundland. Followed his fingers south to New York. Across a rudimentary patchwork of nations and Indian land to the west coast. It was all Mexico, far as he could see, and no towns.

'Not on here. Yet.'

'Didn't say it was. Asked you to show me where you thought we was.'

'Couldn't say, sir.'

'Boy, don't call me sir. My father was a bullocky, not a laird.'

'Mister, what do I call you then?' Sam not meeting the man's eyes.

'And don't act like I'm a laird either. Look at me when you talk. You're a free man now. My name is Thomas Keane. You call me Keane.'

'Yes, Mister Keane. I go by Sam Bellamy, lately of Van Diemen's Land, but born to the Swan River colony. Transported when I was eleven.'

'The point I was making with the globe.'

'Yes, Mister Keane. There's nothing on it.'

'Was all Mexico but a year ago, this town called Yerba Buena. Now it's newly American, called San Francisco, and soon to be part of the Union. But peopled by men from across that globe. That man whose head I uncoupled—he was wrong. It ain't Spaniards here; it's Chileans. Russians. Chinese. Brought on the Pacific Ocean. Every kind of European that has colonies in the Pacific. Some blacks. Plenty of Mexicans, or Californios, as they call themselves. And us, who the Americans call Southlanders, in big numbers.'

'Come for the gold.'

'That's right, come for the gold. Up beyond the Sacramento Valley, out on the American and San Joaquin rivers, and all the little streams run off 'em...'

Sam listened to the man whose eyes never rested, scanning across the maps on the table and occasionally glancing back at Sam to make sure he was paying attention. At first there was a weariness in Thomas Keane's voice, suggesting that this was a speech he had made many times before, and Sam supposed that this was true because of all the new arrivals. But the longer Keane spoke the more his voice changed, and Sam recognised it as the voice that the Magistrate used when he wanted to sound fatherly, and Sam knew that the speech was for his benefit alone. He wanted to ask the man about his mother, and he expected to be asked in turn why he'd travelled over the great ocean, but then he understood that this type of man wouldn't ask that kind of question. In any case, Thomas Keane was taking an interest in Sam, and was trying to educate him, and so he had better listen and not interrupt.

'... There's a race goin among common men to get the easy gold, before hard-rock minin becomes the preferred method, and us Australians got a good start. Ten pound steerage I paid, and near two month to get here from New South Wales; six month and one thousand dollars to get here by wagon train or across Panama from the eastern American colonies. Why there's barely no women, and hardly no children, or boys like you, yet. But plenty of men, the kind who can pack up and leave. American deserters from the war with Mexico. Whalers and sealers tired of the Pacific trade. Settlers from the western Spanish colonies. And just lately arrived, as cabin passengers on the better steamships and clippers, from the Old Country, and the richer states back east—the plain old adventurous. Some of them have wit, and some of them're stupid like children. That's where you come in. You got any vices?'

Shook his head.

'Boy your age, I believe you, excepting one or two. You look at everything, and you always got questions behind your eyes. So ask them.'

Sam thought again of his mother and began to form the question, but the look in Keane's eyes was sharp. That particular matter was for Sam's benefit alone, and here was the leader trying to help him, and he realised that he wanted to impress Keane, and so he asked the question that he supposed was natural of a boy his age.

'Those men making mortars next door?'

Keane smiled, nodded. 'We're arming ourselves, because The Hounds are up to something. They're an American gang, deserters from the Mexican War, who want to take what we have. Our gang, we don't know what they're planning, but something's coming. Anything else?'

'What does it go by, your gang?'

Keane laughed, and the sound was pleasant to Sam. 'They call us many things. Sydney Ducks when they want to mock us, or Sydney Coves mostly, on account of that being one of the names for the quarter you find yourself in.'

Keane next told the story of the early months. How when he first arrived there were a few hundred Americans and some US soldiers stationed at the Presidio barracks, fresh off the border war with the Mexicans. Keane had gone upriver into the mountains around Sutter's Mill like everyone else, looking for the yeller. But his friend got a leg crushed in a rockfall, and they drug him back to San Francisco, and even after a few months absence the place had grown with the new arrivals flooding in from the Pacific Americas and Australia mainly. And how some of The Hounds, lately outnumbered in their own country, soon realised what the coming of foreigners meant for their own aspirations. In particular, the bandy-legged Southlanders with manacle-chafed wrists and ankles, stripes on their backs. Set barefoot upon the shoreline armed with cruel knives and the instinct to survive. Men who had journeyed for the gold but didn't care how they came upon it. For whom the stories of the Californian interior, where freemen slaved to extract the yeller while being plagued by hunger and cholera, held no fear but no interest either. Who looked around at the port streets so similar to those in the Australian colonies but for the notable absence of peelers.

A town without a constabulary. A town without masters. A town for the taking.

And take they did. Mr Keane a freeborn man like Sam Bellamy who had also fallen into captivity. Who also had letters. Who in the caring for his wounded compatriot, with a few trusted friends, began robbing gold dust from merchants who refused their protection, and soon began bushranging into the hinterland. Who bought this their first groghouse in the midst of The Hound's territory and who, in response to the warfare enjoined by The Hounds, by way of targeted murder, had slowly diminished their number to the point where the Americans were now a rabble, plundering the poor Mexicans that lived in wattled hovels on the fringes of town.

Keane talked of his exploits in plain language. None of the grandiloquence that Sam expected from a war leader, although there was a bitterness in his eyes whenever he mentioned The Hounds, until he checked himself. 'Samuel, I'll provide you with board and employment. You can work as a scout, to be schooled by Patrick Ryan, with an eye to the pocket heavy with gold dust and an ear for the loudmouth and braggart. You can tout at the stagecoach muster for new chums with the glint of foolishness in their eye. Was there anything else you want to know?'

'I just want to thank you, Mr Keane, for taking an interest in me, and for offering me a position with your fellows.'

Keane's smile told Sam that the formality of his speech was amusing. The man sat back and huffed on his pipe, curiosity in his eyes, waiting for the question that Sam really wanted to ask and that he seemed to know was coming. 'Mr Keane. I don't know if your influence extends to knowin about mollies and their movements, but I got to ask you about...'

There were angry boot-steps in the hall, coming closer, and Keane raised a hand until there entered a red-headed giant as pale as Sam and equally dirty.

'The Hounds are at the Mexican camp. Our men are situated on the rooftops of Sydney-town and in the streets. The armoury is empty but for our favoured pieces.'

Up some stairs and a ladder, and they were on the shingled roof, a leaden walkway between the twin gables. Five other men were crouched and smoking, dressed in a motley of corded trousers and coats of different leather. One of them passed Keane an eyeglass, who grunted and passed it to Sam. The eyeglass was heavy, but when he trained it lengthways over the blocks of two- and three-storey buildings and the squatters' shacks to the perimeter of mud huts, Sam could see the dozen horsemen in their tattered uniforms charging through the distant encampment with whips raised and cavalry swords descending in silver arcs onto men and women and children running everyway through the tracks. Sam stopped his scan of the Mexican camp, and watched what appeared to be a man humping a well, until the man finished and without pulling up his breeches reached down and took the ankles of a skinny woman and tipped her headfirst down the well, while a child not more than three or four batted his legs, until the man took up the child and sent it after its mother.

Sam put down the eyeglass because of the sickening in his belly. Dempsey's reign and bloody murder appeared to have been merely a foretaste of this new world. It was a massacre that Sam was witnessing, but the men around him appeared disinterested, some of them even grimly amused.

'You can bet this latest campaign is due to Dudgeon's goading,' said the giant redhead. 'Stirring his men for action with an easy slaughter. I'll toss you for him.'

'Done, Mannix,' replied Keane. 'He's had it coming, and I'll be glad to turn him off.'

Several blocks away on a sloping grass cantonment were gathered a hundred men or more. One among them was waving his hat, speechifying from the raised platform of a dray-cart. Even from a distance, Sam recognised him as the Australian who'd raided the whaler. The man replaced his hat and jumped down into the crowd that began to march out of the square toward the Mexican camp.

'That's the Australian man who boarded our ship,' Sam said.

Keane made a look of distaste behind billows of tobacco. 'He's the travesty that goes by Mitchell Walker Esquire, and who's no less criminal than ourselves, but lacks the honesty to proclaim this. He's grown fat charging poor men felonious prices for ordinary goods, and cares not whether they starve as a result, and wonders why they turn to crime. Walker has lately formed a vigilante group which aims to limit our future numbers by raiding ships and turning them back, and, I hear, openly killing Australians who bear the lash and iron-stoop.'

'Now might be the time,' the redhead muttered to Keane, who turned and faced the ocean, but shook his head. 'The wind isn't right. But I agree. It'll need to be soon.'

Sam wasn't about to ask. He felt his separation from the dog, who he could hear whining at the foot of the ladder, and then there was a hand on his sleeve. Keane, looking hard at him.

'Boy, you're shaking and it ain't cold. You better eat.'

On his way down the ladder the wood-frame of the building began to vibrate, and Sam held onto the ladder and stopped his descent. But it wasn't his hunger or a trick of the mind. The saw-boards in the bare walls were trembling against a swelling cushion of sound.

The men in the stairwell laughed. 'It's not an earth-shake,

son,' said Keane. 'Clement has taken to his hurdy-gurdy. You're in for a treat over supper.'

'You're a strange one, Keane, if you think that a treat,' said Mannix. 'There's a reason the redcoats pipe men onto the battlefield, which after all is nothin but a floggin of the ears.'

'Not where I come from.'

The sound rose beyond them as they went lower into the building. On a stool in the corner of the groghouse, an old man with a shiny pate and grey whiskers was bent over a contraption that was half bagpipe and half accordion. The dog kept to Sam's ankles as he took the bench indicated by Keane, where the others also sat and removed their coats and rolled up their sleeves. The sound of the instrument was a fierce warlike drone that rolled and grew, and made their chests tremble. It was an infernal sound, but over the course of minutes, in his weakened state Sam began to feel a kind of strong emotion that brought tears to his eyes, and that he hid by pretending to wipe his mouth on his sleeve. But Keane nodded and his eyes were also bright. The other men grumbled and ducked their heads when the old man launched from the dirge into a manic finger-play over the keyboards that sounded like fifty mad fiddlers setting fire to the air, before he slumped, eyes closed, and returned to the drone in a posture of prayer.

Sam looked to the faces of the hard company but none of them spoke or discouraged the player with looks or gesture. An earthenware pot straight off the fire with its base covered in peels of glowing cinder was placed on the table by the Ancient in the black tricorne hat, who returned with a loaf of bread the size of a pillow that the men set upon. A scree of tin plates was cast down the row, and Sam took his own and a ladle of stew and a chunk of bread, and with the relieving of his hunger, and the pressing of the dirge, the tears in his eyes returned, and Sam hid them by passing bread to his dog and staring into his plate. The only words spoken during the meal were addressed to Sam by a sceptical-looking youth named Barr with sailor's tattoos and iron rings in his weighted ears, who leaned into the noise.

'That dog of yours. Would you share with it your last crust?'

Sam nodded, because it was true, and he had done so, but the youth didn't seem appeased in his suspicions. 'And after your last meal was gone, would you slay and partake of your hound if needs be, to survive?'

Sam looked at the youth who was reading him closely. He was on the verge of replying that yes, he would, because he'd thought it often, but the boy nodded because he'd seen it in Sam's eyes. The youth returned to his stew, and called for ale as the elderly player reached the peak of his drone and bit again into the swarming sound with another frenzy of fiddle-play.

7

The mirror looked like it was made of smoke, and from that smoke an image of Samuel Bellamy emerged that pleased the Chinaman and made him coo. Sam didn't move for fear of bursting the pins that framed the woollen suit jacket, and the picture of himself better groomed than he'd ever been.

That morning Sam had scrubbed himself in a bathtub until his skin was burnished pink. He had a bellyful of black beans and bread, and smelt like the milk-soap that all the men shared, along with the damp blanket used to towel himself dry in the stable at the rear of the hotel. Sam had the stable to himself and lit the fire and heated the jug, filling the tub and soaking in the water until it lost its heat.

He then retraced his steps through the nearby streets until he found the row of molly-houses where Sarah Proctor was quartered. The buildings were each two-storeyed wood-framed huts, rooved with pine shingles and canvas tarpaulins. They were dingy and damp-smelling and had the air of lodging houses because of all the women's clothes drying on ropes between the balconies. He recognised the molly-house where Sarah was delivered on account of the bright yellow blanket that was hung there in place of a door. Sam carried a posy of red and yellow flowers that he'd gathered up the hill from the settlement, and he held them like a candle whose flame was delicate. He wiped his bare feet on the hog-bristle mat outside the door, and pulled aside the blanket and entered the darkness. What he saw there in the windowless room was not like the molly-houses he'd seen in New South Wales, where there was commonly a table and chairs set aside as a welcoming area, but rather some plank benches that held the shapes of snoring men. The smell was of stale beer and cigar smoke and mouldy linen. Sam heard the ceiling creak, and he could see light drizzle down through the cracks in the floorboards. Ahead of him was a large room separated into stalls by wooden posts, in the manner of pigpens, each given privacy by a hung piece of canvas.

There was no sound coming from any of the stalls, and so Sam took hold of the rough-hewn ladder that did for stairs and rose into a small gap in the floorboards above him. He heard the sound of voices and smelt brewing tea. The light from the front balcony was sufficient to observe the dozen women sleeping on mattresses on the floor of an open room with a brazier in a corner. There was no chimney for the smoke to draw and the room was stifling with the smoke from the wood that was wet and green. There were a couple of women on the balcony that he could hear, and so he rapped his knuckles on the floorboards, clearing his throat before announcing himself. There was no response from the sleeping shapes, with only a foot or an arm exposed here and there, and so he climbed off the ladder and into the room.

'Sarah? Sarah Proctor?'

He walked toward the light where the women had stopped talking, although he made a slow progress because he had to step over and between the sleeping shapes, so crowded were they across the floor. Then the doorway was blocked by a woman whose silhouette he recognised beneath the sleeveless cotton shift and whose hands were on her hips. Sarah Proctor raised a finger to her mouth and ushered him toward her. He followed her out into the weak sunlight where she sat on an upturned wooden bucket and indicated that he should sit on the identical bucket beside her.

There was nobody else on the balcony beside Sarah, and Sam tried to hide his alarm because she had been talking to herself in two voices, playing the part of herself and another, whose voice had sounded younger and chiding. But Sarah showed no awkwardness, and he sat beside her while she stared at him. There was friendliness in her eyes but also suspicion.

'I don't want nothin material from you, Sarah, so don't worry on that account.'

She looked at the flowers in his hand, and he followed her gaze. The yellow flowers were beginning to bruise, but the red flowers were waxy and shining as though polished. A thorn had pricked him as he climbed the stairs, and the side of his thumb was spotted with blood. Sam had gathered the flowers for his mother but he saw his mistake, and ducked his head in a bow and passed them over.

'Samuel Bellamy, I never... If you was older or I was younger—I believe that I'd eat you alive!'

The image confused Sam, but her sisterly cuff around his ears put him at ease. Once Sarah had sniffed the flowers and smiled, Sam leaned forward.

'Sarah, what you said. You was right that I didn't come to California for the gold. I never told you while we was aboard that whaler my purpose on this shore, because I feared you would use it against me. I apologise for that, but now I got something I want to share with you, and a question I'd like to ask you.'

Sarah Proctor pretended to be wounded. 'There I was thinkin you was makin love to me, Master Samuel Bellamy. Never one for small talk though are you? And no need to apologise for not trustin me with secrets. I'll admit I was scared enough on that ship to have sold my mother's soul if it got me some advantage. You was smart to abide with your whys and wherefores. So speak now. It appears as though I'm well situated here. The other girls is nice and so is Mrs McGarry, the proprietor. You've given me flowers and that is special but more important is that you trust me.'

Sarah pressed her hands upon his own and he let them be clasped while he told her about his mother and how he came to be aboard the whaler. Sarah heard him out and never once interrupted to clear a point, and when he was finished she squeezed his hands and nodded. 'That is a terrible and sad tale, Samuel, but I knew you was a brave boy the minute I saw you. Yes, I can surely help. I'm only learnin the ropes here so to speak, but I can make enquiries about your Ma. I've heard that there are near a hundred Australian women working in this area, and I'm certain that Kathleen McGarry, who seems to know everybody's business, man or woman, will advise me.'

Her words buoyed Sam's spirits, and he promised to drop by tomorrow morning at the same time, because according to Sarah at night it was too busy to receive visitors.

The other women were rousing as Sam left the molly-house, and they blinked themselves awake and brushed their hair, and one of them sang a bawdy song about a priest's passion for a chaste young lassie, who to deter the priest's attentions dressed like a barrow-boy, but that only spurred the older man on. The song made some of the women laugh, even though the singer was still hidden beneath a blanket. Sam retreated down the rickety wooden ladder that he realised was designed to be drawn up into the second storey, to protect the women while they slept.

It was back at The Stuck Pig that Sam received his first orders for the day, which was the welcome news that he was expected elsewhere so that he could get clothed. The old man in the tavern pointed Sam first toward the Chinese streets, where for a price Keane offered protection from The Hounds, and Sam was barbered for free. He watched in the reflection of a gilt-edged mirror the first Oriental he'd ever seen up close, who did him the honour of pretending he had growth to warrant a shave. He came out of that barber smelling like fresh laundry, even though he was still barefoot.

Next stop the bootery, where a Frenchman from British North America made him wash the mud off his feet in a bucket by the door before measuring his foot-size. While Sam watched, the Frenchman cut a pattern from a bolt of brown suede that he braced on an iron foot and stitched to a leather sole with waxed twine and pliers. When the pair was sewed, he laced the shoes with buckskin, and they fitted so perfectly on Sam's bruised feet that he did a little jig that made the Frenchman smile.

The final stop was the Chinaman haberdasher and tailor, with the smoky mirror set into a lacquered black frame, who offered him bitter green tea with pieces of rice floating in it and a pipe of tobacco while Sam watched the sewing of his grey woollen suit, complete with waistcoat and two collarless cotton shirts and three pairs of woollen socks. The Chinaman pointed to bolts of coloured felt on a rack of hardwood-shelves and invited Sam to choose a colour.

'Sydney-town man like the slouch hat. You choose; I make you one good hat.'

The Chinaman spoke so much like the mocking imitations of Mannix and the others back in the groghouse that it made Sam think he was the instigator of the joke.

'Where you keep your knife? Nice new suit, no cutting with knife in belt no good. You need sheath, I give you sheath. On belt or strap under arm. You choose.'

Sam showed the single-edged hunting knife that Keane had given him.

'Put that one on belt-sheath. No need for dagger sheath. Good one.'

Sam stood on the carpet in his new shoes, and looked through the window of the haberdashers to the street crowded with Mormons in black suits, and Orientals in belted smocks, and dusty Australian miners in pelts come from the hinterland for the gambling and whisky and mollies. The Chinaman's hands prodded and pressed, and with his mouth full of pins and bowl-face and ponytail, he looked like a creature from a children's story about djinns and dragons. The Chinaman wore a western suit of simple black cotton, but the notes of familiarity only forecast the alien in him. The smell of the Swan River blacks was smoky and sour, but this man and his lair smelt of fish and some kind of herbal unguent that Sam couldn't name.

'You sit there, and smoke. I sew it now. Not long, you see.'

The Chinaman bowed his head in deference but Sam wasn't buying it. The Swan River blacks cracked dumb when a white man spoke to them direct, then laughed among themselves at the false impression they had drawn, and went back to doing what they'd been chastised for. Same way the old lags on the whaler hid their true face from Dempsey, biding their time. For they had learned that manner of dissembling on the chain, although no white overseer was ever persuaded from anticipating the retaliatory blow. The Magistrate George Moore had explained it to Sam after witnessing the hanging of two blacks on a tree by the river. The hangings had been ordered as an example to the men's kin, who were herded there and forced to watch. He described how the warriors were proud and defiant until they saw the rope. The terror of the clansfolk was pitiful to witness, but also a salutary lesson of how the British penal code worked on the single hard truth that the only man who doesn't pretend, and doesn't lie, is the broken man.

The Chinaman seemed to understand the importance of pretending by his manner toward Sam, merely a boy—but a boy sent by Keane and therefore a fellow of Sydney-town. Sam's role was to pretend a confidence by virtue of his race, itself a lie and a performance that the Chinaman was playing along with. But while it felt good to pretend, Sam suspected that he'd never be like Keane and his men. The Swan River blackfellows had always treated him kindly, knowing him the son of the limeburner murdered to avenge the slaughter of one of their own, in accordance with their law. Sam grew up playing with black boys in the blacks' camp, and although they hit him and each other when roused to anger, they were never cruel, and Sam never felt a moment of fear among them. But the young wards in the

Vandemonian Boys Home had picked him for a weakling, and terrorised him from the first day, in a manner that made Sam suspect that he was born wrong and so marked out.

Perhaps it was this apprehension that turned Sam from the Chinaman at his cutting bench, scissors slicing through yielding cloth, toward the dusty sunlight playing across his arm on the windowsill that opened to a side alley of bright green grass. A passing shape, thin and small, in a filthy homespun nightshirt belted at the waist. The conical hat made of reeds. A softwood yoke across the shoulders at whose end swung cane baskets. A Chinese boy the same age as Sam, but as soon as he thought this, he saw the lie. As the boy approached the side door, the posture of his shoulders changed, and the way the yoke was thrown suggested not only frustration, but a girl sloughing off something that disgusted her. Her face was filthy with smudges of soot and grease, but the markings looked hand-applied. Their eyes met; her's black and accusing, reading the surprise in his own, and thinking nothing of it. Saying nothing either, she tipped the hat onto her shoulders and entered the haberdashery side-door. The Chinaman at his table cocked an ear and seemed relieved, then looked to Sam, who stared at his feet. When he looked up the Chinaman was still staring at him; the little savage in his new boots and drawers, reading for the truth that Sam had witnessed the girl disguised as a boy.

Chastened, but hoping for another glimpse of the girl, Sam leaned on the windowsill. There began a banging and clanging of pots, and the scraping of a spoon in a pan. The Chinaman grimaced but continued at his work, sewing the seams of the trousers by hand, his bulging eye only a few inches from the cloth. The banging continued, and then the smells of a soup coming to the boil, something like boiled dumplings and the scent of a bitter herb. Sam kept an eye on the alley, glancing at the curtain separating the shopfront from the rooms, but there was no sign of her.

He'd been surprised on his reconnaissance through the town by the number of men who'd met his eye, smiled and even greeted him; the sight of a boy in the streets unusual enough to be welcome. So different to Australia, where he'd been just another urchin, a thing of suspicion and contempt; where he'd received the kindness of strangers but also considerable cruelty. How different therefore for the Chinese girl, who had to hide herself, although whether this was prudent or because of her father's over-protectiveness, he couldn't say. Sam didn't know the way of Orientals, although he resolved to know her.

The Chinaman's shoulders were tense as he tied off a thread. Sam packed the Chinaman's pipe, long and slender with a brass stem and some kind of resinated bowl. He'd learned to smoke dried cane stems at the Boys Home in imitation of the cigars that the master smoked, although he'd never smoked real tobacco. But it was time that Sam learned to smoke, and so he inhaled the Chinaman's tobacco in sips that didn't hurt his lungs, and exhaled the blue wisps of smoke until the smell of it filled the room and the light in the streets began to fade, and the Chinaman left his labours and began to rummage in the corner where he'd flung Sam's trousers, which were little more than rags. He approached Sam ducking and smiling, but his eyes were hard.

'No finish today. You come back tomorrow, I have ready for you. Yes, sorry. Sorry. You take.'

The rancid cotton was greasy to his touch, but Sam nodded, stood into the tattered legs, tied the waist-string and lifted the knees where his skin showed through. On his tail the patches were also torn and frayed, and his new drawers of whitest cotton were bright against the soiled exterior. He looked a ridiculous figure, with his new boots and shirt beside the ripe cloth of his old garment. He turned from the smoky mirror and tucked his knife. Reached out his hand to the Chinaman, to thank him. The man stared at Sam's outstretched hand, a novel or perhaps unkind gesture to him, Sam couldn't tell. More head-ducking and a hand indicating the door. Sam glanced at the curtain but it never trembled. He took his leave with the promise of a midday return.

Across the plaza square was the wine saloon that Sam sought and which was notable for being well lit in the gloom. The establishments around it were mostly dark and shuttered, including the muster-station where the stagecoaches arrived, and the mail-house and several other government buildings whose porches were given over to loitering and conversation.

To get to the saloon, Sam had to pass a row of gambling establishments with names like El Dorado and The Tin Star that were little more than candle-lit tents packed with drunks. The gambling in the tents was precisely as Keane had described—men lining up and not even bothering to sit at table to play the games of faro and monte, but standing on drunken legs and betting bags of gold dust on the turn of a single card.

Sam continued across the plaza square and entered the saloon and introduced himself to the proprietor, a florid man with a bowler hat and powder-grey sideburns. He wore an apron like a butcher. On the shelf behind him were spirits of a kind Sam had never witnessed, in greens and blues and magenta, as well as the familiar amber of rum and whisky. The floorboards looked scrubbed to the point of being abraded, and the place smelled of carbolic soap. The publican took in Sam's appearance and the track of mud his boots had left and gritted his teeth. He tried to smile but the mangled expression dropped when Sam opened his mouth.

'Quiet,' the publican hissed. 'In here, you're an American. My clientele, you understand...'

But Sam didn't understand the American, and looked around at the men in dark suits and top hats and the occasional woman in a tentlike dress and bonnet, each of whom were regarding him askance. None of the women looked like his mother, and in the harsh light they each resembled unblinking birds of prey. Thanks to every hard surface in the saloon, the publican's silencing of him was magnified and audible to all. Sam turned to the rows of pretty-coloured spirits and watched the barman goad a giant silver tureen with cranks of a handle until out of the tap spurted a clear but fizzing liquid that filled the glass in seconds. This was passed to Sam as the publican leaned close.

'You can't come in here dressed like that. And Australians are unwelcome anyhow. Keane knows this and I grant that it's a test of myself and perhaps of your ability to follow orders. But these gentlemen who are mostly the town burghers are liable to string you up if you offend their sensibility anyways, especially in front of their womenfolk, primped for society as they are. Your position is outside the front door in the alley. Any potential customers for Sydney-town I'll direct your way. Tell Keane that I don't need to be observed, especially the day after a hanging. Take this drink and when you're finished, place it on a fencepost. Don't come in here unless you're properly suited.'

The whole sermon delivered in soft tones that reminded Sam of the Welsh speech, but there was no mistaking the seriousness of the American's counsel. To make sure, to Sam's back he addressed words to the effect that a drink of soda for the parched throat of an urchin was a kindness that he hoped wouldn't offend the present company, who Sam could see were still deadly in their examination of him.

He took his place on the corner-post, where a horse-rail ended and the alley smelt of piss, and listened to the gambling shacks across the way, where cheers punctuated by groans and the sound of fighting and laughing ebbed and flowed on the wind. The posts and boards of the saloon were all of unseasoned timber, and smelt of pine-sap and already rusting nail-iron. The saloon was owned by Keane, with the American his proxy, and

Sam's employment was to keep a watch on the plaza for faces marked by an enthusiasm for the mollies and gaming tables and cheap whisky to be had in the waterfront streets.

It was cold in the shadows without a coat. Sam wrapped his arms about his chest and longed for the company of his dog, who was with the elderly musician in Keane's groghouse. Across the plaza, illuminated by the candles and fires of hawkers and loungers, Sam made out the repetitive creaking of a signboard or hoarding in the chilly wind. It was only when some men stood beneath the signboard and held aloft fiery torches that Sam understood that the heavy shapes were the corpses of lynched men, devoid of hats and boots, three of them on creaking ropes beneath a storehouse gantry. The men and their torches moved along the duckboards across the plaza and the hanged men continued to twist in the wind. Sam could no longer see the hanged men, but he wasn't grateful. It seemed worse knowing that they were there, silent in the darkness, and he was relieved when a party of horsemen rode at speed into the square, making a circuit of the plaza before they came to rest at the saloon. Newly wreathed in the clots of steam emerging from their snorting horses, and around the kerchiefs knotted over their mouths, the men were so coated with chalk-dust that they had the appearance of leather-clad skeletons. Their watery eyes stared from black wells at their leader, who dismounted and strode to the windows and peered inside at the gathered gentry and spat on the boards.

'Boys, there's more stimulation to be had in humpin my boot than among the horse-faced pew-loungers in there. We might entertain ourselves at their expense but the menfolk are already drawing their weapons...'

Sam stepped from the shadows with his hands in the air. The ghostly man drew his revolver and it was the only part of him not white. 'Whaddyer want?'

The accent a sinuous growl. Sam didn't doctor his own.

'There's gamblin places over the plaza there but this ain't the quarter for pleasures of the kind you're searchin'. Follow me down the hill.'

The man looked suspicious. 'To Sydney-town? I've been warned, as have we all. For the reputation of your kind is little better than the gypsy whores whose whispers in a sleeping man's ear are said to cripple his virility, should he ever stray.'

Sam saw his mistake plainly, but no remedy suggested itself. The men were soldiers, dusting themselves off, and behind the powder masks were faces as mean as any Sam had seen on earth. He put his hands on his hips, pretending a mischief that he didn't feel.

'It ain't your manhood or even your souls we're after, boys, it's yer money.'

The men thought this a great joke, and indicated for Sam to lead the way. One of them walked his horse beside Sam with an arm around his shoulders, and occasionally patted his head. It was excitement that Sam read as the native emotion among the group, and he envied them their easy solidarity, although they stank worse than their horses. One block away from Sydney-town he began to see familiar faces and looked for some of Keane's company to warn them.

The air was colder by the ocean, and the smell of fish, rotting seaweed and sewage was strong. The merchant shops were mostly boarded-up at this hour, and their porches given over to street-groggers and, from their accents, Australians with nowhere else to go. He heard a revolver cock behind him and the men's laughter tailed off.

From the alleys and porches, dark eyes watched them descend toward the docks. Sam could feel the hunger in those eyes. Men in slouch hats leaned on horse-rails and smoked pipes in the glow of campfires set against the muddy borders of the street crossings. This was called Pacific Street, but like all of the street signs in that precinct, the poles had been cut down and turfed into the muddy holes that were said to be fathomless, and where donkeys had drowned in liquid mud and some drunks too, according to Keane. The Australians had dragged abandoned crates, packing cases and heavy timbers from the port and thrown them in the mud pits, but the sinkholes just drank them up and thirsted for more.

Sam indicated for the riders to follow his footsteps around the edges of the worst drains. In single file they continued toward the shoreline, while the loiterers stared from the darkness and willed them to fall.

The Americans didn't seem so ferocious now, their nerves strained with watching the alleys and shadows. Sam imagined them veterans of Indian wars, well used to the hellish semaphore of silence that forewarned every enemy attack. But now the sounds of the Australian groghouses could be heard, and the men spat and began to smile, and whoever had cocked his revolver uncocked it and the man beside Sam slapped his back. It was a fiddle playing a shanty to a singalong of many voices, in competition with a piano and squeezebox from further along the shoreline, and now there were gunshots and laughter and singing, and somebody was playing the spoons, and elsewhere a choir of ukuleles ran down a medley of national anthems at a comical pace.

They rounded the corner, and Sam let the men take in the length of the shoreline street, with its welter of sounds and hundreds of people in the packed roadway between the establishments. The men seemed undecided, or someway hesitant, so Sam took the bridle of the nearest man's pony and indicated they should follow. He weaved through the tottering drunks and loiterers, and other men gathered in silent communion, whose eyes stared into every face and toward every pocket so that they might eat. Sam looked behind, and the Americans had formed a wary line, and their eyes too looked into every face. Sam paraded the Americans past Keane's groghouse, and the tattooed youth called Barr who'd questioned him earlier about eating his dog tilted his head toward the stables at the termination of the street. Sam leaned toward the nearest American and told him their destination. The American nodded but his eyes were warlike. This was no place to secure a horse or pony when their packsaddles and leather wallets were laden, and where men of all ages were gathered waiting for an opportunity to thieve, and not even hiding that fact, but professing their notoriety with desperate eyes. From the smoke of the groghouse emerged the dog, which by some miracle of nature had picked Sam's scent among the stench of the carousing number. The dog looked into the crowd and saw Sam and took two steps forward, but turned tail and went back up the steps. Like Sam, the dog had survived by reading the faces of men. He went down the steps again, but again retreated to Barr, the tattooed youth, who nudged him away with his heel. The dog followed Sam instead with his eyes, remaining on the porch above the capering drunks that parted to let the Americans through with smirks that suggested all manner of entrapments.

The man whose pony Sam led took back the reins, and drew his revolver, and looked down the line to where the others did the same. Even so, they followed Sam to the livery barn where he rapped on the high plank door. His mind was now on some kind of commission, so that he might build a store of coin. The barn door creaked, and a hulking gnome with a blacksmith's leather jerkin and iron tongs ushered them into the darkened hall. The barn floor was covered in wet hay, and in one corner was a makeshift fire service with barrels of water on a dray-cart with iron wheels. Beside stood a draughthorse, looking at them over a canvas nosebag. The men patted their rides and whispered to them, but didn't remove saddles or suggest as much to the farrier beyond tossing him a silver coin. They followed Sam back out to the streets, and in silence followed him up the steps of The Stuck Pig, where the dog began a strange dance that Sam ignored upon noticing that the Americans had forgotten him already. But the tattooed youth, with sleeves rolled up over his biceps, and wearing a pistol in a holster over his chest, stopped the American party and pointed to Sam. The nearest American grunted, and seeing that his way was barred, pulled out a leather purse on a string from inside his trousers and unleashed the neck and passed Sam a silver dollar. The dog was leaping on Sam's haunch, and he turned and clamped it in an embrace while the beast licked his hands and shivered.

8

Sam and Clement the old musician reclined with their boots toward the round-bellied stove. The seams of the stove glowed red. The dog slept beneath Sam's chair, having spent the day in Clement's company. The warmth of the stove and the resin-smoke that drifted from Clement's pipe made Sam both sleepy and awake. Clement had ordered Sam to drink a medicinal glass of rum, mixed with milk and honey, and he'd drunk it down.

After leaving the American soldiers, Sam had returned to the brothel area, against Sarah Proctor's advice, and he was still haunted by the experience. At that late hour the noise and drunkenness at the brothels was even worse than on the shoreline street. Hundreds of men were lined up outside each of the molly-houses, and down the duckboard paths. Sam thought of Sarah, and possibly his mother, receiving the men one after another, throughout the long night, and the picture of it made him feel ill. There was an angry air among the waiting men who were from all points of the globe. They dressed and spoke different, but each had the same look, and that was frustration at having to wait to fulfil their needs.

Sam made a promise that he wouldn't mention to Sarah that he'd visited the street during the night. Still feeling bad, he instead returned to the familiar environs of the tavern, to sit with Clement while he smoked his resin. But even in the tavern, with his dog beside him, Sam felt distant from the crowded and noisy tableau of drinking and gambling, with the rumbling and shouts and repetitive whorls of the fiddler on stage. From their raised position by the stove, they could see the entire floor.

There was a line out the door that led to twin tables with a dealer playing on one table faro and on the other table monte. Sam didn't know the games, and it seemed the gamblers didn't either, because the purpose seemed to be to slam down your wager in the form of gold coin or bag of dust, and stand back and wait for the turn of a card, and if you won then to bet again until you'd lost everything. Clement explained that there were faro and monte games to be had on most streets, and in American saloons near the plaza square, but the Southlanders made sure to spread rumours that their dealers were the luckiest in the territory. Because gold digging was an occupation defined by luck, Clement said, most miners were crazed with superstitions designed to bring them good fortune. Dutchmen and sailors were considered especially lucky companions, and a Dutch sailor the luckiest of all, but your ordinary man needed to take his luck where he could find it. To make the Southland dealers appear lucky, they'd planted men in the lines out the door, and the dealers made sure to reward their big stakes with big rewards.

There was gold dust visible on the boards beneath the dealers' tables, and Clement told Sam that every morning the old man in the tricorne hat was paid by sweeping up the boards and panning out the dust and that, despite his appearance, the Ancient was one of the richest men on the street.

There were other tables playing poker, and other games Sam didn't know where the participants were sallow and steely-eyed and looked like they lived in their chairs. The tattooed youth Barr stood shadow-framed beneath the lintel that led into the alley, eyes keen and cosh-ready. At the first sign of trouble he waded into the throng and struck out with the leaden purse, and didn't stop until the victims were unconscious, dragging them out by their ankles and tipping them into the street. Nobody seemed outraged, and Barr never once drew his pistol. There was no sign of Keane or Mannix who, according to Clement, still anticipated trouble from The Hounds, and were off making preparations.

Sam's eye returned to it—the patch of floorboard where Dempsey's blood had run out his neck, now laid over with sawdust that was stamped in wine-coloured boot-prints. It was barely two days since Keane had ended the Irishman's tyranny, but under the influence of the rum it felt like an old dream.

If Sam expected Clement to be knowledgeable about the women of Sydney-town then he was disappointed, although the old man was sympathetic when he learned where Sam had been.

'Samuel, if your mother is on that street then I hope you find her soon. They say that a miner ages a decade every year on the diggings, but I count many mollies among my friends and it's no different for them. Time is speeded up in this new colony, on account of the hard work and the money, and the spree that every miner depends upon to look forward to while he's labouring in the dirt. I don't know of any such woman as you've described, but I'll ask around on your account. If she's here then we'll find her soon, but my counsel is not to get your hopes up, even if you find her. Hers is a hard life, and she'll be hardened on account of it. Although the money is better than any other kind of job a woman can do here, just like a miner needs his spree, so too a molly needs her comfort, and for most that comfort is found in the laudanum bottle. I was intending to teach you how to pickpocket in the safety of this tavern, but that can wait. Try to put what you have seen tonight out of your mind.'

Sam nodded and listened to the balm of the old man's talk. Clement wasn't a lag like most of the Australians, but a sailor who'd jumped ship in China, and lived there on the Pearl River with a Celestial wife and harvested tea and grew a taste for the opium resin. He claimed that he didn't drink, because his stomach was painful, and the resin assuaged his many old wounds. He had a kindly face although weathered beyond repair, and his eyes were sharp with an intelligence that voided only when he rubbed his ruined leg, and shifted its weight by hand.

There was a patient ritual associated with the smoking that seemed pious in that raucous company. Clement tenderly rolled a ball of the black stuff in his fingertips, and heated the ball on the end of a sawman's nail, then laid it in the pipe and smoked it dry. The pipestem was brass, and the hot smoke smelled like manured dirt, which Clement exhaled in long clouds that kept their shape under the ceiling. Sam's head spun, and he closed his eyes and opened them again, and fingered the gold nugget that Clement had given him as his first touch of the yeller. It wasn't his to keep but only to meditate upon. He liked its weight and colour even though the nugget was misshapen like a severed ear. Sam stared at the nugget cradled in his palm, and its glow was brighter than a flame, and its weight made him want to secrete it in his boot.

Clement laughed. 'Gold is the storybook of our kind and always a reflection of its owner, truer 'n any mirror.'

Sam made little sense of Clement's statement, but understood that the old man's discourse was a product of the resin affecting his mind, because his own drunken thoughts were tending toward the unusual.

'That is alluvial gold and these here,' Clement whispered, 'are alluvial people. You an' me included. Pushed this way an' that in the darkness despite all gravity, tumbling down shimmerin rivers and imagin ourselves motive with an individual's will. When the alluvial's gone, a whole other kind of man will arrive. Rock miners. Industrials. Men of so-called substance. You will know them by their methods and their manner and their machines. As for these men here,' casting a withered hand, 'they come here looking for the yeller but in actual fact they're lookin for something more precious, even though they are most of them stupid as donkeys and don't know it yet.'

Sam could feel the old man's eyes on him but he couldn't break his gaze upon the gold.

'Son, it won't mean nothing to you, but in that ancient empire of China, I studied in the native script the teachings of the Mahayanan sage Nagarjuna, and Bodhidharma, the founder of Chan teaching, which is my preference as far as these things go. They're as different in practice as night and day but the common principle is that desire is our weakness, our sadness and our burden. Take that gold there in your hand. Now cast your eyes over this bedlam congregation and read therein the general expression.'

Sam did as he was told. The rows of men seated on benches drinking and smoking. The men lined out the door with foolish grins and bags of dust and those at table playing cards. The Ancient behind the bar. The upturned faces of the drunks splay-legged before the fiddler and fife drummer, their eyes closed. The old man called Dirty Tom McAlear who slept with a child's look on his face and made his living eating the dirtiest things offered. Upon satisfying this boast, Dirty Tom was paid with coin by the miners who laughed and watched him eat garbage and drink from spittoons. It was said that he'd been continuously drunk for seventeen years. Beside him was the man called Oofty Doofty, whose age was indeterminate because he made his living as a sideshow to Dirty Tom, by receiving money for being punched in the head, and whose face was one livid bruise, but who had allegedly never been knocked out.

'I would say they are content. Some are outright happy. Even rapturous.'

'Rapturous eh? Boy, you know some words.'

Sam ducked his head. The sweetened rum had made him bold in his language, but the old man clapped his shoulder.

'Boy, that kind of flowerin speech isn't nothing to be ashamed of. You have a sensibility for words and more too, I'd hazard, and you'd best hope that life doesn't wring it out of you. But as to my question, and your answer, which I'm in agreement with. If anything, you understate the matter, although what you've described is the reason I myself am here. The quotient of ignorance is no less in this new dominion, but it has a different tenor and a different taste. Back in old Australia we was all under the yoke. There was the lash and the stock and the gallows. There was always eyes on you. Even that vast Australian bush is full of eyes. But here, my friend, in this lawless domain, it is different.'

Clement wet his lips with a glass of water, but strangely didn't swallow. Wiped his whiskers with the back of a claw. 'And here is wise old Clement, talking turkey, as the Americans say, with a stripling. But you are a good listener, son, which suggests a measure of wisdom, and as for the others gathered here in this circus of inebriation on this distant shore, son, *rapturous* is precisely the word. They come here following the yeller but what they are really following is their heart—no longer in conflict with itself. No longer torn between onerous duty and their heart's desire. Drawn to a flame that will destroy many of them, but in the meantime what you are witnessing in these streets is both rare and precious in the history of our species, even as it is manifest in turmoil. Do you ken what I'm saying, son?'

Sam shook his head, but watched the glowing nub of resin in Clement's pipe as he drew upon it in little sips that filled his lungs with the dung-scented smoke.

'I speak too fast, perhaps, but I believe that you're capable of following my elaborations, the heart of whose meaning is this. You would not believe it from a cursory view of this ragged company, but more so than anywhere else, in this remote town, we are subject to a synchronising with the general philosophic of our times. Lately even sober gentlemen have begun to find civilisation tiresome, and seek instead the thrill of adventure. We welcome them to these shores because in their naïve yearning they are our bread and butter. The scions of the rich and powerful in particular. And Keane has you in mind for some of this work, and that is why I am speaking with you of this matter. This is not a sermon but a school lesson, do you understand?'

Sam was listening but his eyelids had fallen until he regarded only a narrow band of sulphurous light and shadowy movement. He had never felt so good in his life. His body was silent and still, and in the deprivation of clamouring sensation his mind was free. The old man grunted at Sam's nod.

'Keane and I arrived on the same clipper, and slept in the dirt by the shore. We found gold up on the American River and made a fortune until my leg got crushed. Which is why I need this redeeming smoke. But Keane carried me on a mule-cart back to this town, where I presently recovered, and where he refused to leave me marooned and solitary. So he turned to his old ways of bushranging. It was my coin that acquired his firearm, and his arm threw fire that first day and every day since. We don't think it laudatory, but to keep us free, in the words of Mad King Lear, "we'll do such things—/ What they are yet I know not, but they shall be / The terrors of the earth." '

Sam's eyes opened, not to the scene before him, but into a memory that was perfect in its clarity. Seated at the Magistrate's table, late at night, the old man scribbling in his diary while Sam shared the candle-flame. Sam spoke, without hearing himself speak, and the words came from a great distance. 'Still sways their souls with that commanding art / That dazzles, leads, yet chills the vulgar heart.'

Clement roared, and clapped his hands. He gargled and spat, packed his pipe with tobacco. 'You ken the words of Byron the rancorous cripple. Good boy. And were he with us tonight, I would teach you how to fleece him. You are indeed a good listener, Samuel Bellamy. But I have discoursed more than my throat can bear. Now it is your turn. What do you believe? You have lived a life, I can see that. What is it that you believe, having learnt what you know?'

Sam thought to return Clement to the issue of his mother, but he took a moment to ponder on the words and in his drunkeness they were lost to his mouth. The thought of his mother was an apparition that could vanish like smoke around a grasping hand. But while he was thinking of his mother, the memory of the snake returned, and he watched it enter the Magistrate's wattled hut. Sam was alone in his cot, staring out to the yard, where muddy boot-prints broke the rind of silvery frost that led down to the river.

In the trees outside, wattlebirds hawked in their throats and ravens sang out their broken-hearted songs and a chill fog sat heavy over the woodland. Sam was perhaps three or four, and too young for chores and schooling.

The typhoid had nearly taken him as it had taken so many, but the fever had broken. His body was rimed with salt where poisonous sweats had burned the liquids out of him, and his arms were bandaged where the doctor had tapped draughts of his poisoned blood. It was a trial by ordeal, and he'd overheard the Magistrate's wife, who he never managed to call mother, saying that the mongrel Hibernian blood of the Glasgow slums had, in the manner of like for like, seasoned him against the miasma that seeped upland from the river and carried the disease into their huts.

It was true that the serpent abounded in those parts. Where the blacks dug into the muddy riverbank to prise out turtle. In the wetland swales where frogs gathered. On the bald domes of baking granite that bunched like curious eggs in the foothills. On the tracks worn smooth over millennia by clans passing through to the Avon Valley. The scores of serpents, seeking out sun-heat and easy food. Pythons in the trees and the black snake underfoot. The blackfellows ate the pythons but in keeping with their curious aversion for the mussel and the oyster, they refused to eat the black snake. When it entered their camps they beat off their dogs and talked to it like an errant child. To them the raven was a familiar and so was the black snake, likely an uncle or the spirit of a shape-shifting *maban* or medicine man.

Sam's black friends had told him of the dolphins that upon

chanted enticements would gather in the riverine bays and herd schools of fish toward their hunters' spears. Or how the old women chanted until an emu entered their camp, and fell down dead beside the ready fire. Evidence of the serpent's alignment with the blacks' enchantments was the snake's disappearance, around the coming of the first winter rains, when the blacks too disappeared from the great coastal plain and ascended onto the ancient plateau, where the lashing southerly wind was lesser and the kangaroo spread across the grassland tended by fire.

The snake didn't enter the hut like the snakes of summer, each of them curling around the doorframe and flattening along the dark wood like the shadow of a knot. The animals had no ears but were attuned to the slightest tremor, and their red-glowing eyes were angry. The snakes of summer lifted their heads when they neared water, or the native mice that lived in the reed-cladding. They changed the temperature of a room. Their concentration when they turned to you was sufficient to shock a man into stillness. When aroused, their heads arose in a weaving dance, and a hood resembling a burnished cloak shrouded the jewelled eyes and flickering tongue.

But this snake did not slink along the walls. It drew its full length into the sunshine within the doorway, the largest of its kind Sam had seen. It was five yards long and fat as Sam's thigh, sleekly black and glistening with dew. It did not taste the air with its forked tongue because it knew by some intimation that Sam was alone in his cot. He remembered it from his dreams; the serpent who watched from its corner outside the hearth-light, as the Magistrate placed the severed head of a black warrior murdered by settlers on a dinner plate and centred it on the table by candlelight. Thinking Sam asleep, the Magistrate painted the head in his notebook, dipping his bleeding brush in water, blowing on the pages. The Magistrate paused in his meditation of the warrior's head and instead began to compose, scratching the pages with a goose-feather quill, following the notations with little chirrups of sound until his song was complete. He whistled, then sang it back to himself, a choral piece in the manner of Purcell, and seemed pleased. That night while the Magistrate slept, and Sam watched rigid with terror, the snake entered the old man's bed and, unlocking its jaws, began to sheath itself upon the man's head, consuming him in inches painful to watch, until there was only snake.

The Magistrate was troubled enough the following morning to leave off his labours in the vegetable garden, but Sam never mentioned the snake. Now it watched him, mighty in its silence and poise.

'*Wara*!' Sam said, as he had been taught, but the word never left his lips. The snake shifted its bulk, and lifted its head, and something broke inside Sam, although there was no sound. '*Noorn*,' Sam whispered, the serpent's name. And the snake answered, recognised—shivered its flanks, began its silken glide into the bush.

Sam's eyes opened, and his head rocked. Seconds had passed, or hours. Clement took his glass and gargled, spat onto the boards, looking out over the crowded groghouse and nodded to Barr, at his position by the door. He turned to Sam and leaned close.

'Boy, I said this was schooling. Tell me, can you feel anything in the air?'

Sam shrugged himself upright. The drinkers were drinking. The gamers were gambling. There were shouts, guffaws, scraping chairs punctuating the silence. The fiddler, guitarist and drummer had gone silent at a nod from Clement. One by one the dozens of men on the floor began to look around, nudge one another, then look around some more.

Sam cleared his throat, and spat. 'Somethin's comin.'

Clement nodded, wiped his moustaches and slipped out of the blanket draped over his shoulders. He wore a knife at his belt and opened his vest to show Sam the smooth-bore pistol.

'I can smell danger forthcoming and so can the men around you. Let us see what we shall see.'

The man Patrick Ryan emerged in a leather vest from behind the blanket-draped doorway bearing a musket, at whose end was fixed a glinting bayonet. Behind him, Mannix the red-haired giant, toting a rifle, his neck strung with bags of powder and ball.

Clement laughed. 'Patrick, he does favour the musket and bayonet, for its reach. He was caught once between reloads, it ended in a knife fight, and never again.'

The two armed men sat astride a bench along the row from the Americans Sam had brought to the street, who were looking around to increase their number. Several of the company in the room cashed in their chips for gold dust spooned into leather sacks and made to leave. Not a word was spoken, but it was precisely as Clement had prophesied, with more armed men arriving from behind the curtain and more men leaving and nothing but the thickening air to suggest the reasoning.

Barr had turned from the doorway and leaned into the alley, his pistol cocked and primed with ball and powder. A rifle was placed behind him by another man dressed in pelts, who set about priming a musket with a long tamp. He was himself armed with a fowling piece whose barrels were black and octagonal, and lined in his belt were a dozen of the flechettes that Sam had seen upstairs.

Clement had been watching the preparations with the expression of a doting uncle. He turned to pack away his favoured pipe and accessories, which he slipped inside one of his boots.

'This is more than intimation, my son, as I first thought. This is intelligence. There are enemies among us. My advice is for you to take a corner. And this. Keep your finger off the trigger, for the sake of your health and mine.'

Clement examined the bore, pan and lock of his pistol with

a practised eye, then passed it to Sam. 'The corner. Always a corner, with eyes on the doors. You have one shot. Shoot between breaths. Calm thyself beforehand. Shoot, then run.'

But Sam didn't move from his seat. His legs felt long and heavy. When he tried to stand it seemed as though the chair and floor were weighted against his back, and he sat again. The dog repeated Sam's action, although kept its eyes on Clement, who helped the musicians pack away their instruments behind the stack of firewood.

When the wall exploded and the pelted man beside Barr clutched his throat and peered down his nose at the jagged spear of pine embedded there, and Barr climbed off the floor where he had been blown by the mighty percussion, and the next blast of the fowling piece from next door opened up another great hole in the brothel wall and the Australians dived to the benches, Sam was still at his seat beside the glowing stove.

The remnant American party had taken a spray of buckshot and they too rolled a bench and reached for their pieces. There were five of them, and Sam saw Mannix nod toward Patrick, who indicated his agreement. Neither of them fired, saving their ball for the Americans in case they turned on their hosts. But mostly the Americans swore and wiped blood from their pitted faces and looked for means of escape. There were shots from up and down the street and down the alley and from behind the benches and the room filled with smoke and the stink of saltpetre. Barr was on his belly using the dead pelted man as a shield, and the spears of flame from the fowling pieces and muskets and rifles were like sulphurous lightning, and Sam was deafened and gathered the dog and scuttled on his knees behind the stove, whose iron belly rang out with the bashing of shrapnel and buckshot.

He pressed his hands to his ears and closed his eyes but his eyes and nostrils retained the images of fire and the stink of brimstone.

And then it was quiet, and his eyes were open. His hands shook and the dog shivered beside him.

Barr hefted the pelted man's shotgun over his forearm, peered into the gun-smoke. Turned and waved the others past him, who flitted like ghosts between their building and the next. Some shots were fired, while Mannix and Patrick helped the Americans to their feet, and indicated they should leave the back way. Clement emerged from behind the woodpile.

There was cheering from the street. A face powdered black from firing emerged inside the frame of the blasted brothel wall, and nodded. Held up a hand indicating five dead, every man in the room still deafened. A hand clamped Sam's shoulder and he looked up into Clement's face. Saw not weariness but excitement. Sam was led behind the blanket and down some stairs into an alley that smelt of wet grass, then into the street where a briny wind blew off the ocean and men with torches surrounded a kneeling man dressed in the black frockcoat of a minister. Sam's hearing began to return, and he looked to Clement's lips and made out the words, 'Dudgeon. The Hounds' General.'

There were now hundreds in the middle of the road, and more coming. Men and women spilled from the clustered ale and dram and bawdy houses that rose and fell down the street in motley formation like a row of broken teeth. Accents from the counties of the British Islands and the homelands of Australia. Faces illuminated by torch and whale-oil lantern and the full moon that cast a chalky pall over the proceedings. Clement pulled Sam aside, and in his wake the Australian leader Thomas Keane entered the firelight, bareheaded and grim-faced, the great revolver drawn. The Hound struggled against the pairs of hands that fixed him to his knees. He was not wounded or dirtied or cowed. There was defiance in the American's face, although his fate was certain. He spat at Keane's polished boots, and tried again to rise, shouted something lost to the jeering crowd. Keane raised a hand, and the crowd fell silent.

'You can shoot me like a dog, or you can give me the chance—'

More jeering and hoots of ridicule. But the American wasn't begging.

'— to fight…on equal terms.'

Keane smiled, and struck a match off his canvas sleeve. 'You might win the battle, but you've lost the war. What's the point?'

'That is a victory I would cherish, above all mine others. And then your seconds might shoot me down.'

Keane looked around at the shaking heads, but he didn't measure his response against their own. 'It's true enough. If I fall, another will take my place. But The Hounds are gone, and I would die happy. Give him a weapon of his choosing.'

Keane cocked the mighty Colt, and held it to Dudgeon's head. The American looked to the armed men, avoiding their faces, seeking out his favoured armament. Saw Patrick's musket, and made come hither with an urgent hand. Patrick nodded to the men whose hands were upon the American's shoulders, and indicated he should rise. The crowd murmured their apprehension, knowing the musket as a piece with a true aim. They parted in a fearful silence, and fell away against the horse-rails and doorways and plank-board steps. Patrick marched Dudgeon thirty yards into the gloom, the bayonet at his belly, and waited for Clement to cease his whispering to Keane, who stared impassive. Then Keane held up his pistol and shouted, 'I will match the musket's single shot, and then, if no man is fallen, we will take to it with knives.'

He braced himself where he stood, knees slightly bent, feet planted. The great silver Colt mounted across his forearm, his eye trained along its length, to where Dudgeon calmly stood, the musket raised to his shadowed face, both of them made eerie in the moonlight by their whiteness.

Clement pulled Sam behind him, and stood forward, walked to a distance equal between the two men. Raised a white kerchief above his head.

Dropped his arm, and stood back.

Sam not breathing, and no one beside him either. No shot ringing out. Both of the combatants waiting for the other. Keane shifted his weight, and waited for the killing-ball, and when it didn't come, dropped his stance and stood inviting, arms a-stretch.

The musket fired, and Keane didn't flinch. Neither did he fall. He raised the Colt back onto his forearm and sighted quickly, the American pointing the bayonet toward Patrick, daring him to approach. Keane fired, and the muzzle flame and the recoil lifted him, even as the American was lifted, and spun, wrenched onto his face in the dirt. Patrick approached and took back his musket, wiped its stock on his shirt. Saw the nod from Keane, and buried the bayonet in the American's ribcage.

Keane was immediately beset. Cheers and slaps on his head, back and shoulders. Kisses from women. Two men tried to lift him, but he shrugged them away, tolerating further enthusiasms until the groghouse steps, when two of his number barred every man who followed. He did not turn to his admirers, even as Clement took Sam's arm and guided him down the alley, toward the side entrance.

In the wrecked hall, the Ancient in the tattered redcoat stood unmoved, his tricorne hat tilted in its regular gesture of mockery toward its former owner. Sam was passed a mug of porter, which he drank, surprised to find himself cleansed of his earlier intoxication, excepting the humming warmth of his body that wanted him to be still. He helped the men replace the furnishings, standing chairs and lifting tables, sweeping the broken glass.

Keane sat by himself, and nobody approached him. Only Clement patted him as he approached the cache of instruments, and hefted the hurdy-gurdy, took to the nearest stool and balanced his feet. Looking at Keane's bowed head, the Colt still clasped in his friend's hand, the old man began to fill the bag with his breath and soon commenced his warlike drone, filling the hall with an ancient sound. Keane's shame when he met Sam's eye apparent. Not for the combat, or the killing, but for the invitation of his own undoing, the making of himself a willing target. He looked away then, and closed his eyes, gave himself wholly to the dirge.

November 1849

9

The dog bounded across the mudflats so mad and powerful that it appeared to glide upon the silvered surface broken by spurts of sand and water. The three seagulls that were its quarry seemed part of the game as they wheeled about at the end of the beach and flew back along the shoreline so that the dog likewise skidded, and turned toward Sam with crazed eyes and bared teeth, even as the seagulls continued to hover and caw and mock.

Sam watched the dog's adventuring and worked his toes into the mud and felt around for the cockles. The water was shin-deep, and when he captured a mollusc between his toes, he lifted his foot and passed himself the cockle that he placed in a sack over his shoulder. He'd learned this manner of harvesting back on the Swan River, and rightly guessed that the Californian shoreline might offer a similar bounty. At the base of Goat Hill he'd also set crab pots made of scavenged wire in the deeper water baited with fish-head and tripe. There were always big swimmer crabs in the pots when he pulled them in, and their claws were large for the task of getting about in the bay's strong currents. On the rocks about the waterline was crusted a layer of mussels and oysters that he removed with his knife, and they also went into the bag with the cockles.

It was difficult work at the beginning of Sam's day, but he didn't complain because it was peaceful down on the water at that hour. The gentle light on the amber shallows. The wraiths of mist over the forest to the north. The pelicans on the rocks that observed his silent progress across the mudflats until the sun rose over the hills and the pelicans lifted into the sky and the mist burned away and there came the first stirrings of life from the town beside him.

Sam had been in the American colony for three months but there was still no sign of his mother. Rather than journeying to the mining camps of the interior, Clement had counselled Sam to maintain his position with Keane's gang and instead save his money, and learn the skills of survival in this new world. It was hard advice to follow when Sam thought of his mother out there in the diggings, but according to Clement, the pace of the goldrush was such that towns were pulled down and packed up overnight, and moved entire from valley to valley, and there were now hundreds of thousands of people swarming the hills and all of them moving. The chances of finding his mother out there were small, and in the meantime what Clement said was true—Sam could save his money and otherwise keep a weather eye on the comings and goings at Sydney-town.

The other reason that Sam collected the mussels and crabs and cockles and oysters was because shellfish soup formed the main part of his diet. He was lodging for free at Missus Hogan's establishment, which was the name of the hotel he'd found himself in that first morning in San Francisco. The sign down in the muddy courtyard never made it to the front wall of the hotel, but within a few days of taking over the building for Thomas Keane, everybody in Sydney-town knew about Missus Hogan and her lodging house.

Missus Hogan provided Sam lodgings in service to Keane but also on account of Sam gathering the materials for her soup. The only other favour she asked of Sam was that he serenade her while she ripped the beards off mussels and cracked into the private homes of the oysters and lifted them off their sculpted beds and tipped them into her broth. Often when Sam sang his hymns for her, the dog began to croon its own language, and then it was common for the men in the rooms to stand in the hall and listen, and on occasion to enter the doorway of the kitchen if Missus Hogan was amenable.

Sam hoisted the rattan basket weighty with swimmer crabs and shellfish onto his shoulder and felt the water sluice down his back. The dog got underfoot and he nudged it away and listened to the sad gassy hissing of the crabs as they crawled over one another and waged war in a futile attempt to flee the basket.

The morning was cold and the water colder, and Sam coughed and hawked into the rippling waves because the new habit of smoking hadn't settled with his throat and lungs. He looked across the bay that was crowded with ships whose masts were empty because the sails had all been turned into canvas tents and trousers. There was near a thousand ships in the harbour, and most of them were abandoned because the crew of every boat had rushed off to follow the yeller as soon as they arrived. At night you sometimes heard the terrible crack of a new ship entering through the Golden Gate and crashing into an abandoned vessel, because there was no light aboard the crewless hulks, and there was hardly room to get between them anyway. The whole scene resembled a terrible battlefield, or a graveyard of ships, or a dead forest of masts and spars, and the only men who lived out there were the pirates who preyed on the new arrivals, and those men who'd returned broke and sick from the goldfields and couldn't find a place to sleep on land.

Sam quickened his pace as warm burrs of sunlight caught the rim-line of the nearest hills in anticipation of the fresh bread that would soon emerge from Missus Hogan's oven. He was also eager to make a circuit of the nearby groghouses to see if anyone had dropped coins overnight. He was sometimes lucky with a silver dollar or a nugget wedged in a floorboard. He secreted this treasure in the leather purse that hung on a buckskin strap around his neck before heading back to The Stuck Pig, and his regular morning employment of sharpening the knives and bayonets in the armoury, using first a pedalled rotary stone and then a whetstone. If Sam did a satisfactory job he was allowed to take out a rifle or a revolver and practise shooting into the side of Goat Hill, while the dog kept at a distance because he hated the ugly percussion and ran in little circles in the middle of the track with his tail between his legs and wouldn't meet Sam's eye.

The tideline was clogged with driftwood that was tangled in seaweed, and always the hardest part to climb with the heavy load of shellfish, and Sam braced his feet in the loose sand and shifted the basket from one shoulder to the other. Seagulls spun in a tight loop above his head, still cawing and mocking, and the dog howled to them and danced on its back legs and leapt at them if they came too close. There weren't many people on the shoreline street at this hour, but over by the docks there was a new company of men disembarking down gangplanks toward the jetty. The men coming off this steamship weren't Australian, but looked to be Chilenos, or Peruvians, because of their colourful hats and their overlord who stood among them in fine clothes and with a short whip directed the barefoot peons to carry the heavy packs and trunks over to a wagon and lay them there.

The newly berthed steamship was named SS *Oregon* and was well known because it sailed the Panama–San Francisco route. There were a few Americans among the migrants, and by their condition Sam could tell that they weren't wealthy but were ordinary young men. Like the new arrivals of yesterday, and the weeks before, the Chilenos and young Americans didn't waste any time but instead began to troop off the docks toward the plaza square, where they would most likely continue straight out the other side of town toward the nearby hills. Most virgin gold-seekers couldn't afford the paddleboat upriver to Sacramento, and this daily migration of many hundreds who lacked maps usually meant following the man in front, and the churned mud track that disappeared down the peninsula.

Back on the shoreline street, Sam followed the dog past the

horse stables and down the alley to the rear of Missus Hogan's. He kicked open the gate and edged sideways into the muddy courtyard. The smell of the privy was strong behind the wall of mildewy sheets hung to dry in the yard where the mud was green-tinged, and sucked at Sam's toes. There was a wooden bench against the back wall that he hefted the basket onto. He went and collected a pail of water from the horse-trough to refresh the sea animals, before knocking on the rear door.

Mister Hogan stuck his head out, and grunted and was then shoved aside so Missus Hogan could eye the catch. She smiled and winked at Sam, who went back to the trough and stripped off his shirt and began to wash the fishy juices off his shoulders and hands and legs. He ducked his entire head in the trough and washed his hair and face and neck, before drying himself using an old horse-blanket special for the purpose. Beside him, the dog got up on its front paws and drank from the trough in a delicate way.

Inside Missus Hogan's kitchen Sam warmed himself by the hearth-fire, and drank a mug of tea while the soup pot came to a boil and a loaf of soda bread cooled. Mister Hogan peeled potatoes seated on an old barrel and whistled some Irish song. The sun was barely risen but he was already drunk, although it was true that Sam hadn't seen Mister Hogan in a sober state at any time of day or night.

Missus Hogan entered the kitchen and unheeding of the snapping claws took hold of the crabs and dropped them into the cooking pot. She wore an old patterned dress and a heavy canvas apron stained all the colours of blood and jam and pickle. She rested her great boots on the edge of her stool and began to separate out the mussels and oysters from the basket. When she finished, she dropped great handfuls of cockles into the stock while casting a disapproving eye at her husband who was staring at a patch of dusty light instead of peeling.

Missus Hogan began to hack into the loaf of bread and pass

the slices to Sam, who placed them in his lap and reached for the plate of dripping.

'There's deer-stew in the clay pot by your feet, Samuel. You're welcome to take it to share with Clement, and there'll be soup here ready for your return. In the meantime, when you've finished eating, that second loaf should be baked plenty if you'd assist me by getting it out.'

Sam swallowed the last of his bread and dripping and wiped his hands on his soaked trousers and knelt and opened the oven door. With some blackened tongs he drew out the loaf and placed it on the cob. The soup came to a boil beside him, and as the steam began to rise to the ceiling, as though summoned by the smell, he heard the muttering and grumbling and hawking and bootscraping of Missus Hogan's lodgers arising and getting dressed.

'Here come the Devil's Army,' she said. 'Concealing their lizard wings beneath frock-coats, and their horns beneath hats.'

Sam grinned. 'You wish me to set the table?'

'No lad, the first one down is the genuine hungriest. He can array the plates and spoons for the rest of the curs.'

The residents of Missus Hogan's lodging house were Australians of the criminal persuasion. Their schemes were varied but they each fenced their stolen goods to Missus Hogan against the price of their rent, and for as little as she could pay. They brought her goods such as pocket watches, and silver chains and wedding bands, and silver tobacco boxes stolen by cunning or force in the better streets to the north of the plaza, which Missus Hogan kept in an iron strongbox beneath the floorboards of her kitchen. She showed the cutthroats nothing but contempt, in order to keep the prices low, but still they loved her as a representative woman of the Southland who many called Ma. The braver ones even teased her around dinnertime, but the image of her working a butcher's cleaver against the flank of a goat or deer usually put them to a respectful silence. According to Missus Hogan, Sam shouldn't trust none of them, seasoned as they were in the arts of charm and deception, but who were likely to abuse him for a girl if given the chance.

Sam left the kitchen to the sight of Missus Hogan sharpening her cleaver while glaring at her husband snoring in his corner. He returned upstairs to his room to put on his suit. His room was as he'd left it, with his bed made and the single chair squared against the wall, just as he'd been trained in the Boys Home. His suit hung from a nail in the wall, and his boots were stood in formation beneath. He took down his suit and smacked off the dust and laid it on his bed, stepping out of his wet drawers and wiping the mud from his toes with a clumped rag. When he was dressed and his bootlaces were tied he drew fingers through his hair. From the small cardboard box beneath his pillow he extracted a gold nugget and three timepieces and a half-dozen gold and silver dollars and placed them among his pockets, then emerged onto the balcony and locked his door. He'd just started toward the stairs when an Englishman by the name of Vaughan stepped out of his room and barred Sam's way. Keeping a wary eye on the dog, Vaughan leaned into Sam's ear and spoke softly.

'Boy, I have a story that I think will be of interest.'

Sam thought only to get past the man, but Vaughan wouldn't step aside. Sam knew Vaughan as a pickpocket, who while resident at the lodging house generally got about in his grey woollen underclothes, whose arse-flap had no buttons. He was one of the men who regularly plagued Sam with their attentions, claiming that he was a stage performer waiting for a suitable company, in that no theatre types had yet arrived on that shore.

'Just a few minutes of your time, son.'

'Mr Vaughan, I got to—'

'I know, boy, but hear me out. I've struck up a friendship with a Yorkshireman, newly arrived and in the company of his wife and three children. Now, would you meet with this man and hear what he has to say? This man intends a school for the colony, and he thinks you a useful addition as both helper and pupil.'

'Sorry, Mister Vaughan, but I ain't interested. Bein indentured was my fate back in Van Diemen's Land, and here I got other designs.'

Sam tried to step backwards but the man's arms held him firm.

'I'll confess to you, Samuel, that the schoolmaster has promised a fee for the introduction, and possibly a position as teacher of dramatics and song. Would you oblige me by meeting him? There's nothing to be lost in declining his offer, but at least I'll receive some coin in my pocket, which I'll gladly share with you.'

There was a mad look in Vaughan's eye, and Sam decided that it was due to the desperateness of the Englishman's situation, and so he nodded and followed. He could meet the Yorkshireman schoolmaster and go direct from there to meet Sarah Proctor.

They departed the lodging house and walked the shoreline street. Vaughan wore his green suit garlanded with a thieved watch-chain as well as a new bowler hat. The groghouses were mostly empty at that hour, and at the steps of The Stuck Pig the old man in the tricorne hat sat astride the plank-boards panning the floor-sweepings with an iron basin, to which he added water from a tankard. He greeted Sam with a toothless grin. Even from a distance of ten yards Sam could see the glinting of gold flake and dust in the sediment. Vaughan doffed his hat but the other man only watched coldly. The dog went to him, and sniffed his trousers, then rejoined Sam and like them peered into the recesses of the groghouses whose doors never closed, and where now blankets were beaten and the general odour was that of gunpowder from the purging of miasma, whose smoke drifted toward the crude shacks on Goat Hill behind them.

They passed the docks that were under construction, and the dog ran to the waterline and sniffed at the dead things lumped in weed and caked in brown foam. Beyond the half-formed docks was the main jetty, lined with merchant ships. Sam assumed the jetty their destination, but Vaughan paused on the sandy shore and took off his hat and waved it at a ship several furlongs out in the bay. He received an answer in the form of a shout, and presently two men clambered down some netting into a dinghy.

Sam backed away a few steps, confused. That ship he knew to be a merchant vessel who plied the Sandwich Islands route, where the richer men sent their shirts to be boiled and starched and ironed. Sam knew this because Clement had joked about the merchants who because of the shortage of domestic help in the city, thought it preferable to send their dirty washing on a journey that might take one month, or even more if the shirts went to Shanghai, such was the importance of appearance to a paper-collar gentleman.

'What's goin on here, Mr Vaughan? I don't see no schoolmaster hereabouts.'

Vaughan occupied himself inserting some snuff in his nostrils while the dinghy approached, and when finally he turned, he seemed about to speak in friendliness then thought better of it, and grabbed Sam and pinned his arms. He was strong for such a small man and grasped Sam about the throat so that he couldn't shout. The dog growled, and began to dance around them as the dinghy cut across the longshore current and rode the wash, and Sam could see the men grinning.

So he was to be sold, and made a shipboard slave.

Sam began to twist and stamp his feet on Vaughan's shins, but that only made Vaughan lift him off the ground and tighten his throat-grip, and now Sam couldn't breathe. The dog danced around and lunged in, and took a hold on Vaughan's knee, and Vaughan grunted but didn't shout. Then there was a mighty clap, and some of it caught Sam's ear, and suddenly he was facedown in the sand. There were more slapping blows and Sam was winded and the dog snuffled his face, and behind the dog he could see the dinghy had turned away, and was making back to the ship. Sam was rolled over and he looked up into the bruised and skewed face of Oofty Doofty, whose eyes were large with excitement. Sam groaned, couldn't hear what Oofty said because of his deafened ear, and he looked over and there was Dirty Tom McAlear sitting on Vaughan's chest. Vaughan was retching under the weight of Dirty Tom's notorious stench, and Dirty Tom saw that Sam was watching and punched Vaughan in the face and Vaughan went quiet.

Sam left them on the beach while Oofty guided him across the shore, and into the street, then up the steps into The Stuck Pig, where the Ancient who'd sent Oofty and Dirty Tom to observe Sam's position awaited him with a mug of tea. The old man didn't say anything to Sam, but passed the mug of tea and patted Sam's shoulder and went back to his panning. One look at Vaughan and he'd understood the man's nature, and therefore his likely enterprise.

Sam sat quietly at an empty bench, angry because he'd been so stupid, even after Missus Hogan had warned him. He finished his tea, and nodded his thanks to the Ancient, and called the dog and went out into the streets. He walked up toward the crowded plaza square. His eyes were sharp on the faces as the voice of self-reproach continued in his head.

As was his usual custom, Sam next stood across the road from the Chinaman haberdashers and watched for signs of the Chinese girl, of which there was none.

On the porch beside him there was arrayed three tables where men played vingt-et-un, and he had a clear line of sight across the street and down the alley where he'd first seen the girl. Sam hoped for nothing more than a glimpse of her, while in the meantime he occupied his fingers with Clement's schoolwork—picking his own pockets of the timepieces and coins, slipping fingers inside the jacket where the heaviest timepiece sat clipped with a silver chain, although today his fingers too seemed angry, and he could feel them inside his pockets and that only made him angrier.

He doubled his concentration while practising the various manoeuvres taught to him by Clement in the tavern: the fishing for chain and gentle lifting of the watch from a vest pocket; the making a pincer of his hand so to extract a fat wallet from a jacket or a back pocket; the insertion of his middle fingers into a forward pocket to lift out a coin in the manner that the Chinese ate with their twin sticks, and always the governing principals of patience and nerve and a ready eye on avenues of escape. When Sam could pick his own pockets without noticing, then he would be ready to practise on the drunks in the tavern, under the armed gaze of Clement or Barr, who would both intervene to protect him.

Sam eyed a drunk man watching the turn of cards beside him, first employing Clement's advice to identify whether a quarry was worthy of robbery. This man was swaying in his boots, and his hands looked rough and reddened by hard work, although his clothes were not the red serge shirt and canvas trousers of the recent arrival but the fine broadcloth suit and plug hat of the successful miner. There were gold rings on each of his fingers, and Sam was sure gold necklaces inside the paper-collar shirt. Because he was feeling angry and a little reckless, Sam nudged the miner behind the knee as he had been taught, and stood back ready to apologise. The man staggered round and Sam caught the glinting of gold teeth, a newly common practice, and a heavy gold watch-chain at the man's vest. Sam steadied the man by taking his forearm, as he'd been instructed, and distracted him with practised words of contrition, although he didn't move for the great gold seal that hung from the man's neck on a thick gold chain.

The miner's eyes were red and his breath was foul, and Sam stepped away, and apologising a final time with raised hands backed onto the street. There had been something in the miner's eyes as he looked down at Sam's face, and he pressed his fingers against his throbbing cheek and felt the swelling around his eye. The puffed skin had gone silky, and Sam knew that the bruise would blacken. He had gone but a few steps when he heard jeering and cheering, and saw ahead the Englishman Vaughan, knee-deep in the muck and entirely naked, hobbling up the thoroughfare. The townsfolk parted to let him through, and Sam joined them to observe the man whose hands covered his privates, his hair plastered over his face, and then the silence as the Englishman passed and Sam like the others saw the terrible welts and red stripes across his back.

10

It was too early to report to the American harbourmaster in his cabin at the end of the jetty, who knew what was in the hold of every ship. As Sam did every morning, he left the churned streets and headed down the rows of molly-houses that lined the blocks inside the Australian quarter. As always, Sarah Proctor was sitting on the ground floor porch of her brothel on a rocking chair with her legs in the sun, smoking a cigar. She wore rouge on her lips, and her newly long hair was combed out and warmly glowing, but as Sam bent to climb the steps he saw that Sarah too had a black and swollen eye.

'Lookit you, Samuel Bellamy. Did someone catch you stealin, or did you likewise walk into a doorknob?'

Sam grinned and waved away the enquiry, and the dog rushed to Sarah and buried its head in her lap, staring fondly at her, pleading for a scratch.

'You're just in time. I was set to preparin breakfast.'

Breakfast for Sarah Proctor was a mugful of her favourite drink of hot chocolate, boiled on a brazier like they boiled tea in Australia. The raw chocolate was bought in great chunks from the markets of the plaza and cost very little as it was sourced from Mexico. Sarah drank her chocolate laced with rum, but Sam drank the muddy brew in a tall mug mixed with cream, which was a luxury item due to the lack of dairy cows in that territory. Every few sips she spilled some on the boards for the dog, who sat before her and whose eyes followed her every move.

Sam had learned her ritual of making the chocolate, and while the dog continued to nudge its nose between her legs, and rest its head on her belly and look up at her with beseeching eyes, he knelt and took up the block of chocolate and began to scrape it with his knife. When there were sufficient scrapings he tipped them into the pot that was already filled with water. He struck a match and held it to the newspaper and kindling that was ready in the brazier, and when the fire was crackling he placed the pot on the fire and watched it carefully in case the flames went out. He wiped the two tin mugs with his finger and nodded to Sarah.

'You want me to add yer rum?'

Sarah Proctor passed the bottle that she'd cradled in her lap and which was near empty. Sam poured the rest of the bottle into her mug and put it beside his own. He took his regular position on a low wooden stool and mimicked Sarah's posture by putting his legs out onto the railings and inclining his face into the sunlight.

'A doorknob you reckon?' he asked her.

Sarah winked with her good eye. 'You should see my opponent. Wicked Amy we call her. We all got our favourite town men, and it's an agreement that we don't steal them that's regular customers, but she won't never listen. Sometimes she needs remindin but she saw it comin and got me first.'

Now Sam looked at her closely, and like every morning, Sarah shook her head, and that and the pang of disappointment he felt was enough to tell Sam that she'd had no luck finding his mother, and that they needn't speak of it further. He knew that Sarah worked till dawn, and that her nights were rough and long, and so most mornings they didn't talk much but drank their chocolates and watched the street and every manner of strangeness to be found among the dress and customs of the folk from all regions of the globe. Their experience of Anderson Dempsey's tyranny on the American whaler was a bond between them, and their ritual of sitting in companionable silence was what he imagined a brother and sister might do.

Sometimes Sarah's friends came into the sunshine to join her, and they played with the dog, and teased Sam and messed his hair, and spoiled him with little treats of hard candy and silver coin if he wrote a letter to their sweethearts back in Australia. They were mostly young women who spoke in a manner of code when they didn't want Sam to understand, although on occasions he heard them quarrelling in their quarters upstairs and their anger was something to behold. Sarah then nudged Sam with her bare foot and told him to get.

On three occasions in those first weeks Sam was reluctantly drawn to tell the story of his father's butchery at the hands of the black warrior. Sarah's hope was that the particularities of the narrative might trigger a recollection in one of the dozens of women who came to listen, until she eventually forbade their asking on account of Sam's discomfort. It was his secret, shared only among the women, for Sam hadn't told any of the Coves apart from Clement and Keane about his reasons for being there, and no other had asked.

But the women, by and large, thought the search for his mother a romantic quest, and in particular favoured the story of how he'd made passage to San Francisco. The women would sit closer, and listen, and none of them looked sceptical because they each had a story that was similar to Sam's own.

The women leaned in to hear his quiet voice, and he told them how he'd persuaded one of the overseers at the Vandemonian Boys Home to investigate his mother's whereabouts in the colony. Sam had learned that his mother had been granted her ticket-of-leave three years previous, and according to all reports had journeyed to Sydney in the company of a sealskin merchant. With the overseer's permission, Sam wrote a letter to that merchant and learned that his mother was off 'whorin on the Rocks'.

The following week Sam wrote another letter, this time to the overseer, apologising for his treason, then broke into the superintendent's office and stole a silver watch and chain, and a silver letter-opener, and five shillings in change.

He made for the Launceston port directly, with nothing to eat but a loaf of bread and the knowledge that the merchant's clippers sailed regular to the New South Wales colony. He slept in a cave in the nearby gorge during the day, and at night he went down to the docks. When the clipper made port and was loaded with sealskins he slipped aboard and hid himself in the hold amongst the reeking cargo, and stowed away for the week it took to make Sydney. He was so hungry that he chewed the sealskins, and ate raw flour, and licked the condensation off the rough wooden ribs of the ship as it rolled through the waves.

At the port he was discovered by a sailor, and beaten, but not turned over to the peelers on account of his parting with the silver letter-opener. He bought bread and biscuit that first night, and slept in bushland on the edge of the settlement, and by day enquired around the brothels after his mother. He was by and large treated kindly by the colonists, although the sick feeling that developed over that first week was the understanding that his mother mightn't want to be found. After all, she'd been free for three years and had made no enquiries back in the Swan River about her children.

One night Sam made friends with the dog, who appeared beside him on the shoreline while he stared into the black waters. Sam was at that moment pitiful crying, and the dog arrived at his side like it was summoned by his sadness and desire for company. The dog was merely a puppy, starved and lame where it had been cruelly mistreated.

Sam carried it back to his camp behind the tree-line and shared his dinner and they were loyal partners ever since. The Sydney Rocks was a frightening place at night, and from their hill they looked down at the eerily lit shacks and narrow sandy tracks and listened to the fiddle music that was punctuated by shrieks and roars and things being broken.

Sam continued his enquiries until all his money was spent, and then he saw the advertisements for California, and he learned about a woman who might be his mother, because she had red hair and her story contained a history in Van Diemen's Land and the Swan River colony. But she was gone weeks earlier, he was told, with a band of other mollies. Asking around at the docks he learned with barely an hour's notice that an American whaler was departing for California, and that it was taking passengers. He didn't like the fearsome aspect of the crew but decided to abandon his country and his worldly goods at his camp, and everything that he didn't carry in his knapsack. He sat there and felt sick with nerves until he finally approached the Captain, and offered the silver watch as payment, and then he and the dog were pointed toward the whaler.

So began the story of Dempsey and his tyranny, although it was Sarah Proctor who told the other women about the mutiny and the murder, and their eventual escape onto the shore of San Francisco, and Dempsey's execution at the hands of Thomas Keane.

At the termination of the story some of the women would pat Sam's arm or ruffle his hair, and some of them offered their own stories, to which he listened with the equal patience they'd offered him. They otherwise consoled him, and made pretend love to him if they thought him unhappy in appearance, and laughed when he blushed, so easily overwhelmed by the power they had over him.

But there was never a hint of recognition, or any recollection of a band of Sydney mollies under the charge of a madam arriving in a party. None of the women said what Sam understood was on their minds, on account of the rumours of the many ships that had sunk on the way to America.

The water came to the boil and the dog stood back in fear of the hiss against the rim of the pot that it knew was coming. Sam stirred the chocolate a final time with a fork and used a cloth to protect his hand while he tipped the brew into their cups. It was only now that Sarah Proctor opened her eyes. She took her cup and put her lips to it and gave him the barest smile.

'Tastes good, thank you Samuel. I been breakin my fast on this bottle on account of not bein able to sleep. And no, I ain't gonna tell what happened with Wicked Amy. There's nothing but shame and stupidity in the tellin for all players. But I will say that you look mighty fine this morning. Where is it you're headed next?'

Sam shrugged, and looked down into his mug. The thin brown water on the top. He swirled the mug and drew up the sediment and put his lips to it. He knew that despite her affection for him, Sarah envied his position as a man of Sydney-town, who went wherever he wished and did whatever he wanted. In actual fact, he didn't do what he wanted, but that was how it looked.

Down on the street a middle-aged woman paused and looked their way. She was dressed in the French fashion, wearing high leather boots and a flounced skirt of green velvet, and a red caped jacket with bell-shaped sleeves, holding a parasol in her gloved hands. The moment that Sarah saw the woman her face changed, and she leaned forward and started to sneer.

'Hey darlin, are you lost? I think you gone and walked down the wrong street.'

The woman was proudful in bearing but she still blushed, looking around and pretending she hadn't heard. Sarah rose to her feet and doubled the volume of her mockery. 'Don't tell me you're givin it away, love! Don't tell me you're makin that mistake? Come up here an' join me for a rum. I'll set you straight about a few things. I can see you is lost and mistaken in your directions.'

Sarah's call was taken up by other women down the street, some of whom began lewd whistling while others made love to the woman with shouted endearments. The well-dressed visitor turned and fled as fast as she was able, using her parasol to pitchfork the mud when she slipped.

Sarah's face remained fixed in anger until the woman was gone from sight, then she winked at Sam with her good eye.

'We can't be entertainin tourists like we're monkeys in a cage, Samuel.'

'I understand.'

The flush of anger was gone from her face, but her eyes were still alive with an odd light. Now that he knew Sarah better, there were often unguarded moments like this when he looked at her and saw the child that she'd been in her features, and those moments made him feel even more tender toward her.

'Samuel, you didn't tell me how you got your own shiner,' she said, not looking at him.

'I'll gladly relate that story to you, but first, tell me again about London,' he said. 'Them summer days when you'd go out the commons with your sisters. Tell me about them birds and animals that you'd see.'

Sarah Proctor laughed, then started on her hacking morning cough brought on by the hot cocoa. She drank down the rest and tipped the dregs on the boards for the dog, then settled back on the chair and drew her skirts up higher so the sun touched her knees.

'Well, we only went on Sundays, see, because...'

11

A downy grey chicken feather was crusted in the muddy rim of Sam's right boot. He bent in his chair and prised it off and looked around the room. The Mayor's clerk had gone, and Sam tucked the tattered feather under his seat and resumed his posture of sitting and waiting for the Mayor to call him. The Mayor was in the office next door, but it was no grand establishment like you would expect. The two-storey sandstone building smelt like it used to be a barn, and the planks of the old wooden staircase were loose in their carriage posts and there was no balustrade either. The walls were cracked because of the earth-shakes, and the deeper cracks had been stuffed with mud and straw. Even so, Clement had ordered that Sam wear his best clothes for this delivery, and Sam had dutifully scrubbed his face and hands with carbolic, and ladled icy water over his back to get rid of the smell of crab and cockle and mussel. The delivery to the Mayor was a promotion for Sam, and he wanted to make the best impression.

The sitting room was dark beneath the joists and beams and shingles of the exposed roof. There were swift nests up there and spider webs that in the weak light appeared like finely spun glass. Sam could look past his feet through the floorboards onto the cobbled ground where the Mayor's clerk in his black suit was boiling a kettle in a corner hearth whose chimney was made of river stones.

Like the Mayor, the clerk was a Mormon and dressed in a black suit with a white shirt and black tie. He smoked a cigar while he waited for the kettle to boil, running a hand through his long hair. He looked up at Sam and spat on the floor, shifting on his haunches. He hadn't been friendly to Sam upon his arrival, and his expression told Sam that this wasn't going to change. A swift landed on the chair beside Sam and stood there on its delicate feet darting glances around the room, ignoring him as part of the furniture. It flew to a corner and retrieved a piece of straw from a pile of sweepings, and flew back into the roof and began its shrill chorus. Sam closed his knees around the leather bag that was the purpose of his visit. It wasn't heavy, and so likely didn't contain gold, and nobody had told him not to look inside but he didn't anyway.

After dressing himself and eating his daily ration of shellfish soup at Missus Hogan's kitchen, he'd gone to Clement in The Stuck Pig and received his orders. The old man was grave in manner because Mayor Bannon was, he said, one of the most important but also most dangerous men in the colony. Clement retained the leather bag while they sat on a bench-seat because he could see that Sam was eager to do his duty.

'Don't be fooled by the sobriety of Bannon's dress and speech. Like some painted king, his actions cannot be predicted.'

And so Sam waited for the Mayor to open his door. He lacked a timepiece, and instead measured the length of his waiting by the number of times the family of swifts returned to the sweepings pile and gathered material for their nest, and the fact that the Mayor's clerk had now smoked three cigars and had drunk two mugs of coffee downstairs.

Presently the clerk climbed the stairs. He thumbed cigar ash in the sweepings corner, looked at the leather bag and indicated for Sam to follow. There was no handle on the Mayor's door and the clerk merely pushed it open to the reveal the Mayor, not praying as Sam had assumed, or studying from his holy book, but reading the newspaper with a vexed expression while the loose pages were cast about his desk and across the floor.

Mayor Bannon was a big well-fed man with black moustaches

and angry brown eyes, and huge red hands that he beckoned toward Sam, who approached and proffered the leather bag. Bannon didn't open it but placed it under the table while he looked Sam up and down. Clement had schooled Sam toward adopting the posture of someone resolute, but also respectful and impressed by the dignity of the man's office. He held Bannon's eye for the appropriate measure and then looked away and put his hands at his belt and waited. Apparently satisfied with what he saw, Bannon nodded to the clerk, then returned to his reading of Sam.

'Are you a Christian, boy?'

'I was raised so, yes sir.'

Bannon looked sceptical. 'I'm not given to proselytising, but on the matter of nationhood I except myself. You'll make a fine American, son, I can see that. For we need white men in this territory. But in the meantime, is it true that there are blacks in your colony called New South Wales? And if so, how did they come to be there?'

Sam had been advised to humour Bannon, and to not rile him, and so he pretended a thoughtfulness that he didn't feel. 'I assume they've always been there sir. Beyond that, I wouldn't hazard—'

Bannon held up a hand and cocked his head like he'd caught a nearby sound. 'Curious. For the redskin natives of this land are certainly descended from a lost tribe of Zion, of which there are others still strayed from the shepherd. Would you say, based upon your observances of the black men of your homeland, that they too might contain the holy seed and derive their ancestry from the sacred land of Israel?'

Sam looked to his boots, which had left prints of dried mud. 'I couldn't say, sir.'

'... because if you even suspect that they carry the holy spark, it behoves you to return to your native land and bring them back into the flock, wouldn't you say? And for this purpose I can supply you, should you be called.'

Sam thought of Thomas Keane in his own office, feet up on the plank-table, smoking his cheroot and watching Sam through the blue-grey smoke. Keane was a convicted bushranger and known murderer who hid nothing of his exploits and declared them fully.

Bannon on the other hand was a church leader and mayor who ordered murders and lived by tithing the criminal elements of the town. If he suffered from the censure of his Mormon God then he didn't show it in his speech or his dress or manner.

The clerk behind Sam coughed and scraped his boots and Bannon looked at him and took some kind of signal that he should desist in his speechmaking. He offered a cigar, which Sam pocketed, bowing and taking the cotton satchel proffered by the clerk, who was even more mean-looking up close. Sam thanked the clerk and turned and thanked the Mayor again, and went out into the sitting room and put on his hat, and watched the family of swifts race around the perimeter of the roofline so fast that the beating of their tiny wings made a baffled sound that followed him down the stairs and into the street.

12

Sam knew the contents of the satchel and saw the sheaf of papers with his own eyes when he arrived at the cabin built onto Goat Hill.

He was puffed after hiking up the dirt track. He paused to take a view of the cove, with its ghost fleet of marooned ships and the haze of wood smoke over Sydney-town; at the sight of the canvas shantytown behind the plaza square and the old Spanish Mission across the flatlands to the south. He knocked on the cabin door and was invited to enter by a gruff voice.

Inside the cabin were three men working who were Keane's best forgers. They occupied a table that was brightly lit by whale-oil lamps despite the sunshine streaming in the open windows. On the table were different kinds of inks and feathers and stamps and blotters made of calfskin stretched and nailed into place. The three men were equally old. Two of them were identical brothers who wore spectacles and barely looked up when he entered. Sam passed the satchel to the grey-bearded man who was their leader and whose nose resembled a turnip dug from the field. The man fastidiously wiped his hands against his apron and then opened the satchel, and slid out the sheaf of papers and grunted his approval. He took up a magnifying glass and bent over the first paper that was a blank title deed stamped and signed by Bannon. Forgery was a lucrative business in the new colony, and these lags were Keane's favourites because they were expert in crafting facsimiles that authorised ownership to mining leases in the hills, or to town plots, which were sold to gullible new arrivals. Bannon supplied the official forms, and these scriveners filled out the claims with perfect cursive script of the government type, so akin to the originals that it was impossible to tell who legitimately owned what and with no way of settling the matter excepting by warfare.

It was plain from the manner of the three old men that they regarded their craft with the utmost seriousness. The old man with the bulbous nose looked over the papers one by one, grunting his satisfaction and then carefully turning the page and leaning once more into the clear light cast from the nearby lamps. Sam took his leave, carefully shutting the cabin door behind him, not lingering over the view because he was eager to be reunited with his dog, who was with Clement and would be pining for him.

The dog was good at forgiveness, and sat with its snout wedged between Sam's thighs, and looked up at him with loving eyes, its tail beating on the floorboards while Sam scratched around its ears and the favoured red ridge upon its forehead. They had dined on the tavern stew, which the Ancient simmered in a giant pot behind the bar, and which never ran out because it was daily replenished with whatever was at hand. The stew today contained navy beans, meat, potatoes, carrot and chunks of navy biscuit that even after hours of stewing was tough to chew. Sam gave these to the dog, which he gulped down, and asked for more with a little whine that was a precursor to his regular burst of outright howling, and that all the men thought a great joke.

At the table with Sam was Clement, stringing a fiddle with catgut, and Keane, and two Irishmen who were from New York, drinking rye whisky and becoming loud in their teasing of one another.

Clement leaned closer and indicated with his chin the two New Yorkers. 'Those two Irishmen are emissaries from a New York political party who call themselves Democrats. We don't trust Mayor Bannon to hold the course, and so Keane is treating with these Democrats to support the Australian cause when elections come. The Nativists, who support the merchants, and the Democrats are bitter in their enmity, and each employ henchmen. That man Charlie Duane with the red moustache is the right hand of the Democrat leader Patrick Casey, beside him. Casey's not a bad sort of man, but watch out for Duane, he's a killer. They both get to drink free in Sydney-town, and you'll be seeing them at our poker tables, where their winnings are guaranteed. That is the price of business, which is another way of saying that it's the price of democracy.'

Sam watched the henchman Charlie Duane pick his teeth with a fingernail, then drink from his glass of rye and gargle and swallow. Sam looked at him closely because of Clement's description of the man as a killer. Sam had lately known plenty of killers, and he was always looking for something constant in them. Some look in their eyes or mark in their expression. Some feeling they caused by their presence. But there was nothing about this man different to any other, excepting perhaps a certain arrogance in his movements; taking up more space than he needed, and drinking like there was a fire inside him that needed dousing. Keane on the other hand sat quietly, like he always did. Every killer seemed to be different, and that was likely because what Clement said about killers was true—that they were only killers because they'd learned that killing a man was no more significant than blowing your nose. This understanding was more deadly than the act of killing itself, according to Clement, especially in the hands of a king or a general or a pope, because if killing felt like nothing, then so too death was nothing. One death or a thousand deaths or a million deaths—each and together meant nothing.

Duane wasn't a big man, but his grey woollen three-piece suit was new and the green top hat that he wore was also new and cocked back on his head. He caught Sam watching him and wiped his coppery moustache with the back of his hand and raised the same hand in friendliness. Sam responded in kind although they were only feet apart, because the Democrats leader Patrick Casey was expounding upon some point that he punctuated by beating his fist on the table. He wasn't angry, and in fact appeared to be telling a joke, although his singsong voice didn't match the hardness in his eyes or the tension in his limbs or the set of his jaw.

Then they heard the familiar sound of knuckle on bone, and turned as one and there was Oofty Doofty, who sat with a crash on a stool and toppled off backwards and fell silent on the boards. No man had ever knocked out Oofty with a single blow, and that fact guaranteed his income, but there he was, unconscious on his back. The players at table laid down their cards, and the drinkers hushed, and all looked to the man who had launched the blow. He was tall and clean-shaved, and dressed like an American in polished boots and woollen suit, but when he spoke it was with an Irish accent.

'He said I should hit him. And I but tapped his forehead. I meant him no harm.'

Dirty Tom McAlear was at Oofty's side, peeling back his eyelids. He looked hard at the tall stranger, but said nothing.

'He's here. Yankee Sullivan!'

The tall man turned at the sound of his name. It was Charlie Duane, risen from his seat and spreading his arms wide. 'Boys, this is Yankee Sullivan, the American boxing champion, who like yeselves hails from the Southland, come over to work with us on the elections.'

But Sullivan looked past Duane to Thomas Keane, smoking a cigar and smiling. 'Tom Keane, is that you? I'm fresh off the Panama boat, and I heard there was a Thomas Keane to be had in this establishment, but I doubted the news.'

The two men of equal height and stature embraced. Keane called over Clement, who rose and put away his fiddle. Sam watched the introductions and in particular the hands belonging to the fighter, which were large and scarred. Sullivan caught him watching, and winked. Soon they were all drinking at table; Sam fetching the refills of porter and whisky, with Sullivan calling for a pisco punch, which he'd heard was the native drink of San Francisco. Sam had to retrieve a bottle of the Peruvian spirit from Hell Heggarty's dram-house down the street, and some fresh pineapples from the plaza square, but by the time he'd returned Sullivan was drinking whisky like the others, and Sam passed the cocktail makings to the Ancient, who looked at them askance and stowed them away.

Sam took his position on the bench. While collecting the pisco from the dram-house he'd witnessed a private moment between the wild Irishman Hell Heggarty and Keane's man Barr, both of them inside the shadowed doorway. Heggarty was the bigger and older man, and he held Barr in an embrace from behind, his arms gentle-clasped around the younger man's waist while he nuzzled Barr's neck. Both of their eyes were closed in a kind of rapture. It was the tenderness of the embrace which surprised Sam, who lingered outside the doorway rather than disturbing them. For a full two minutes the men stood, saying nothing and leaning into one another, as though every moment was precious. Sam knew that men used other men as women, because he had seen as much in the Boys Home, but he didn't know that there might be love. He felt surprised by this knowledge but also betrayed. The adult world that he remembered from Australia was full of masks and disguises, but it wasn't like that for the people of Sydney-town.

The understanding triggered in Sam a determination to act, to show them what he might become. He slid closer to Duane on the pretext of refilling his whisky, keeping his place beside the Irish Democrat whose glass was emptied every few minutes. Duane was turned in his seat, adopting the posture of one preparing to interrupt a conversation and make a point of his own, and only Keane and Clement noticed Sam's position. Keane embarked upon describing his memories of Yankee Sullivan while they were sixteen-year-old boys on the run together in New South Wales, surviving for three months as wharf rats and housebreakers before they were recaptured and sent to different jails. But even while he talked he was warning Sam with his eyes.

'Boys,' said Sullivan, turning to Casey and Duane. 'Thomas Keane was my brother back in New South Wales and you have chosen your ally well. Never have I known a cleverer or fiercer man—'

But Charlie Duane, who'd been drinking freely, as Sam predicted, began to talk over Sullivan. 'Boys, you likely won't know how once upon a time this madman sailed incognito from New York to London, from where he'd been so cruelly transported those many years ago, and successfully challenged the British champion, Hammer Lane, for the crown-title and a purse of one hundred pound, before the English learnt his true identity and he had to smuggle himself back to old America.'

The blood was hot in Sam's face, and his heart was thumping, but he leaned his left elbow onto the bench the better to listen to Duane, and ignoring the warning look in Keane's eyes let the fingers of his right hand trace the bottom hem of Duane's broadcloth jacket. The problem was that Duane was animated in the telling, and sitting up and down a few inches. Sam's fingers found the side pocket of Duane's jacket and tested the opening by walking it open with a scissor movement. The weight in Duane's pocket sat on his thigh, and the opening was under no tension. Sam's fingers slipped within and his fingertips traced the twine-bound handle of a leather cosh and beside it a small leather purse with a snap button. He tested its weight with his two fingers and it was heavy. He knew that if he dropped the purse it would land on Duane's leg and alert him. Duane stood up then and Sam saw the response in Clement's eyes, which was to reach for his pistol, but the Irish Democrat wasn't ready to cease his memorialisation of Yankee's heroics.

Sam caught the glance from Thomas Keane to Yankee Sullivan, who shrugged, because the tale was true. Keane shook his head and smiled, but the smile was pinched because he was still looking at Sam, who had the purse now in his fingers and slid it down his shin and onto the toe of his boot. He then put both his hands onto the bench and refilled Duane's whisky and kept his hands above the table where everyone could see them.

'Now, Yankee, to the matter at hand,' said Casey. 'Tom Keane here will find you a place to live and eat among your countrymen and recreate according to your appetites, but in the meantime, how do you fancy putting those fists to work?'

Yankee Sullivan looked at his hands, and made them into fists. The action appeared to hurt him, and he grunted. 'Sure, if there's takers I'll take them, and their money too. But let's go now before I drink myself to foolishness.'

A cheer went around the table where dozens had gathered to see the big man, who stripped off his jacket and shirt and removed his boots and socks. Sullivan's back was junked with cruel scars, and so were his arms equally marked, and there were the familiar rings of proudflesh at his wrists and ankles where he'd suffered the irons.

The men stood to drink, and Sam nodded to Clement and Keane, and bent down to his feet.

'Mr Duane. Does this belong to you? It was on the ground here.'

Sam held up the leather purse and Duane's face blackened and his eyes went fierce as he checked his pockets. He looked at Sam and at the purse then back at Sam again. He spat on the floor and made a fist, and the men around the table stiffened. Sam tossed the purse to Duane and thereby broke the man's posture of attack, but Duane's aggression was just a ruse, weighing the purse in his hand and winking at Keane.

'The lad's under training?'

'He is, Charlie, although...'

'No offence taken, Thomas. It's good to be reminded.'

And with that he tossed the purse back to Sam. 'Boy, it's yours. You earned it. There's forty-three dollars in notes within and seven gold eagles and the purse itself is made from the nut-sack of one of my enemies back East. It's brought me good fortune, and may it continue in your ownership as a marker of your apprenticeship attained this day. Come here and embrace me like a son.'

Sam looked to Clement who nodded, and Sam accepted the embrace from the older man who leaned down and hissed in Sam's ear.

'You return that purse to me as soon as we're alone or I'll gut you and throw you in the Bay.'

Sam flinched, but pretended the threat was not made. He still felt elated at stealing the purse, and his heart beat strongly, and his skin tingled with the pleasure of his first success. When he turned, Yankee Sullivan was beside him, kneeling among the backslapping to stroke the ears of Sam's dog.

'This is the native Australian dog, is it not?'

'I don't know, sir. I found him in your old haunt, at Sydney Rocks.'

'Boy, will you tend to me today, with water between rounds and a cloth to wipe the blood?'

'Yes sir, I will.'

'Good lad.' With that Sullivan leaned closer and said, 'Give me the purse to return to the brute. I know him well. If I return it he may forego his revenge.' Sam passed the purse and Sullivan stood amid a new round of cheering, and headed toward the block of dusty light that marked the doorway into the crowded street.

Sam followed once he'd secured cotton slops from the infirmary upstairs, and a stoppered jug of water from the bar, heavy enough to make him stagger the several blocks to the plaza square, where already a crowd of several hundred had gathered. Mollies from Sydney-town and workers from the nearby streets stood beside the regular sailors and miners and itinerants while Casey stood at a loading dock and proclaimed the arrival of the Southlander champion who would take all comers on this square. He offered a purse of five hundred dollars for any man who bettered Sullivan by way of pugilistic combat. This stake cheered the crowd, who looked among themselves for a willing opponent for the Australian, standing barefoot in the mud within a cleared space of several yards while the crowd jostled for the better position.

Presently, a giant Russian sealer stripped himself down. He too was cruelly scarred, and his black moustaches glistened from the clear spirit he drank before raising his fists. The move was a ploy however, and he put his head down and charged Sullivan, who stepped aside and then the crowd closed in and Sam couldn't see. Sullivan must have won, however, because the next time the crowd cleared, Sullivan was trading blows with an American, distinguished by the red sash at his waist and Oregonian hat, which was shortly dislodged from his head.

There was no pause for water or cloth despite Sam's presence, and one after another Sullivan fought every comer throughout the afternoon and into the darkness. The crowd barely abated or lost voice, and it hurt Sam to witness Sullivan's exhaustion and the sneak attacks that new fighters made to Sullivan's kidneys as he bent over and caught his breath. Finally a gunshot sounded, and it was Keane and his colt raised, shrouded with gunsmoke, calling an end to the bout.

Sullivan was hefted onto shoulders and sagging drunkenly was carried out of the plaza square toward Sydney-town. Sam followed with the dog at his heel, the cloth unused and the water shared only with spectators.

Sullivan was taken to a Kathleen McGarry molly-house. The notorious proprietor guarded him with her famous truncheon, which she waved at all who dared follow. The crowd dispersed along the shoreline street and into the groghouses where the festive atmosphere and marvelling at Sullivan's endurance continued long into the night.

Clement came to Sam at The Stuck Pig. Instead of chastising him for robbing Duane, he congratulated him, although his voice was grave.

'You know you must return the purse.'

Sam nodded. 'It's done. Sullivan conveyed its return.'

'Good lad. Although you should leave this tavern, and keep your distance until Casey and Duane have sobered up. Go now to Mrs Hogan and request her to make up a room for Sullivan. Go now, and don't return tonight.'

Charlie Duane and Casey were seated at their table and counting their takings. They were still drinking freely, and as Sam passed he caught the cruel glint in Duane's eye, who immediately stood and broke a bottle upon the edge of his bench and turned to the nearest table and plunged the broken bottle into the arm of a sailor and stood back and laughed. The sailors rose as one but were soon dispersed by Keane's men, because they didn't want the American hurt on their home territory, despite his being the aggressor. Sam took that as his cue to return to Missus Hogan, who beamed at the news and berated her husband into assisting her to clear her best room of a Welshman's belongings. He was a pickpocket who she never much liked, she said, and whose possessions she threw into the alley where they were set upon by men from the street.

18

Sam held the quill and pressed upon the page as another gust blew through the doorway of the tavern. It made writing difficult but at least Keane was patient with him. Sam's benefactor sat on a bench seat and drank his coffee from a tin mug and smoked a cheroot. He looked into the face of the next supplicant and waved for him to begin, although it was clear from his expression that his reading of the man in woollen undershirt and braces was complete before the miner opened his mouth.

The man began his tale of woe, and Keane nodded and eventually cut him off with a raised hand when he tired of the story. Now it was Keane's turn to speak, which he did by asking a series of questions. Yes, the miner answered, he had a trade. He was a fellmonger before his transportation, and a stoneworker throughout his years of slavery. He could tan any hide or build any chimney.

Keane looked to Sam, and that was the signal to start writing. Keane reached into his purse and withdrew a golden eagle, and passed the coin over, and gave the name of an Australian brickmaker who needed labour.

The miner was grateful, and took the coin and stood beside Sam. He gave his name in a shaky voice. 'Bevan Gillespie,' he said, and then he thanked Keane one last time and was gone, and it was the next man's turn.

Sam recognised the sailor from earlier in the week. He'd been enslaved by an English captain and forced to work the passage from Boston to San Francisco before he'd jumped ship. Keane had given him money for clothes and a revolver, and here was the man returning that money to Keane after only two days.

Sam was only now beginning to understand how the society of the Coves worked. They were mostly the original Australians who'd been in the colony for six months, and worked in a gang of two dozen men, who were commanded by Keane and Mannix, depending on the manner of crime. Keane no longer participated in the armed robbery of money-boxes from within the town, or bushranging the inland tracks where gold was transported by stagecoach and mule-train. That was Mannix's preference and he had his favoured men. Keane instead looked after the Coves' interests in the shoreline streets; collecting tribute from merchants and Australian businesses, and paying off councillors, the sheriff and Mayor Bannon. It was Keane who ran the teams of forgers and confidence men that plied their trade against the greed and gullibility of the newcomers.

Sam put down his quill and looked over at one such unfortunate, a middle-aged man with a bald head, a mutton-chop beard and pale watery eyes, who sat on his own at a corner table and stared miserably into his empty ale mug. It was Clement who had played the lead hand in the drawn-out game of fleecing the newly arrived gentleman from Boston. The man was first played the oldest trick in the book. On his second night in San Francisco he was seduced by a molly, and in the midst of his pleasures, another man claiming to be her husband had kicked down the door and threatened the Bostonian's life and demanded recompense for his humiliation. The man was then handed over to the Coves' regular card sharps for further parsing. Finding himself in debt, he was then suborned into a deception incorporating the man's good name in the establishment of a sluice-mining company, designed to draw investor money from the eastern union, based upon fraudulent mining leases and property papers. The man was tolerated in The Stuck Pig because of the bounty that was soon to be realised, and he was given a daily stipend that he drank within the hour, but he was a pathetic sight with his despairing eyes and flinching at every sound.

The gold-seeker next before them was an eerie-looking fellow with grey skin and black bags under his eyes, and fingers that kept clasping and unclasping his cabbage-tree hat. He made his argument for charity, and took his gold coin and offer of a free meal, and agreed to head to the docks where he was needed to work on a bullock-team. Keane made this final pronouncement and turned to Sam, and winked. Because of the muddy streets with their treacherous slides and bottomless sinks, working on the bullock-teams was the job that Keane favoured for those he disliked most. The man he sent was a schoolteacher back in New South Wales, and was malnourished and gaunt after weeks of humping his pack, but despite his begging showed a clear disdain toward Keane. Keane and Sam shared a smile because they knew that the man would be back the following morning, having learnt a hard lesson.

But Sam didn't understand the teacher's disdain toward Keane, because Keane and Clement were two of the finest men he'd met. When the teacher was dismissed, Sam gladly accepted Keane's invitation to join him for coffee and a plate of stew. The dog sat on the bench-seat beside them, and ate off its plate like a man, and Keane rewarded its superior table manners by patting its head.

Today's bag of gold dust was for the town clerk, who was paid off every Friday. Sam clucked to the dog and they set off through the streets toward the plaza square. It had rained overnight, and there was a mule-train loaded with tea-chests that was bogged just outside the Australian quarter. The first pair of mules in the train were buried to their necks in a sink. It looked like they were swimming in the mud, and their eyes were rolling in their heads and their mouths were frothing with exertion and crazy fear. The other mules were refusing to go backwards. There were fifty or so men with nothing better to do than watch the spectacle, and the driver and his labourers were arguing with the crowd, who were beginning to jeer.

Sam skirted the crowd and continued up the street and nodded to the shopkeepers that he knew. He was given an apple by the Jewish dry-goods merchant, Schloime Harris, whose store on the corner of Pacific Street was the first that pilgrims off the boats encountered. He stocked all kinds of things that a miner could need, and plenty they didn't. The prefabricated wooden shed was crammed with goods and even on the outside walls there were ropes hung with whips and harnesses and ribbons and sashes. Old Schloime spent most of his time outside on the street smoking and watching, until a ship came in and then his spruiking could be heard from a block away.

Sam bit the apple, which was spotted with bruises and tasted floury but was a rare treat. As he did every morning, he approached the porch opposite the Chinaman's tailor shop, his fingers in the pockets of his waistcoat practising his future craft, and his hat cocked so his face caught the sun. But there was no sign of the girl, and Sam finished eating the apple and passed the core to the dog, who chomped it down. Next Sam stood for a few minutes in the alley beside the haberdashery, right beneath its single side window, smoking a pipe with his hat cocked and his hand in his pocket, hoping that he didn't look as foolish as he felt.

But that didn't work either, and so Sam went into the Chinaman's shop to collect his new shirt. He had ordered the shirt two day's previous, his third in as many weeks. He had four shirts now, and three of them had never been worn, but there he was in the Chinaman's parlour again, unbuttoning his waistcoat and suspenders, shedding his used cotton shirt while the Chinaman unwrapped the new shirt to test its size. The Chinaman was no fool, and lately spoke gruffly to him, making sure the interior door was shut. From behind it the muffled sounds of domestic chores, and once, a snatch of song that made the Chinaman wince and clench his jaw. The man now held up the new shirt for Sam to try on. He caught Sam's glance at the door, and muttered in his language and stood watching Sam robe, his arms folded, his chest proudly cast.

Back outside the haberdashery, the dog sniffed at Sam's trouser legs and fell in behind. Another customer entered the shop, and through the smudgy window Sam saw the Chinaman occupied with his bowing and scraping. Instead of taking his usual route up to the plaza square, Sam went again down the side-alley, and seeing no movement behind the window entered the rear yard of packed dirt and cages of Muscovy ducks, and a single pig staked in a corner. The pig grunted at the sight of the dog, who went rigid with one paw raised. Sam knelt and patted the dog, and looked about the dirt. He saw a gravel scrape in some hardened mud beside a puddle, and prised loose a pebble. With one hand on the dog's ears, he cast the pebble against the rear window, and waited. The fog had misted the glass, but the sound was clear against the thin pane. He tossed another stone underhanded, and then another, and finally those eyes peered out at him.

They weren't angry, but neither were they conducive to offering the invitation that he hoped for. Sam didn't know what to do next, and found himself grinning foolishly, scrubbing the dog's coat with a vigour that made the animal lean into him. The dog started looking at the pig again, but not like he wanted to eat it, instead play. He stamped forward, and ducked his head. Howled a little. Sam was so absorbed in getting the dog quiet that he didn't hear the door open. She was already beside him when he noticed her. He stood, and found himself imitating her father, ducking his head, taking off his hat and running a hand through his hair. The girl was taller than he, and dressed in a cotton smock that reached to her sandalled feet. Long hair tied in a braid over one shoulder. Her eyes bore an unmistakable friendliness, but she wasn't looking at Sam. Lifted her smock and folded her legs into a crouch, reached a pale hand and scratched the dog's head. The dog glanced at her but kept its eyes on the pig, trying to mesmerise the creature that only had eyes for the girl.

At this the dog set to whining.

Since the girl scratched the dog's ears, Sam ruffed its back. 'That porker don't speak dog, silly. Why don't you direct your attentions to this 'ere new friend you've made.'

She looked under the dog's belly to its privates. Said, 'What is his name?'

A sweet kind of English like he'd never heard. Not bowed under the weight of accent. Plainly spoken, but music in it. She looked at Sam for the first time, and her eyes were friendly. Shy, like his own. A clear intelligence there.

'It doesn't have a name. It stays with me anyways. I just got to whistle. You want to give it one?'

The suggestion made her smile. 'You want me to whistle?'

Sam's confusion obvious, backtracked through his words. 'No, you want to give it a name?'

She didn't stop smiling, and her teeth were pretty. Two sharp incisors, crowded around her front teeth. 'Did he come with you, across the ocean?'

Sam nodded. 'Yes he did, though I can't say he enjoyed the passage, once he ate out all the rats.'

'Then I shall call him Bo. Like a wave.'

'Aye. Like a wave.'

'You don't like it?'

Sam blushed. 'No. I mean yes. It's ... pretty.'

'Pretty name is good? For a boy?'

'I mean *you* are.'

The words felt like they'd been sloshed out of a bucket. Hadn't meant to say them, but was glad he did.

She pretended that she didn't hear, her eyes on the dog, whose fur she rubbed, the dark-red groove between its eyes.

'Goodbye, Bo...'

And then she stared at him, and there was expectation and humour in her eyes. And he understood, amid a new blush.

'Samuel Bellamy. That's my name. Lately of Van Diemen's Land.'

'My name is Ai.'

'Ai. Aaii.'

He felt like he wanted to keep saying her name, till he caught the music in it, the way she had. But he already felt a fool. 'You going to tell me what it means?'

But she'd already turned, and in three quick strides was through the door. The sound of a latch. And the dog setting to whine again. He took it gently by the scruff and guided it round his legs, pointed it at the alley, and followed.

There were gamblers all the way up to the plaza square, on the porches of the various shops where sharps had set up tables that dealt monte and faro and vingt-et-un. Men lined up despite the hour, and drank whisky in little glass jars that were sold for a pinch of gold dust, or ten cents or whatever could be traded. Sam walked past them, and the workers constructing new wooden buildings to replace the old canvas tents. Sam had to sidestep into the churned thoroughfare at one point, and get his boots muddied to the ankles, because a carpenter tore off a tarpaulin from a pile of freshly milled planks and discovered five miners sleeping beneath it who had crawled in during the night to escape the rain. The carpenter shouted and kicked the wood, but was otherwise temperate in his actions because the miners looked hard men, and were sick with drink or perhaps the ague that was going through the town. The miners braced their feet and grimaced into the sunlight, and the foreman stood there and waited for them to scarper.

The town clerk was a thin Mormon of indeterminate age in a

grubby black suit with ink-stained fingers and jaundiced eyes. There was always clamour in the clerk's offices, as newcomers and dusty miners sought his attention to register claims, and draw up deeds, and lodge complaints against claim-jumpers. Sam caught the clerk's eye and the man left his besieged counter and met Sam on the rear steps of the government building, next to the red-brick commissariat that resembled a fort. Sam passed him the felt sack of dust, and received in turn a ledger-page listing the names of new merchants who'd registered town-site leases, and where they were staying. This intelligence would be passed on to Keane and his men, who would invite the merchants to accept the Cove's protection, but if refused, would initiate their various ploys of parting the merchant with his savings. There was no bank in the town, and so equally valuable as the currency of gold dust or coin was the currency of information that led to the locating of the hoards and caches and personal stores of the wealthy, and every morning at Keane's table there were informants who were paid to deliver this knowledge to the Coves.

Sam returned to the plaza where the wind riffled the canvas tents and snapped at the pennants strung on guy ropes between the establishments. The dog followed at his heels as he called out hellos to the men that greeted him as he walked toward Sydney-town, the name of the girl Ai on his lips, saying it to himself again and again in the manner she had taught him. Her name was beautiful as she was, and put together, her name and her face was like a crack of light in his day, and even the cold wind on his face was a refreshment and a friend.

14

As usual around midday, Joseph Borden could be found beside his rainwater barrel on the baker's porch. Sam waved and made his passage toward the Australian, down the muddy track that was called Pacific Street, edging around the sinks and puddles and keeping to the planks and duckboards. Borden held up the ladle, which was his common greeting. He wore his regular leather trousers, and a canvas shirt under a leather vest and oilskin slicker, and a wide-brimmed hat in the Oregonian fashion which he never removed. His moustaches were long and grey, and belied his young man's eyes and clean white teeth that showed in his smile at the dog's recognition of their friendship, sidling up to Borden and offering its flank for a scratch. Borden lifted off the wooden lid from the barrel and dipped his ladle into the freshwater and passed it to Sam, who drank deeply then offered it to the dog, who did the same.

Borden was a man who Sam stopped to talk with regularly, but on this day there was a reason for his taking the porch. Sam had assumed that it was a matter of time before Sarah Proctor's friends heard something about a red-haired Scotswoman transported from the Swan River colony, and who'd taken on molly-work in New South Wales. But he was wrong, and Sam didn't know what to do next, except that Borden was someone who knew his way around the territory of California, even though he was a Vandiemanlander who had settled in Melbourne, and was the first to leave that shore when the news of the gold rush was published. Like most men, Borden lived in a canvas tent pitched outside the row of streets that followed the semi-circular shape of the bay. There were thousands of these tents, lit from within by whale-oil lamps and candles, and at night the hillside resembled a constellation of golden stars set against the darkness.

Other men lived in the hulks of the abandoned fleet out in the bay, and risked death at the hands of the area's notorious currents when swimming to and from the shore, or fashioned rafts out of the cannibalised wrecks and made a living transporting salvage. Joseph Borden was one such man. Although he lived on land, during the day he ferried men from ship to shore, and broke apart the abandoned ships, and sold the finest wood and brass fittings to builders so that the town's nautical origins were made daily apparent in the scavenged circular windows and the skirts, architraves and barge-boards of the new edifices built further up the hill.

In between work and sleep, like most Australians, Borden sat around and conversed with whoever passed by, from his position on a stool beside a salvaged wine barrel now fashioned into a rainwater vessel. He collected the rainwater with the permission of the baker whose long sloped roof was natural for the purpose. Freshwater was hard to come by, despite all the rain, and more expensive by weight than either beer or rum, and Borden sat with a ladle and sold his water or traded for food.

He sat now and scratched the dog's ears in the way that the dog favoured, so that its nose was beside his own, eyes closed and leaning into him. Borden's eyes were however on Sam, and there was caution in his voice.

'Sacramento is no place for a boy. The anti-Australian feeling is strong in that river-port, where the streets are straight and the minds narrowed by open Nativist resentment. The lynching of Southlanders is common, and so there are few Australian mollies at work, and I should know. Better for you to remain in this embayment where you're safe among your countrymen, and where the opportunities for a clever boy are greater.'

The advice wasn't welcome, but Sam respected Borden's knowledge of the colony and also the forthrightness of his opinions. At first he'd thought Borden a pest, whistling to him as he passed and offering him water, but lately Sam looked forward to chatting with the short man who knew the interior and many of its people.

Borden kept away from Sydney-town for reasons he wouldn't explain, but knew Keane and Clement and asked after them. He'd sluiced for gold alongside the two Coves up on the mountain rivers and creeks, until the snow melt had inundated the best shores and most gold-seekers had turned instead to dry-digging in the hills nearby, which Borden wouldn't consider on account of it being like 'searching for a drop of freshwater in the biblical ocean'. And yet even though Borden had turned his back on the interior, he still retained that look about him that reminded Sam of the faces straight off the boats—enthusiastic and excited and optimistic.

This was, according to Borden, because the gold-bearing land he'd pored over in the Californian hills reminded him of similar land he'd traversed back in Victoria, and not far from Melbourne either. His plan was to return upon the first possible ship, to begin his explorations unmolested by thousands of rival miners, and all the foolishness of the gold mania around them. Borden had learned the hard way that the reality of gold-seeking was different to the promise, and he offered that advice freely to all who paused for a ladle of water in those alternately dusty and muddy streets. There were many thousands who'd died up there, he said, waving a hand at the clouds to the east, broke and broken and never a priest to say a word over their graves. One man in ten, he reckoned, passed out of the world in that fashion, and still they kept coming. That would end, Borden assured Sam, when the measure of disappointment outweighed the dewy-eyed optimism that governed the new arrivals.

In the meantime, it was his missionary responsibility to help that disappointment prosper by declaring the truth to any who'd listen. Sam looked at the faces of the men Borden preached to as they stood in the street, but universally they shook their heads and thought him a fool, a blatherer made bitter by failure or even worse—a man who'd manufactured his own bad fortune by speaking ill. As every man knew, bad luck was contagious, and those who suffered it were best avoided.

Borden didn't care about the ill feeling of those he considered ignorant, and that made Sam trust him.

'Is there anywhere else I can look? What about the town of Los Angeles, which I saw on Thomas Keane's map?'

Borden shrugged. 'In truth, I haven't been that far south, but I hear that it's a small fishing village. Nothing there for a ... your mother. But there is one other possibility in this town that is unlikely, and tragic if it's true. If I was searching for a white woman strayed from her kind, I'd suggest looking in the shanties among the sand dunes to the north of Goat Hill, where many Chileans identifiable by their domed hats seek asylum, and blacks and Indians and all breeds in-between. There are white women out there, some plying their trade in the service of niggers, I've been told, but I've never seen this myself. They are the mad ones, they say, cast from our society but too valuable to be imprisoned in any bedlam lockup. I hope to God that your mother isn't in that company, for it sounds like a living hell, more so than any regular molly-house. If you go, take your dog and arm yourself, for there is no law that applies to you where there are no whites to observe it.'

Sam was silent while he let the information sink in. The possibility that his mother might be mad, or enslaved. He considered asking Borden to accompany him to the shanty-town, because of the dangers spoken of, or Clement or even Sarah Proctor, but decided against it. In his mind he always imagined coming upon his mother alone. She would know him, and they would be together.

With that, as he did every time they parted, Borden passed Sam the ladle and he drank deeply from it, and it tasted sweet and metallic, and he passed it back to Borden who placed it under the dog's nose, and laughed as it gulped and went cross-eyed, and licked its lips and padded in a circle around the ladle until the great spoon was licked clean.

It was said that on occasions Thomas Keane slipped out of town in a disguise that concealed his long hair beneath a Mexican hat, or a sailor's woollen skullcap, depending upon who told Sam the story. Keane was wanted throughout the territory for his bushranging exploits, although Clement explained that Keane's absence was actually because he'd taken a lover—a newly arrived French Madam who'd set up an establishment in French-town, one that Keane described as furnished in velvet and dark woods and that brought a touch of class to the settlement. Keane was lately absent several days in a row, and Mannix was gone raiding into the hinterland with Barr and several others. Clement didn't mind when Sam asked for time to explore the northern beaches behind Goat Hill, where Borden had described the Chilenos as camped.

The dog sprinted past Sam as it realised they were leaving Sydney-town, heading round the base of Goat Hill and into the scrub. It had rained for two solid days and nights, and it was good to leave the muddy tracks and clamber round some rocks toward the sand dunes. The dog skittered over the boulders above the waterline, looking back to make sure of Sam's following. New smells and new ground. Sam clucked his permission and the dog climbed the rocks, and disappeared into the coastal heath, while Sam clambered over seaweed drifts and hitched his knapsack and leapt to the sand.

It was a relief to get out of the weather, and he trudged the first swale where the wind whipped at the peak of the dunes and a thin tracing of sand migrated down and caught in the roots of the grasses and bushes whose leaves were pliant as he plucked them and worked them in his fingers. The leaves smelt of salt, and in the sheltered swale Sam might have been back on the Swan River but for the detritus of squatters in the scrub around—shreds of clothing and empty cans of beans and meat and bottles of medicine and rum.

There were the older scoop-footprints at the base of the dune, but with the wind blowing a curtain of sand it was hard to believe that hundreds passed daily along this track. Soon the discarded goods consisted of live provisions, scavenged from the unwanted crates and pallets on the dock: cans of navy beans and brined beef and sacks of flour and cornmeal too heavy to carry the final distance to the camps.

There was shortly a thin smoke on the wind, and he recognised the fuel as the familiar saltbush scrub from the fires at home. The dog struggled in the deep sand to the top of a dune and disappeared over the summit and there began the sound of barking but not from the dog. A gunshot broke the muffled silence and the dog sprinted back over the dune and tumbled and leapt until it rejoined Sam, whereupon it hid with its ears back and tail pointed down.

Sam continued along the floor of the swale until the ground hardened and the pale aggregate sustained a bed of salt grass, while two small dogs the size of harbour rats patrolled the ridgeline and yapped down at him and the dog. He could see the smoke now, and around a final drift of sand he emerged into a small valley where the crusted mudstone supported a village made of salvaged packing woods and tea-chests, and canvas flies strung between the low trees.

There were hundreds of these makeshift dwellings, and an equal number of men and women, but the governing atmosphere of the place was silence, and a kind of secretiveness, except for the barking of the two hounds that now sped toward them and gathered in a furious barricade of teeth and snarls and shivering. The dogs were the ugliest Sam had ever seen, and thought themselves the stature of wolves by their actions, but were miniature enough to fit in his jacket pocket. The dog looked to Sam and took his lead by ignoring the two things, and trotted beside him as they entered the camp. There was no sign of the musketeer who'd fired at the dog, but one by one the inhabitants of the camp ceased their labours and recreations and turned to watch him come.

Clement had told Sam that a majority of these sand-dune dwellers were Chilenos, or Peruvians or Mexicans, routed by The Hounds from the townsite proper, and that the dunes were a refuge because no white man would live there due to the lack of fresh water and the sand that flowed in antlike migration around their cots and entered their mouths and eyes and ears.

Sam looked into the faces that were stilled by suspicion, and he felt his heart beating faster, and he covered the dagger-blade in its scabbard with a conspicuous jerk of his jacket. Most of all he tried to avert his gaze from the rows of black eyes, so as to not give offence, although the swarming in his chest and the pressure of blood in his ears and the awkwardness of a white boy patrolling through their camp while pretending to be invisible was too unlikely, and he glanced at the faces that were unanimous in their condemnation.

The two ugly dogs were called off. The only sound now was the wind at the top of the dune, and his footsteps crunching in the gravel. On griddle-plates were patties of cornmeal, and stews of various concoction, and hanging from the stunted trees were chandeliers of drying mackerel and legs of gammon pork, and around the tents were herbs and vegetables potted in tins and canvas bags.

Despite the possessions, the camp looked like a good wind would carry it away, and Sam remembered the routing of these people by The Hounds from their previous situation, and his already tentative steps became doubly self-conscious as he searched in the shadows for a white woman with red hair like his own. But there was no such woman, and Sam realised with a spike of shame that Borden's story of fallen white women living in slavery amongst the refugees was an abject rumour, and a further insult to these people, who were many of them healing from injuries likely inflicted by the very same rumour-mongers.

It was the sight of the camp's end in a cul-de-sac before a giant dune that sank his spirits further. An old woman with a brown moon face and crinkled eyes smiled at him, and for a moment he saw himself as she saw him—a skinny boy made fearful by their silent observation of his passage. He tried to repay the smile, but managed only a grimace, and so instead ducked his head in thanks for her kindness, and continued toward the mighty dune that rose above him.

There was no exit from the camp and there was no alternative to climbing it other than returning the way he'd come, but that thought filled him with dread. No man had lifted a hand against him or spoken harshly and the dog was similarly unmolested, although the hundreds of eyes had unbalanced his ambition.

He began to climb the sheer sand-wave, and the dog slogged ahead and turned to watch his awkward passage on his hands and knees in the boggy sand. A sparrowhawk, or harrier of some kind hovered above the dune's crest, and seagulls could be heard cawing and scrapping. In the bowl of white sand the weak sun was trapped, and he began to sweat in his collar and woollen suit, and his boots filled with sand. He turned and looked over the camp, and not one of those inhabitants had paused in their observation of the strange boy's passage through their morning. The dog was gone now, and Sam walked on his hands and feet the final twenty yards up the slope without stopping or looking back, feeling the ocean breeze on his reddening face, finally slumping over the crest and scrambling out of view.

The relief he felt at escaping their solemn observance was

magnified by the view that awaited him. Height was the first impression, because the dune banked down to a bluff, where gnarled and ancient trees stood into the weather, so fixed and so permanent that when the wind blew in little gusts off the ocean their dark green foliage, which was pinelike with little brown nuts, trembled not at all, unlike the salt grasses which swept this way and that.

The dog patrolled the perimeter of the bluff, and whined at the terns and gulls spaced along the wet rocks below. Sam slid down the dune and sat upon a rock covered in a bright green punk-moss that was dry and tinderlike. Catching his breath, he gulped in the sea air and emptied his pockets of sand and then his boots. From his knapsack he withdrew a bottle of Borden's sweet rainwater, and drank it, and called to the dog to accept a splash in its mouth. He had some dried meat, which he chewed, and shared likewise with the hound, who swallowed the jerky whole and asked for more with big sad eyes.

Sam clucked him and away he went, back to the cliff-side where he resumed his whining and pacing above the birds. The sun broke through for the first time that morning, and Sam angled his face into the sunlight, and drank it up like a flower. So comfortable was he in this position that he kept his eyes closed, and listened to the surf glissade along the reef, and the dog calling the seabirds to a feast of which they would be the meal, and the head seagull ignoring the dog by asserting its suzerainty over the number with brutal caws.

Sam laid himself upon the rock and crossed his bare feet, and spread his arms Christlike to take in the sun-warmth. Red and green starlights crossed his eyelids, and he imagined the Chilenos behind him eating the cornmeal and dried fish, and playing on their stunted instruments, and dressed in their conical hats and colourful blankets.

His mother wasn't among them, and his regret was manifold

beyond the purpose of his trek, extending into the unfortunateness of his fear of communicating with the Spanish-speakers and learning something of their ways.

It was a great comfort to Sam that he now regarded Clement as his kindly grandfather. He had lately told the old man as much, and he was equally grateful to consider that he and Sarah Proctor were like brother and sister. But among the rest of the Coves, Sam was barely tolerated, and expected to be a listener and observer. San Francisco was beginning to feel like a home, but that home was just a few buildings and a few streets, and none of them contained his mother.

The only way to escape his despair at this fact was to look upon the vista with a deliberateness that was trained in him. Clement had told him about the thinkers of China, who sought the truth about the nature of things within the fathomless depths of themselves, and Sam's response had been to imagine how such a notion would be received among the Swan River blacks, and one man in particular. This man was tall and scarified like all the men of his generation. His grey hair and beard spoke of a life before the coming of the whites in 1829, although he demanded that Sam call him Clive, which was a name given to him by the explorer Grey on their journey north of the colony, and which had some phonetic resemblance to his proper name. The blackfellow Clive was a leader of sorts, and always encouraged Sam within their camp as a speaker of English beyond the regular pidgin. All of the camp boys looked up to this man, and followed him silently down to the river in particular to watch his spearplay and listen to his song.

But it was amid the campfire smoke that Clive occasionally grabbed Sam's chin, and pointed him toward something in the trees: a breeze whose whispering was like children's laughter, or a koolbardi magpie whose sentinel position in the dark canopy bespoke a watching back at them; or sometimes nothing but a recognition of the tree itself, whose stateliness and presence became magnified the more Sam stared until it seemed ready to climb out of the ground.

Unlike the pious in church, the blackfellows kept their eyes open when they prayed, the better to keenly observe the world around them, and Clive was no different when he chanted his couplets and clapped his sticks. This was no reflection upon an inner space, but a meditation upon the world itself, and the same manner of looking had become ingrained in Sam, because whether among black or white, that territory on the Swan River was the most absorbing place that Sam had ever known.

He opened his eyes. The visitation that greeted him seemed a reward for his reflections, and he smiled in recognition. Upon the rock beside him was a lizard whose sleekness described an ability to burrow through sand. The lizard blinked, twitched its head and bobbed its feet as though dancing, or performing for him. Beyond the perspective of Sam's own crossed feet, a family of birds he couldn't name, but from their plumage and size guessed to be honey-feeders, were gathered in the nearest tree, hopping from branch to branch and scraping their beaks on the dry bark like a barber stropping a razor. Sam adjusted his focus, and there in the blue waves was a single dolphin, whose slow-spoked roll seemed a language for the mood of the ocean itself. Behind the dolphin was another peninsula, and he understood that he was facing north and that the strait before him was the famed Golden Gate and entrance to the bay.

Sam sat upright, and wiped his eyes, and the lizard scampered off the rock and the birds ceased their chirruping. In looking for the hound, Sam turned to find a great wave of fog bearing down upon the strait from out of the distance, a vision that in its scope was akin to the rolling storm-fronts whose pulsing grey faces moved over the Swan River and resembled a floodwater reaching to the sky. Advance tendrils of the fog floated spectrally over the waves, calling behind to the great grey follower that had no ceiling and no border that could be measured by eye. The Golden Gate opened up to her, and for a moment the sunlit colours of the peninsula became soft and vivid, and the dog appeared at his side, and together they watched the fog cover the sun and soundlessly enter the bay, and it was like they had been raised into the clouds and looked now upon some mythical landscape of the gods, from where the scurrying of humankind might be observed and mocked.

Sam whistled, and the dog joined him on the rock and accepted his embrace. For the vision of the clouds come to earth had brought tears to Sam's eyes, and he didn't want to be alone. It was moments like this that he often thought of his dead father and his brothers, or his mother, as someone to share his apprehensions of the mystery, but on this occasion his thoughts ran directly to the Chinese girl, Ai, and the memory of their meeting yesterday. In particular, it was the sight of the fogbound ocean and the tender way the air settled upon the bright green leaves of the branches that returned him to the image of her shucking off the softwood yoke those months ago in the bright green alley, with the soft light and the damp air shrouding her shoulders, and the barest glimpse of her pale neck and face turning to him, her angry eyes. He'd returned to this image often, and in every recollection Sam focussed upon those eyes, and on every occasion the eyes became less angry, sharing his own longing for company. What he had witnessed in her eyes yesterday was confirmation of his first impressions: a sorrow that was a kind of understanding of him.

He laughed at himself then, and the dog cocked its head, and when he kept laughing the dog nuzzled his ribs in search of his hand. For Sam understood what was happening to him, and it was not the first time. It was his own secret, how easily he loved, first with a little blonde girl called Adelaide when he was five or six, whose smile kept him awake at night, and later a black girl two or three years older than he, whose large brown eyes and pink tongue and wheezy chuckle occupied his mind for close to a year when he was ten years old, and who expressed her own affection by wrestling him to the ground. His childhood infatuations, expressed in pining fantasies of kissing and holding hands, could only be relieved by his being in the company of the beloved, just like in the poems the Magistrate taught him to recite. The thought of visiting Ai was a similar pleasure but also a kind of burden, principally because he hadn't seen her since their meeting yesterday. He had waited this morning on the porch across from the Chinaman's shop, but the side door onto the alley was closed, and the Chinaman glared at him through the windows and shook his head.

In mockery of himself and his foolishness, Sam wrestled the dog's head into an armlock, and chuckled, and began to put on his boots. He hadn't been able to habituate himself to the wearing of socks, and so the boots smelt of his rough feet, but the dog didn't seem to mind, and could often be found asleep with its nose buried inside. The dog watched him tie the laces, and followed Sam down the rock. There was a footpad along the crest of the bluff that meant avoiding the Chilenos' camp. Sam nodded his head, and the dog took off in advance of the fog toward Sydney-town where the bald skull of Goat Hill could be seen in the distance.

15

In this way Sam entered his thirteenth year. In truth he hadn't noticed any changes in himself. He still lacked hair on his privates and his voice hadn't thickened. More noticeable was the changes in the dog, which had grown to the height of his knees, and as Yankee Sullivan had suggested, with its reddish fur and great head bore some relation to the native dog of Australia. For it rarely barked and mostly sang, especially when Clement played his harmonica, which all the men thought a great entertainment. The dog followed Sam through the port streets and waited in the thoroughfare while he delivered his messages, and collected Keane's tithes. It growled when people tried to move it along or leant down to stroke its ears, baring its teeth and raising its hackles.

One morning Sam was asked to restrain the dog on a leash tied to a bench in the Stuck Pig, due to the arrival of a clipper chartered by Keane and paid for by his own coin. It was a cloudy morning but they knew that the boat had arrived because of the Goat Hill semaphore operator who was himself a Cove, but also because of the cartwheeling seagulls who followed every ship through the Gate until they berthed and began emptying out the hold. The gulls hovered and scrapped and the smell of the docks was always sour with stale fish and the tubs of boiling pine pitch used to caulk the ships against the return journey. Half of Sydney-town was down the docks upon hearing news of the ship's arrival, and many of the men were Australian miners who had come from the hinterland. Sam could tell which miners had struck gold because of the number who'd taken on the American fashion for wearing red sashes around their waists, and gold jewellery on their wrists and in their ears and around their necks. These men looked like pirates with their long hair and old rifles and polished boots, and Sam looked among them for the reason of their gathering, and as soon as he saw the ship's cargo he understood the order requiring the dog's quarantine. Above deck were dozens of horses that sniffed the cold air, and looked out at the miners with calm disinterest as they were liberated from their wooden cages and led down into the throng.

Ponies and horses were hard to get in the colony, and prices upwards of five hundred dollars for a good Californio pony wasn't unusual, and also the reason why the Coves' stable was always under an armed guard. Sam recognised the Timor ponies and walers from Australia, calm and dignified even among the dozens of hands reaching to pat the beasts and welcome them ashore after the sickening journey.

There was a festive air on the docks, and many men were singing. Sam looked among the miners and heard the tinkling of silver dollars. Some had already opened their bags of gold and were proffering these to whoever would listen as they began making a case for a particular horse.

Most of the men in the red sashes, Sam knew, were rich for the first time in their lives, and those who could never afford a horse back at home thought themselves raised up in the world. There was only so much gold jewellery that a man could wear; only so many rings and bracelets and necklaces placed on fingers and wrists and neck before a man looked ridiculous, and the new suits that they bought were no real measure of status because all were equally muddy.

The men leading the horses through the crowd ignored the offered money and the shouts of frustration, but all of them fell silent when the hold was emptied and a space was made among them. It was Keane himself who rode the block-and-tackle hoisted crate where inside a giant black beast glowered.

The gantry crane inched lower. When the crate settled, and the door was prised open, Keane stood before the horse, singing to it quietly. He laid a harness over its noble head, and fed it a carrot and guided it onto terra firma.

It was a fine thoroughbred, the first in that territory, and the men stood silent in their appreciation, for they knew it to be a nervous creature and worth more than their lives were it to spook and harm itself. Keane took off his slouch hat and bowed to them all, then raised his hat and proclaimed that the name of the Australian mare was Black Swan, and Sam looked around and witnessed tears in many homesick eyes. An armed escort of four men cordoned off the mare, and made a passage through the streets, and thereafter the hundreds of men followed with the reverential expressions of pilgrims.

Sam retrieved the dog from the groghouse, where he learned that the horse was destined not for Keane's own use, but for the town of Los Angeles, where a wealthy American had made a bet with a wealthy Californio that a good Irish thoroughbred could outpace the best Spanish pony. Clement chuckled at that, commending his own foresight in suggesting to Keane that he import the horse for one of the richest and most powerful men in the territory, despite the cost to himself and the risk of the long sea voyage. He demanded that Sam keep his dog away from the stables, at least until the mare was gone.

The dog now followed Sam into the Chinese Quarter, sniffing at the air and the footings of buildings. Wood smoke mingled with the heavy fog that drifted off the ocean, moving like a sinuous thing among the streets and alleys, pressing against the shingled roofing and pine-boards and leaving a silvery dew over every surface. Sam had the bag of gold dust for the town clerk in his waistcoat pocket, and his knife sheathed upon the buttons of his suspenders.

The gate down the side-alley next to the Chinaman's shop was opened, and that meant that Ai had tied up the pig and it was alright for Sam to visit. When the gate was shut, she'd told him, the old man was working in the back room and Sam had better keep away. She didn't appear afraid of her father, but the matter-of-factness in her voice suggested that she trusted Sam to use his common sense and listen to her advice.

He peered around the edge of the gate and checked that the pig was tied. The dog peered around the gate beneath Sam's legs too, and he imagined how they looked a funny couple, trying to appear natural and yet so furtive in their movements. The pig snorted as it always did when it saw the dog, and Sam tossed it the piece of bacon rind that he took from Missus Hogan's kitchen. So that the dog wouldn't feel jealous, Sam passed it some venison jerky and called it to heel while he gathered up some pebbles, although this morning like most mornings he didn't need to toss them upon the window. Ai's face appeared beside the curtains, and the door cracked open.

He took his seat beside her on the back steps. It was a position that she favoured, for what reason he didn't know, except that when he remained standing Ai would pat the seat beside until he joined her. It was probably because of her labours and having to stand all day, although he didn't know if this was true. Often they didn't talk much, and Ai seemed happiest during those times, stroking the dog's face and Sam just happy anyway.

But today she was silent in a different kind of manner, and he knew that it was because she had something to say, and likely because she'd rehearsed an answer to an earlier question of his. He'd learned that Ai was from a village near Canton, but as a child had been sent to the city. Sam had looked on the globe in Thomas Keane's office at the map of China and there was Canton, right down on the southern edge of the empire, wedged in among other kingdoms that he'd never heard of. Ai's silence deepened until she sighed.

'We didn't bring any books with us, and I tried to paint you a picture, but it wasn't very good. So I'll just tell you about it...'

Sam didn't know what Ai was talking about but he wasn't about to interrupt her. He glanced sideways and saw that her brow was notched in concentration, and when she looked at him she laughed, and that was because whatever it was that she was planning to describe had made her shy.

'It's alright Ai,' he said. 'We don't have to talk if you don't want. I'm just glad for your company. I'd like to hold your hand if you're willing, but we don't have to do that either.'

'No,' she said. 'You asked me about Canton. I don't know the history of the city, but I lived with the English, on a small island that was surrounded by a fort. There was a ... war before I lived there, between the English and the Canton people, but I don't know why, except that whenever Chinese people talk about it they are angry.'

'Did you live in a big house, with the English?'

'Yes, it was a big house. With many servants. The master was a merchant. I don't want to talk about him.'

'We don't have to. We can just sit here.'

'He had three daughters, who were my friends.'

'And you learnt English from them?'

'Yes, the mother taught us. She was Mrs Casboult. She let me and my sister and some other children attend their lessons, although we weren't allowed to talk, just listen. But we would practise among ourselves when we were working. We were spoken to in English and were allowed to speak in English.'

'I didn't know you had a sister.'

He was a fool sometimes. As soon as Sam shut his mouth, he knew that it was a stupid thing to say. Ai's sister was likely dead or missing, just like his Ma. Ai leaned forward and placed her face alongside the dog's face, her eyes hidden from him.

The streets by the plaza were busy as any other day, crowded with dray-carts delivering timber and bricks, and the frontier birdsong of hammers hitting nails and saws biting at planks of wood. But now as Sam approached the plaza square he found himself part of a stream of people flowing there in such numbers that he had to shorten his steps, to avoid treading on the heels of the men in front. As they got closer to the plaza he heard the sound of an Australian voice that was full of rancour. Sam cut sideways along the nearby porches and climbed over bannisters until he made the front porch of the saloon owned by Keane. Like all the other porches, it was crowded with onlookers, although in this case men and women clutching mugs of beer and glasses of soda water. Sam nodded to the American saloon-keeper who looked over Sam's attire, and the demeanour of the dog, and nodded his permission to join them.

It was the Australian merchant, Mitchell Walker, on a dray-cart, shouting through his hands over the raised faces. Beside him were five or six other men with fine suits and watch-chains in their waistcoats, and pistols in their hands. Each wore a species of top hat, and moustaches and mutton-chop beards.

Sam stood among the gentry on the saloon balcony and made his own space, although his head was still occupied with the memory of Ai, and her silence after he'd raised the matter of her sister. She was never able to sit with Sam for more than ten minutes at a time, and half of that time today was spent with Sam trying to think of something to cheer her up. He'd finally got up the courage to stand before her and dance the haymaker's jig, tapping his right foot twice and his left foot once and speeding it up and slowing it down while he whistled the tune. That broke Ai's sadness, and her smile and the curiosity in her eyes told him that the dance was a novelty to her. With his heart beating faster and blood in his face he'd put out a hand for her to take, and to his surprise, she'd taken it and he gently lifted her so that she stood opposite to him. He didn't let her hand go but changed his grip and bowed to her. This too was clearly a novelty and she smiled and nodded her head in mimicry. He put her hand on his hip and he began to whistle a tune in three-quarter time whose name he didn't know but which he'd learned from the Magistrate whistling in his garden. Sam demonstrated the first three movements of the waltz and that was when Ai began laughing with pleasure.

His daydreaming was interrupted by an elbow to the ribs. He looked up into the face of a gentleman whose eyes were roused by passion, and some of the men beside Sam murmured their agreement at Walker's chastisement of his countrymen.

'Pillagers, respecters of no laws, parasites from the extremities of the earth. A pox on this here settlement, whose future mustn't be waylaid by a band that daily fills the street with corpses, where decent men lately fear to promenade, and resist sending for their loved ones out of fear of what'll befall them if matters aren't rectified...'

And on he shouted, until the barman winked at Sam and rolled his eyes. Leaned toward Sam and muttered, 'Words wasted on this mongrel assembly who're mostly present because they thought to see a hanging—' The publican's words were cut short by a bearded man with a cane, who held up his empty mug.

There was no way Sam could get to his destination, the government buildings across the square. And so he waited. Walker held up a sheet of paper and pointed to the picture of Mannix and asked who among the crowd would extricate the outlaw known as Mannix from the heart of Sydney-town if the sheriff remained unwilling. The same outlaw who had lately, it was said, taken to an even more nefarious trade than plunder and murder. Namely depriving ordinary men of their freedom—men of all nationalities lured to his saloons, who drank spirits laced with opium and who awoke far out at sea, shanghaied in other words, and locked into unwilling service to a new and unscrupulous shipmaster, and all for a tidy commission. Walker's answer nothing but a few murmurs. To further his point, he read out the crimes committed in the previous month. Some thirty-three murders. Innumerable armed assaults and burglaries. Crimes against property and person.

'My own wife, accosted in the street by two ruffians who stole her purse and threatened violence if she resisted. My own wife, who in our previous benighted home lost her three children and husband to murder at the hands of black savages, who sought on this shore the opportunity for a new society of free men and women, absent the convict stain. Who has convalesced in our home only to be newly reminded of the violence that stalks every territory where a strong hand is lacking, and by strong hand I mean the hand of swift judgement, the justice of tar and feather and noose. For my wife's heart is newly broken, and I am resolved—'

The beating in Sam's heart drowned out the ugly voice. He felt light-headed, and liable to fall. It was the mention of Walker's wife. Lost her three children and husband at the hands of Australian blacks. The number of times Sam had been goaded to tell the story of his father—it meant that the murderousness wasn't common. He pushed his way to the front of the balcony and looked for signs of Walker's wife, but there were no women in that furious company. Only Walker, pacing the dray-cart and growling at the hundreds of heads beneath him.

'Immediate action is required and, to whit, my peers have sent a letter to Monterey, demanding that the company of soldiers stationed at the Presidio outside town, who only venture here to enjoy the fleshpots of Sydney-town, be garrisoned right where I stand before you. And that they parade in this square. And that they train a civilian militia in the ways and means of warfare. And that they patrol with said militia until every rogue is taken from the streets. And if this isn't sufficient, I have suggested that we burn Sydney-town to the ground. Look around you.

Everywhere you see improvements, and evidence of a town on the rise, that will one day become a great and noble city. But Sydney-town is the identical hovel-strewn locale it was a year ago. It will not be missed, I can assure you.'

Walker stood aside and introduced the next speaker, who Sam recognised as Mayor Bannon, dressed in his regular black suit and bowtie. There were sniggers in the crowd, due to Bannon's notoriety regarding graft, now proselytising on behalf of the vigilantes. But Sam knew it to be a terrible omen. Bannon had thus far protected the Australians, but that protection was now publicly rescinded. Bannon held up a noose-rope as he spoke and waved it to the crowd, which roared as one.

'You know me as the mayor and as a straight talker and pious man, and so I tell you that enough is enough, and that I'll be petitioning the Governor to abide by the letter of the law and refuse the admission into this territory of those with criminal records, as required by the law. And that until such time as this territory becomes part of the Union, and my promises here can be confirmed by my election under the Nativist ticket, I hereby promise that at that time, under the powers vested in me, to ensure that no new leases be granted to Australians or any other foreigner wanting to buy property in this city, and that the current ownership of mining leases will be cancelled and handed without compensation over to Americans only. For make no mistake—this is an American territory, and it will be peopled by Americans, and foreigners of dubious provenance are not welcome here. I know there are many from foreign shores among you, and you are welcome to become Americans, but those who protest my decision will suffer the full force of the law. So I have here in my hand a lynching rope for any American who wants it, at any time of day and night. For until the Governor sees sense, and applies military law to our streets, we must needs look to our own resources if justice is to be served.'

There were cheers and applause from the Americans in the crowd, notable for their red shirts and wide-brimmed hats, and nervous comment and stunned silence from the majority. Mayor Bannon leapt from the dray-cart, and was mobbed by those Americans who'd pushed to the front of the crowd in order to petition for opportunity. Sam recognised some of the Australians from the cove at the edges of the crowd, slouch hats tilted low and making themselves small. His thought was to return to Keane, and tell him of Bannon's threats to burn out the Australians and take their land, and turn over their mining leases to Americans, but that would be done by others. It was grave news, and spelled out Clement's fears that the Nativists would, by an appeal to greed and resentment, triumph over those who arrived before them. Sam whistled to the dog, which lay at his feet, and swung down into the alley, thinking to return the way he came, and thereby make his way across the square to the clerk's offices. But the streaming out of the square on all sides blocked the passage, and the mood among those who weren't American was turning ugly, so he stood in the alley and waited.

The day was heating up, or else the warmth derived from the rank humanity in the square, and so Sam opened his jacket and flapped it around his ribs. In so doing, he noticed a boy his own age, deeper in the alley, looking hard at him. The boy was dressed in rags, like Sam when he arrived on these shores. His feet were bare and muddy; his eyes were hungry. Sam thought him a Mexican, with his brown skin and floppy black hair. He was small and wiry and there was poise in his stillness, looking over Sam's shoulder to scan the crowd. He was moving closer, too, the only change in him, like a trick. He had a broad flat nose and eyes like black stones. Sam knew that look. The Indian boy was nearly on him, and still no change in his face. Nothing in his hands.

Sam raised his own hand in greeting, tried to smile. But there was too much hunger in the boy's eyes. Sam tried to shuffle back toward the crowd but the rutted alley caught his feet. Then the Indian boy was underneath him, although the grimness had gone. Replaced by a humour. Sam drew his knife but the boy stepped back and grinned. Darted in and poked Sam in the belly. Sam held up the knife and waved it at the boy's face. The boy darted in and scratched Sam's face with his fingers. Was enjoying himself now. Saw that Sam couldn't speak, that he was freezing up. Walked right inside the knife's arc and pushed Sam in the chest. Caught him in the rebound off the saloon wall and repeated the action. Sam's voice trapped in his throat. All he had to do was shank the knife. But his hand wouldn't listen to his head. Seemed distant and not his own. The boy said something in his language and sneered, took a hank of Sam's long red hair and stroked it. Leaned in and took Sam's privates in his hand, to check, and stepped back in disgust. Saw the bulge in Sam's waistcoat pocket and dipped his fingers there and pulled out the sack of gold dust. Weighed it and smiled. Gripped Sam's wrist and prised loose the knife from his fingers. Sam's breathing coming in hard gulps. The boy saw this and was shocked, took a few seconds for the smile to reappear. He stepped back and looked Sam up and down, pressed against the wall, held vertical by his lean. The boy looked kindly at Sam then, and the punch he threw at Sam's face was an act of charity, and Sam knew it and the boy knew it, and Sam knelt and spat blood and watched the boy return down the alley and disappear around the corner.

Sam looked back to the square, blood streaming from his nose, bright red on the green weeds. The saloon-keeper, the American, was stationed at the entrance to the alley, alerted by the thumping on his wall. He must have seen the theft, but he said nothing, and returned to the porch and his waiting customers.

Sam found Keane in a war-party with Mannix, Clement, Barr and some of the others, in the armoury. He listened from his position at the top of the stairs as the men strategised on the matter of Walker's threats and Bannon's betrayal. Rather than losing everything they'd worked for at the stroke of a pen, Mannix counselled the assassination of both, but Keane spoke against it. The Military Governor, an infantry general, was coming to inspect the cavalry major and his troops at the Presidio, and because of Walker's importuning, the merchant's name was known to the Governor as a community elder. Murdering Bannon would surely make him a martyr to the Nativists, and see their popularity confirmed.

The other likely consequence of such an assassination would be the major leading his company of troops against Sydney-town. Could they see off a hundred cavalrymen?

Mannix's response was to call Keane a coward, and at this there was thumps on the table, and the scraping of chairs and a tumult of shouts and insults. Sam thought to retreat, but his dizziness saw him waver, reach for the wall and trip onto the floorboards at the top step. Right away Barr was at the door, knife drawn. He looked down on Sam and there was only suspicion in his eyes. He reached for Sam's arm and drew him up, walked him into the armoury. There were more people than Sam had thought. The whole company of Sydney-town who were leaders. The American Democrats, Casey and Charlie Duane, and the fighter Yankee Sullivan too. Some of the women brothel-keepers and groghouse foremen and card-game supervisors. Some of the stevedores who organised stealing at the port. The bomb-makers and arms procurers. The old forgers. Men dressed as miners and sailors. Sam knew them as people he sought to pass on messages. They looked to him as one, his bloodied face and torn shirt. Empty knife-sheath.

Sam watched the kindliness in Keane's eyes abandoned as he understood the nature of Sam's position, relative to the atmosphere in the room and the sensitivity of their negotiations. His benevolent interest in Sam forestalled by the interest of the others. The smell in the room of damp wool and sweat and anger. Barr didn't leave his side, or let go of his sleeve.

'Caught 'im listenin on the stairs.'

They all knew Sam as Keane's boy, but their eyes became the eyes of strangers.

'I came to tell you about Bannon. Him speakin under the Nativist banner.'

Keane looked around at the others, to see if they believed, or cared. He angled his head. 'Get, boy.'

But Mannix put up a hand, his blood still hot. 'How'd you come to a beatin, son? Was you set upon? Was it Walker's men, or Americans?'

Keane staring at Mannix. Sam looked instead at Clement, whose face was encouraging. 'I was robbed of the gold, and my knife, nearby the town square.'

'How many of 'em, and what was their purpose? Ye'll remember their faces.'

Sam didn't answer, because he didn't know what to say, hoping to be dismissed. But his silence was unwise. There was muttering, and Barr took his face and angled it, looked to his wounds. Said what most of them were thinking.

'I know you trust this boy, Keane. But this nose ain't even broken. Not a broken tooth neither. Not a bruise on him otherwise. Boy could punch himself in the face and take the gold for his own. Wouldn't be the first to try.'

Sam tried to shrug himself free, but Barr held tight, turned him to the judgement of the others. Keane raised a hand to silence them, but when he spoke his voice wasn't kindly.

'Was there witnesses? I'd advise you to speak.'

Sam nodded, didn't trust himself, but spoke. 'The American at the saloon, he saw.'

'And what did he see?'

Sam blushed, for shame. 'It was an Indun boy. He took it, and the American saw.'

'How was he armed? How many in his company? And you fought back, so you were struck down?'

It was Sam's silence that condemned him. And the questions that Keane had asked, an opportunity to lie not taken. And the unlucky coincidence of the angered company, now jury.

Keane looked back to Mannix, to resume his discourse. Clement shook his head. Barr took Sam's sleeve and pulled him to the door. Their faces were closed to him, and the hinges groaned as the door slammed shut and the shouting resumed.

16

Sam decided to await his punishment. He helped the Ancient in the groghouse wash dishes, prepare the evening candles, sweep the floor around the feet of the drinkers, then sweep it again. Certain of his relegation in the matter of his employment, Sam prepared himself to make arguments against being cast out of their company. He could work in the stables, with the farrier. He could work with the butcher, making tallow. He could clean or learn the trades of the woodworkers. He could help at the port.

The ceiling began to groan with the weight of feet above them, and the stairs began to creak and rattle. The men and women of Sydney-town entered the groghouse and wended their way around the drinkers and returned to the street.

Neither Keane, nor any of the other leaders emerged. Only Clement, who looked for Sam, calling him to their place by the fire. Sam stood beside the older man and waited for him to speak. To take out his pipe and paraphernalia and resume his ritual of smoking and schooling. But Clement didn't settle, or take off his coat, or indicate for Sam to take a bench. He stood sideways to Sam, and spoke quietly.

'Samuel, we don't care about the gold, or the knife. That's not what the native boy took from you. You ken?'

Sam nodded, thinking instead on his punishment. He could feel it now, the cold and the hunger, returning. He saw clearly how the warmth of Clement's friendship had sustained him these past months, more than the vittles and the blankets in his cot.

'Yes, sir.'

'Son, a man is just a boy who's learnt to perform the role of man. Keane has given you a role, and you must learn to play it. What do you say? Can you learn to play the role? And in learning to play the role, come to be the player? What say you?'

The voice was hard, but the eyes were warmed.

'I can play the role.'

'You cannot return to your former employment of conveying dust. Not until you prove yourself. Perhaps the forging of titles or notables, which is a skill you could learn...'

Sam nodded, and Clement's face softened. 'Sit, boy, and tell me what savagery precipitated such a bearing in you. I knew when we were introduced that you'd witnessed much for a boy your age, but I did you the honour of not prying, and potentially releasing the terrors. But I observe now that you live with them daily, even if you don't ken that yourself. So tell me, son, this above all else. On that first night on this shore, before the butchery ensued in this hall, I asked you a question about what you believed. A look passed across your face that made me fearful. Tell me, what vision did you see, in that moment of dread?'

Clement sat, and Sam took the stool beside him, and leaned close, and he spoke for near twenty minutes before he recounted the dream of the black snake, Clement smoking and nodding thoughtfully but keeping silent.

'The jaws of the black snake dislocated and the beast sheathed itself fully upon the Magistrate, who continued to sleep, while I watched from my cot, the glowing coal of the snake-eye fixed upon me, and I could not move, or cry out, or escape...'

Sam looked to Clement, and there was a concerned expression on the old man's face. Finally, his body slumped, and tears started into his eyes. 'Boy, you had your vision *before* the bloodshed ensued in this hall. Which I don't think a coincidence. My opinion is that witnessing the severed head of the black warrior, and your dream of the snake, which I'd reckon as likely not a dream, are closely related. I don't ken the ways of the blackfellow, but I know something of the interpretation of dreams and what they might augur. That snake is trying to tell you something. What, I cannot say. It is for you to figure. Does that make sense to you boy?'

Sam nodded. The paralysis and terror he felt at witnessing the gorging snake, and in those moments when fear of the violent hand claimed him, were one and the same.

Clement tapped the pipe-ash onto the boards, stared at his boots awhile. He was a long time silent, and it was a silence louder than the rough cursing of the drunks and the first strains of the Irish fiddler, who began to play a shanty with one leg on a stool. Sam thought back upon the words Clement had spoken, in particular his augury of the dream, and he looked once more upon the black snake, meditated upon it, his eyes never straying from the ruby coals of those clever eyes, and for the first time his guts didn't tighten, and his throat constrict. For behind the black snake was the forest, with the dew heavy and the red gum's jewelled wounds and the sunlight on the silvered leaves, and the vision was one and the same.

17

Any talk of alternative employments was forgotten in the dramatics following Bannon's speech, and the Coves set Sam to delivering messages as he always had. Despite the fact that California hadn't been declared a state of the Union, the preparations for an election were underway and these consisted mostly of the Nativists posting messages on shopfronts about the moral hazards of the Sydney-towners and the Chinese and the French, and every person not American.

Sam was tasked to rip down these posters if he came upon them, but this was a dangerous enterprise, and on one occasion he was chased by a draper waving a pistol through the streets until he reached Sydney-town, and there the draper refused to follow. A notorious Cove by the name of Jemmy from Town, who stole and fenced and marauded for Mannix, was shot in the back in the middle of the plaza square, and in the streets there was talk that the Nativists under the leadership of Mayor Bannon had hired the remnants of The Hounds, and were embarking upon a program of assassination, although it was termed extermination by many. Jemmy died in Hell Haggarty's dram-house and Mannix, Barr and some of the others swore mortal revenge.

There were other mysterious disappearances of notable Australians, and when Sam was tasked to attend the adobe prison-house, he learned on every occasion that the missing were not there.

It had long been the custom that when an Australian was arrested, one of the several drunks who earned their living as professional alibi-givers would present themselves at the prison, and the Australian would be released. Now, however, the sheriff warned Samuel to warn Keane, that under Bannon's orders this practice must cease, and that Bannon had placed a Nativist judge on the bench whose instructions were to imprison, exile or hang every Southlander who came before him, and to only accept bribes from Americans. So Casey the New Yorker was put to earn his money as the Australians' champion, but he did this with mixed success. He was the subject of bitter abuse in the city's two newspapers, and occupied himself mostly with getting Charlie Duane and Yankee Sullivan to avenge his good name by way of fists and boots.

Sam was busier than ever delivering and receiving messages in the light of recent events and ensuing rumours. When a Vandiemenlander named John Williams was caught trying to sell distinctive jewelled necklaces and bracelets to a Welshman named Clarke, upon learning that the previous owner of the goods was assaulted and robbed, the Welshman went directly to Mayor Bannon who rather than handing Williams over to the police, sent his thugs to apprehend the Cove and torture him in the mayor's home. Williams turned coat under duress, and named every aspect of the Cove's operations, before his eventual release, confirming, it was said, Sam's employment as collector of tithes and deliverer of bribes to Bannon's countrymen. It was Clement who took Sam aside, and relayed the news that Sam must be careful. He was notable in his employment by leaving Sydney-town, and venturing throughout the city, and was therefore vulnerable to kidnapping. Because he was a boy, moreover, he was susceptible to the breaking of his vows after the certain application of violence. Sam needed to remain vigilant, and keep a watch for spies, and routes of escape. Should he be caught, he needed to remember the lag's covenant that his confession should touch upon elements of the truth while avoiding relevant names, and otherwise delay until his rescue, which was certain as it had been proclaimed by Keane.

It was Clement who schooled Sam, because Keane was lately absent with his Frenchwoman, although this too was dangerous, because away from Sydney-town Keane was liable to assassination. Tasked to deliver the message to Keane that Charlie Duane was looking for him, Sam passed along the wharf-front until he reached Battery Street, and then turned inland toward the French camp. It was his first visit to this location in many weeks, and already the place was different, and precisely as Keane had described. There were the remnant canvas tent lodging houses downhill in the mud, but on a rise up Bush Street there were several new wooden structures that were clearly molly-houses, with sheets hanging off the front verandahs, and one large building made of red-brick, whose balcony was under construction within pinewood scaffolds. The miners in this precinct wore woollen suits, with great bone disks for buttons, and their beards were mostly black and oiled and looked combed as well. There was the usual tobacconist, and purveyors of whisky shots and smoked fish, but also a drapers larger than any other, whose trestle-table shopfloor was laden with wind-rows of cotton and silk and tweed bolts, and a whole table given over to red and green and black velvet.

Sam entered the shop and pretended to linger over a table of silks, while he looked over the direction he'd come to see if there were pursuers. There wasn't anybody he could identify as different to the milling Frenchmen, and the shop-owner was giving him fish-eyes from atop a high stool, so he gave them right back and left into the mud. He looked a final time before entering the plank boardway inside the scaffolding, into the brick building.

The inside of the building was truthful to the rumours of opulence, and even Sam could see that the curving stairway and the dark-wood panelling wasn't locally made or salvaged from a ship, but imported for the purpose. There were pictures on the wall that weren't of women, and the bar-top was made of hammered zinc. The shelves behind were lain with all the drinks that Keane was lately offering in The Stuck Pig, from all points of the globe: absinthe and cognac, and gin and vermouth and sloe gin, and the local favourite which was pisco, and the only thing from South America that was favoured by the miners. There were liqueurs that Sam didn't recognise, and he was standing in the darkness reading the labels when the barman entered from a trapdoor in the floor bearing a barrel of ale on his right shoulder. He was an old man and stripped to the waist, and the whole aspect of his face beneath his nose was concealed behind a long grey beard. But his eyes were kindly, and he asked Sam what he wanted in heavily accented English. Sam was told to ask for Mr White, and when he did so the man lost the friendliness, and shrugged and pointed with his chin to the staircase.

'The Lyon Room,' was all he said.

Sam climbed the stairs, which smelt of new wax, and the plush red carpet-runner was also new, and the whole establishment smelt like no molly-house he'd ever known. There was piano music being played somewhere, and fresh flowers in vases on little tables outside every room. The Lyon Room was at the end of the hall, and Sam knocked and presently a woman replied from behind the door, and when Sam asked for Mr White the door cracked open. The woman was very beautiful, with curly black hair, freshly combed over her bare shoulders, and she wore nothing but a corset and bloomers and her arms were pale and plump and she smelt like flowers, and she had a pocket deringer pointed at Sam's belly.

She didn't say anything but took her time looking him up and down, as though he were a picture, and then she smiled and she had white teeth and her eyes were a warm kind of blue.

'The man downstairs told me—'

She waved the gun like she'd forgotten it. 'Bah, my husband. Come in.'

The boudoir was bigger than the whole Stuck Pig bar-room,

and there was Keane propped up on pillows in a brass bed with polished fittings between two tables laid with flowers in vases. He gave Sam a weak smile, and he didn't look very well. The woman went about combing her hair again, while watching them in a gilt-edge mirror. Keane got two feet onto the boards and sighed but he didn't look drunk.

Sam had never seen his superior with no clothes on. Unlike most Australians, his body wasn't marked with tattoos. There was probably no place on him to mark with a tattoo because of all the scars. Sam had seen the scarring caused by wrist-manacles on Keane's forearms, but in this he wasn't unusual. There were the same burnt-looking welts on his ankles, and his back was junked, but his chest was also striped and pocked with scars that had healed red and shiny, and he had a terrible zig-zag scar across his belly with every stitch visible, and the same kind of scar down one thigh. There were too many scars to count, and some of them were knife-inflicted, and some of them made by musket-ball, but it was Keane's thinness that was shocking, with his belly slack and every rib visible. Keane smiled at Sam and tottered to his feet, and held onto the bedpost, and pointed to a bottle containing a dark green liquid on the bedside table and ushered Sam to bring it. It was tincture of hemp on the label, and Sam passed it and Keane drank off the shoulders of the bottle and gave it back while his eyes watered in the semi-gloom.

'What a sight I am, eh, boy?'

Sam didn't know what to say that was polite, so he said, 'You're sick, Mr Keane.'

At this the woman laughed, but made no comment.

'Aye, Samuel. It's the consumption. Caught in Her Majesty's cold stone hostelries. I'll be lucky to see out the year at this rate. But what brings you to my sanctuary? I trust that you weren't followed?'

He was tying his long hair as he spoke and there was a gurgle to his voice. The woman came from behind Sam and wrapped her arms around Keane, and then there were two sets of eyes staring at him.

'No, Mr Keane, I was careful in that regard. But I got a message from Charlie Duane, to meet him this evening at sunset, at the regular place.'

The woman tut-tutted and kissed Keane's neck. He closed his eyes and went limp in her arms until the woman leant backwards and laid him gently down on the bed, and tucked up his legs, and Sam could see the strength in her arms and in her eyes.

She patted Sam's cheek and straightened his collar.

'He is your hero, no? But the fate of every hero is tragic, and this one needs rest. The tincture is my own patent, and a ready balm, but it requires sleep and time to dream. He will be at his meeting with whatever thuggee you have named, but you must never speak of this or his illness to anyone. Do I have your word?'

She saw it in his eyes, kissed him on his cheek, then turned him to the door.

It wasn't until Sam was outside and in the mud that he remembered his surveillance, and paused to look left and right for the odd note among the Europeans. But there was nothing he could see, and in a kind of swoon himself he began to climb higher up Bush Street, and found that there were tears in his eyes. Clement was old, and Keane was likely dying, and he couldn't trust a single other soul beyond Sarah Proctor on this whole world. It was the sight of Keane's wracked body that had shocked him, and there was pity in his remembrance of the bony torso that was skinny as his own, but his wondering as he climbed the hill was the lack of pity in the Frenchwoman's eyes, and instead a kind of understanding. What Sam asked himself, as he laboured to his next destination, was when his own strong feelings would be replaced by understanding of the kind that she had shown, and Clement too, and Sarah Proctor as well, but was denied him on account of his age. This frustration bred a kind of foolishness in him, however, and despite his orders Sam crossed the plaza square openly with only his hat pulled low to disguise him.

His next destination was Nob Hill, so named by the Australians on account of all the richer folk who lived there, above the noise and stink of the port. Perhaps it was the mood that gripped him, or perhaps the opportunity, but he decided even as he began to climb the bare hill through the miners camps, and the track that crossed eroded gullies, that he would find a way to introduce himself to Mrs Walker of Nob Hill, and thereby ascertain the truth of her story of a murdered husband and children at the hands of Australian blacks. For it wasn't fear of her husband that had delayed him, but more the strategy of his approach.

Mrs Walker's house wasn't hard to find. There were fewer than a hundred houses on the craggy hill, and only one building defended by armed men at its gate: cannibal roughnecks in leather coats bearing rifles of the latest manufacture. Sam walked past the home twice before the giant guard noticed him and cocked the hammer on his rifle, though he said nothing and stared mostly at the dog. And so Sam walked to the end of the street, and climbed the peak of the hill and laid in the heath-bush.

There was a kind of clover thereabouts that he laid upon, and some scraps of cress that he knew were edible. Beside him in a low gully was also a stand of yellow mustard flower growing among red-limbed waxy shrubs whose flower bulbs were not yet open. All the plants and the dirt were damp, even though it hadn't rained, and Sam assumed that the bushes were watered by the fog that hadn't lifted for days.

But the dog wanted to play, and kept stamping on Sam's back and darting away. Sam held it by the scruff and looked down into the rear yard of the two-storey home with a great bricked chimney and a dozen or more rooms. He could see the flagged stone floor, and the copper in the laundry where a woman was boiling sheets. Sam looked more closely at the upper windows, where Mrs Walker was likely to spend her time away from the sights and smells of domestic chores. But there were only the heavy drapes. With his belly on the ground, Sam felt the earth begin to tremble long before the guards and the servants noticed. He stilled the dog who was prone to howl when the dirt began quaking, and watched the shingle roofing bounce and the plank-boards shudder and the stone fence lose its mortar. It wasn't a big shake, but all the servants ran outside and one of them got down and prayed, and crossed herself when she'd finished. The guards looked across the hillside, and Sam ducked his head. When he showed himself again there was nobody in the yard, and he went back over the hill and found the goat-trail that curved down toward the settlement.

In the distance, he could see a mountain range to the south, although its peak was hidden in fog, and all down the peninsula there was more hills than he could count, and each of them was now crested with tracks and wood smoke and homes and shacks rising up the side. Directly beneath him was the Chinese quarter, and behind that Sydney-town. He turned and looked out into the bay and gave up counting the ships when he reached four hundred. The counting was all to take his mind off thinking about the danger he was in. The question of whether he'd be able to prevail if he was captured. The loneliness that would follow if the Australians were purged from the city, and he was once again truly orphaned.

At the back of his mind were thoughts about Mrs Walker, and what she might mean to him, but in anticipating his probable disappointment, he thought instead about the girl Ai. She was at least real in her friendliness, and the memory of her sustained him in those moments of ugliness that were punctual in Sydney-town.

That morning she had received him in the back yard with

the pig, and by now he assumed that the Chinaman was aware, although that didn't amount to permission, and never would. He listened and watched Ai's face come over dreamy and warm while she described the land of her childhood, with its mist-shrouded mountains and highways of cobbled stone, and stories about the creatures who inhabited the great forests.

This morning he had watched her especially closely, in the light of Clement's revelation that Ai was not the Chinaman's daughter or even his ward, but rather what Clement described as a serf, akin to a slave. Clement knew the Chinaman, who he called Chen, because Chen was the source of his opium resin. Chen was, according to Clement, the Chinese equivalent of Keane, with his own brothels and mah-jong gambling houses, even if he pretended to the respectable and industrious habits of Walker.

Clement described Ai's future as Chen's bride, if she wasn't already. Or perhaps Chen would sell Ai when her price was maximised by longer experience in the domestic arts, and her capacity to either please men or bear children.

Sam looked again in his memory at Ai, seeking in her innocent features the hand of mistreatment or disguised suffering, of which there was nothing that he could remember. He thought of the Coves' armoury, and pictured what weapon he would choose and what he would do if Chen was mistreating Ai. Lost in his angry thoughts, when Sam looked next for the dog he understood that they weren't on the path to Sydney-town, but had returned to the street where the Walkers were housed. The cannibal guard watched him come, and it was the guard's suspicion that firmed Sam in his intention to continue to her home.

He told the guard what he wanted, who craned an ear close, and smiled when he understood. The guard told Sam to stay there, even as he clucked at the dog, who cocked its head. The cannibal waddled to the other guard, and spoke, and returned.

The other guard went inside, and a minute later Sam saw an upstairs curtain shiver, and a pale hand, and the curtain return to its place. The other guard came out and the cannibal took his message and returned.

'She don't know no Samuel Bellamy. So you'd better step off. And not return. Or else.'

The Pacific man cocked the gun and laughed. It was hard to know if he was serious or not, but the dog knew, and backed away behind Sam's legs.

Sam crossed to the other side of the street and sat down. There was a picket fence, which was the back fence of a cottage lower down the hill. The dog sat on Sam's feet and watched his face. But Sam just stared at the mansion's windows, and the cannibal seemed content with this distance and didn't say anything and pretended Sam wasn't there. Pretty soon the dog was asleep, and the sun was gone, and the fog closed in from the ocean and there were gunshots from Sydney-town but that was nothing unusual. Sam's stomach growled, but he was used to that too. He was warm in his suit and boots, and he must've fallen asleep at some point, because when he awoke the cannibal was nudging him with the toe of his moccasin shoe.

'The Missus want to see you. In the parlour. You touch anythin or look at her the wrong way, I got orders to gutshoot you. Savvy you?'

Sam nodded and got out of the giant's shadow, following him to the front door. But the other guard pointed his rifle at the dog and shook his head. The dog looked sadly at Sam but was used to it now. The Pacific man knelt and tweaked his ears, and the dog let it.

'Don't do that when I'm gone inside. He won't allow it.'

The man laughed, and stood up, and stepped away.

The door was held open for Sam, and he entered a large room with lime-washed walls and red wallpaper. Fancy pieces made of brass and china on hardwood tables. A painting above the staircase of some ships at harbour. A ceremonial sword in a glass case. A bookshelf with a glass face. Some carpets on the flagged stone, and leather chairs and a leather bench.

He stood there in the middle of the room and waited. Saw the shadow in the stairwell, and watched her come. If Sam was expecting his heart to reach out and touch hers, it didn't happen. She looked like a well-off woman, in an ankle-length domed skirt that showed the crinolines beneath its surface, and ruffles at her waist. She wore a chemise that was the same blue as her satin skirt. Paisley shawl over her shoulders. His own red hair, tied back severely. Painted lips and fierce blue eyes, watching him watch her. With a flick of her wrist she waved the guard outside, then floated toward Sam, her face unchanged. He expected her to stop at a distance but she came in close and took his arm and pinched it.

'What are you playing at?' The Scots accent whispered harshly. 'You'll not get any coin from me. I warned my blowhard husband as much, for he does so like to tell that story. That it would encourage impostors, such as yourself.'

Sam didn't understand because he couldn't see her face. Her strategy was unknowable to him. She smelled of perfume and fireside warmth. Her fingernails pinching a continuous march up and down his forearm. He endured, and waited.

When he didn't answer she stepped back and took him in. Must have seen something of herself, for there was doubt that she tried to hide behind a sneer.

Sam put up a hand, stepped back. He was suddenly exhausted. 'Your three children didn't die at the hands of the warrior. That part is a lie. Ma, I am Samuel your youngest. The only one now alive. Do you wish me to continue?'

She nodded, her face a porcelain mask, all the blood gone, but shining with new sweat. Her fingers trembled in the cage of her hands. He looked in her eyes, searching for the longing that he felt, but there was only confusion. To make her want him, he began to tell the story that he'd told so many times, although the automatic quality in his voice deserted him, and he kept pausing, and looking into her face, until the hope of those moments finally brought tears to his eyes, because there was nothing in hers different from any stranger.

18

Sam didn't tell Clement until a week had passed. A week of slogging through the town to deliver messages to men who were frightened and angry and wavering in their loyalty, who asked him to repeat himself to make sure they heard right. Sam watching over his shoulder for the men who might abduct him, and tie him to a chair, and put a flaming torch to his skin, as Mannix had described it. Keane was still sick, but only Sam and Clement knew the full extent of his illness, even as he continued his cohabitation with the Frenchwoman and delegated his wishes to Clement. Matters came to a head with the arrest of Yankee Sullivan, the champion pugilist and Democrat wardheeler, accused of participating in Mannix's crimes.

Sullivan was innocent, and the arrest was political in its strategy, but its seriousness was made plain with the lynching of one of Sullivan's cellmates, an Australian arrested for piracy in the bay, although he too was likely innocent and never given a trial.

Sullivan, it was said, was shaken by the hanging, and the guards were a torment to him, and both Casey and Duane were frequent in Sydney-town, demanding that the Cove's free their ally from prison. Keane advised a suitable diversion in the form of riotous behaviour, and he and Casey set to a plan, but shortly there was new intelligence, not helpful to their plans of rescue. Walker, the Australian merchant, had hired extra gunmen to escort the stagecoaches and the paddleboat that carried gold and money back and forwards from Sacramento, where there existed a reliable bank. Both the stagecoach and paddleboat had been set upon by Mannix and his men, and there were five American casualties. Even so, the Governor had refused Walker's request for soldiers to be stationed in town. Walker had instead lured many of them to burn their uniforms and take up a civilian role as mercenary for Walker's vigilantes. They were posted around the town square outside the establishments that paid Keane tribute, and they harassed and beat any Australians who looked hard enough to be Coves. The guard detail on the watch house was hired from these mercenaries, and they were well prepared for an attack to rescue Sullivan. There was more talk of lynching, and the rumours made Mannix angry enough to lead a posse of his men into town one night and shoot several of the mercenaries dead, and leave them piled up on the loading dock of Walker's storehouse.

Sam was sent to observe the watch house, which he did from the shadows abutting a storeroom, fearful of every glance and passerby. Having confirmed the timing of the change of guard, he returned to Sydney-town with the intelligence, then was sent to the foremen on the docks, and the dram-house proprietors who each had a gang of hard men in their employ, and were now instructed to prepare themselves for war. And all the while Sam walked those lowland hollows and the shoreline flats amid the constant fear of capture, he thought of his mother up there in her eyrie, watching the town and imagining Sam at his business. The idea that someone watched over him was a new kind of strangeness, and yet his head was troubled because her daily words to him were not a boon but a trial. He sought refuge in Ai's company, because the sound of her voice was enough to cleanse him of worry. He watched Ai and they made conversation, and then one day she let him hold her hand for more than a moment, and the warmth of her skin against his own made his chest near burst with joy. He had to hide his face for a moment. But then he left her and the voice of his mother returned, and his heart was stepped into the mud, and he knew he had to make a decision.

Clement didn't think on it.

'Do it,' he said. 'And do it soon. I'll run it by Keane. But in the meantime, I have a message for Chen that I thought you'd like to deliver in person. Right away, if you prefer. Keane thinks the Chinese useful allies, although you don't need to know the whys and wherefores. Just tell Chen that Keane wants to meet. It ain't going to sit well with Mannix, and some of the others who have an aversion for the Celestials, and like to raid them for sport. They won't hear of an armed Celestial and won't accept the responsibility of protecting them against American raiders, if it comes to that. But Keane thinks it inevitable and I agree.'

And that was how Sam ended up before Chen's tailor shop in the dim light of early morning. He could see smoke coming up the chimney and knew the Chinaman would be at his breakfast, with Ai serving him. Sam went through the front door and didn't knock. He stood there in his fine clothes wearing his new scabbard knife with a whalebone handle and didn't take off his hat. He'd been careful not to trip the door chime, and walked behind the counter and knocked on the dividing wall. It was Ai who opened the door, her hair down and dressed in a long cotton smock and bare feet. He stared at the new detail of her toes, then smiled at her but she didn't smile back. Sam pushed open the door into the room that he'd never seen inside of. Chen nearly choked on his gruel. Got to rising but Sam put out a hand, living Clement's words. Be the performer, in the hope of becoming the performer. Had thought about his words on the way over. Didn't want to seem a mere messenger, so he said it plain, looking into the angry eyes.

'Mr Chen, I got some news for you.'

He said it clearly enough, but his eyes were already darting round the room. Taking it in. He was looking for one bed or two. There were two mattresses, rolled up in different corners. Bit of sheet poking out of each. The room smelt of dried fish and tea and some kind of bitter herb that didn't sit well on Sam's empty stomach.

The Chinaman's face was a blank, but he nodded. Didn't indicate for Sam to sit beside him, on a pillow on the floor. Which was fine by Sam.

'Mr Thomas Keane would like to meet with you, at a time of your convenience.'

Chen looked him up and down. The skinny boy with his lank red hair. Hat and clothes that Chen had made. Who'd seen him in rags when he first set foot in San Francisco, when the Chinaman had been at his own performance of ducking and bowing and scraping. Didn't seem inclined to perform either way now. Just nodded his great round head, looked down into his gruel, took up his spoon.

Sam tipped his hat anyway. Had rehearsed this in his mind too. 'Mr Chen.' Turned to the girl. 'Miss Ai.'

She didn't look happy at the mentioning of her name, or his performance of being a proudful man of Sydney-town. Her head bowed. He waited for her to look up but she didn't.

'I'll see myself out. Good day.'

Sam reached Nob Hill and braced himself for the climb. His thoughts of Ai were put aside as the deeper anxiety came back upon him. What Mrs Walker was asking. The giant Pacific man at the gate lifted his rifle like a drawbridge and Sam stepped under it. Strode up and knocked at the door. Mrs Walker said to visit only during certain hours, when Mr Walker was absent at his business. That her husband wasn't to know. Because of her plan.

She was waiting in the parlour, dressed in a maroon shawl over another of her ruffled and hooped skirts. Her hair was tied in a bun. The smell of rosewater when she embraced him, held him under her arm. Gauged by his level of resistance that he was troubled. Held him away and looked into his eyes.

'It's a hard burden, Samuel, but the only way I can be free, and us reunited. Go south to sovereign Chile. The port is called Valparaiso. I got a list of all the shipping routines, don't you worry. We'll time it just so. Did you speak of it to your countrymen?'

Sam looked grave. 'No, ma'am, I would never. But I got a woman for your companionship, like you asked. Another Australian by the name of Sarah Proctor, come over on the same boat as me.'

'Is she currently at whorin'?'

It was strange the way his mother spoke. One minute it was fancy talk, aped off the gentry she'd served as a maid, the next it was her real self. She wanted a young Australian woman because Walker only hired blacks and Mexicans and cannibals. Didn't trust his own kind, and certainly not Australians. But a young woman, she was lately firm on that. Wanted the company. A young woman like Mrs Walker herself, who still had her looks, was only thirty-and-four years old.

'Yes, ma'am. She is. But I know her to be a kindly soul. She's amenable to sittin with you during the day when you're lonely, and to livin in the servants quarters.'

His mother smiled, and pinched his cheek, drew him into her bosom again. He felt her heart beating against his neck, slow and steady, and it only made him burn for revenge against Mr Walker, who treated her so bad. His ma said she wore the long-sleeve bodice and gloves even on hot days, to hide the bruises that the brute inflicted when he was enraged.

But soon she would be clear of him. Sam like an angel's messenger come to rescue her. The kind of trust between them that only blood could own. What his father would have wanted. When they were free, she would hear each of Sam's stories. Couldn't bear them now, his tales of woe inflicted in the search for her, when she herself was situated little better than a slave.

As she did every morning, his mother led him over to the leather bench where tea was set and held his hand. It amused her greatly, his stories of the citizens of Sydney-town. She puffed up at his bravery in service of Keane, a boy doing a man's work, knowing the ins and outs and characters who inhabited the street and the bawdy-houses and whisky bars.

She liked to hear the life of the streets such as the story of the new groghouse called The Grizzly Bear, named after the giant beast that was tied to a post and had a taste for porter but who hated smoked fish. And the grand new American establishment on the plaza square, with felt-topped gaming tables and half-naked women flying above the gamblers on trapeze swings, and the most famous barman in the Union who made a drink that was flaming whisky poured in liquid fire between mugs. And when she added that it was preferable, in hindsight, that she'd stayed with her own kind in Sydney-town, rather than try and raise herself up in the world, on the arm of a brute in the cloth of a gentleman, Sam consoled her, because her eyes were full of admiration for him and her gloved hands were soft and tender in his own. She never talked of her husband's role in persecuting the Coves, and he never raised it either.

It was only when she returned to her plan that the fear began to gather in his belly, and he couldn't meet her eyes, and she held him firmly and roused him with strong words.

Sam could do it, she said. The day wasn't right, but it was coming. She knew when Walker's reserves of cash were at a peak. He could do it, and *only* he could do it, and then they would be together and free.

She drew him to her again, and began to tell him, again, what he was like as a baby, how she'd nursed him in their hut by the potato field, just as he described it. The colourful parrots of the Swan River raucous in the trees. How his eyes would widen and how without fail the sound made him chuckle. And how she would chuckle, too, because it was parrot-stew in the hearth-pot. His father out in the field, chasing the birds and waving his hat and falling over the ploughed mounds, or down at the lime kilns suffering in the heat, crushing oyster-shell and firing the lime. His brothers crouched beneath trees with hand-fashioned slingshots, which they were too young to use. How at night they sang the songs of home in Glasgow and sat around the smoky hearth with their eyes burning from smoke and laughter. Their bellies empty, mind, but dreaming of the plot of land that his father planned further up the valley. Some pigs and sheep, in that region already cleared by the blacks' firesticks. His father swearing that he'd had his fill of saw and plough, until kingdom come. And Samuel always watchful, always listening. Peering out from his sling on her back while she worked for the master, cooking and cleaning and sweeping the floor, as though it were the finest marble and not compacted anthill sands. And how far have we come, my son, from that distant place, where we thought at times we would be happy, or that we would all starve, to this new land with its numberless breeds of men and every breed in-between. How far we have come, and how far yet to go.

19

Sam stood beside Sarah Proctor with his hat in his hands. Keane and Mannix and Clement and Barr astride the bench seats in The Stuck Pig, faces clouded by the news that Yankee Sullivan, only hours before his forced release by two dozen armed Sydney-towners and fearing his imminent lynching, had opened his veins with a piece of glass, although none of them believed it and each now suspected a spy within, so near was their plan to execution. Charlie Duane had turned riotous at the news, attacking a newspaper editor who'd pilloried him earlier, kicking his head in. He was arrested, and Casey had gone into hiding, and the Democrat cause looked fatally wounded. There was open Nativist celebration in the form of Mayor Bannon speechifying on the plaza square, surrounded by an armed guard of hard-looking mercenaries, paid for by the merchants, who dressed, fed and watered the deserters and billeted them with their own families for protection.

Before them were arrayed cups of sweet tea and dunking bread, but Mannix called for whisky to mourn Sullivan's passing and that is what they drank. Beside Sam, Sarah Proctor stood with her hip cocked and shawl pulled tight. She was many months pregnant. Dressed in a white cotton pinafore with her bare arms all goosebumps and pale white hairs. She was waiting for her orders, just like Sam.

But first the terms of agreement.

Mannix still wasn't clear on it, and Sam could see the frustration in Keane's eyes and set jaw.

There is murder ahead between these two, he thought, sure as night follows day.

But Keane waved for Mannix to continue. The giant redhead lit a cigar and toasted Sullivan and drank his whisky and glared around the table.

'We got a boy and a whore headed where no Cove has managed to get—inside Walker's house. I don't care what they steal but one of 'em's gotta cut the bastard's throat while he sleeps. Then we pursue the safe. That's the proper order of events. I'm in agreement with the particulars but you got it the wrong way round.'

There was logic to Mannix's declarations, but Sam wasn't going to cut any throat, and they all knew it. Mannix stared long and hard at Sarah Proctor.

'If you can't do it yerself, you let me in of a night. I'll be happy to oblige. And slaughter his whole troop of mercenaries while I'm at it.'

Keane shook his head. 'Walker is the richest of the merchants and his money funds the Nativists. We take his money, then we weaken him, and thereby Bannon too. Samuel, what have you learned?'

Mannix sneered at the question.

'The strongbox in Walker's storehouse is made special against forced entry,' Sam replied. 'It's said to be fireproof and bomb-proof. The key is a singular design. He had the whole thing imported from New York. There's only one key that my mother's aware of, and it's worn around Walker's neck. He only takes it off to sleep. Her idea is to pass it to me and for me to steal his cash reserves and any bank notables that can be carried off and hidden, and return the key and the money to her. Walker will cut off her head if he suspects betrayal.'

Mannix laughed, threw up his hands. 'The wisest course of action is to murder Walker and then turn to Bannon.'

Clement shifted his weight and glanced at Keane, who nodded. 'I thought we agreed that murdering Walker, at this time, would bring down the Governor's fury upon us. The Governor takes our tribute, but that won't count for nothing if we make him come down here with troops. Walker's agitation is all for cleaning up the town but we know what the real ambition is. There are Americans who want our business, our profits and most of all our land. Walker will keep. Let him bleat on. People will tire of him and his antics. The gold is still coming fast from the hills. All the merchants are making money. And a thousand people are arriving by ship, every day.'

Clement nodded and Barr didn't disagree. He'd been wounded on their last sortie into the hinterland, and his leg was strapped and stiff with blood. Clement was the doctor and no doubt had been counselling him while tending the wound.

Mannix looked at them and shrugged. 'You think the boy has the courage to rob Walker's storehouse amid an armed guard? A boy who gets disarmed by an *un*armed savage? And when the weakling gets caught, and speaks of our involvement, what then? And I'm not clear on the purpose of the molly.'

'Leave that to me,' Keane said. Turned to Sam. 'If your robbery is a success, is your true ambition to accompany your mother to Valparaiso, as stated? Leave these shores?'

'Yes, Mr Keane.'

'I commend you to that course of action, now that we know what they're capable of—murdering an innocent man in his cell. We can't take the risk of you being arrested, and so I'm pleased you've found your kin. And the molly will be in place, when we have his key, for our further manoeuvres with Walker, or we'll pull her out when you make your departure.'

Sarah Proctor looked at them like they were fools. Talking about her like she wasn't there. Like Sam's mother, searching for a place in the world where she depended upon no man for her wellbeing. Sam's mother hadn't found that place but she was still looking. Sarah Proctor the same. She'd come eagerly at Keane's bidding, and the offer of employment otherwise than working on her back. The dog was friendly to her and wagged its tail at her arrival. She'd packed nothing because she had nothing to pack. The other mollies shared what they had in the way of dresses but there wasn't much to share. Most of the women made extra by stealing from the drunk miners who were their main custom, but that was a dangerous and often fatal employ. And in a month or more Sarah would be too pregnant for molly-work.

She told Sam all this on their way up the hill. He was shocked to find that Sarah Proctor hadn't left Sydney-town in all that time. It was a cold day with a heavy fog and she held the shawl tight over her chest, as well to hide her breasts from the eyes of the men who tipped their hats and leered. For the first time in his life Sam was properly armed. Keane had insisted that Sam carry on his person a single-shot smoothbore pocket deringer. It hadn't occurred to Sam that escorting a woman through the public streets required a declaration of naked force. The gun was small but heavy in his hand, and he held it beside his leg as they walked the muck. Men coming the other way sized him up and glanced at his gun but soon ignored him and fixed their eyes upon Sarah Proctor.

'You've risen yourself up, Samuel Bellamy, in a way that I never would have guessed. Your mother must be proud.'

Sam looked into the face of the next man approaching before he answered. 'That's only an accident of birth. I'm fast on my feet and the best messenger they have. What is it you hope from this arrangement?'

'You have promised nothing; that is true. But I hope to earn enough money to support myself, or to meet a man who isn't a sour-stinking miner. They want their pleasure but they is none of 'em looking for a wife. They come to town then go back to their claims. Say them all, those yonder mountains are no place for a woman, and judgin from the state of 'em, I'm inclined to believe. But I return the question back upon yourself. What is it that *you* hope from this arrangement?'

Sam laughed, for she had read him truly. His mother had made the request but his own motives were real. 'I would appreciate your reading of my mother. You said to me once that despite everything you've seen, and all that you've suffered, that you're young and not yet damaged beyond any real hope. That because of the drinking, and beating, that every molly, at a point not recognised by themselves, crosses some threshold that means that they're unable to be kindly any longer. My mother has suffered greatly and I do not judge her, but before I throw in my lot, and leave behind my position with the Coves, I'd appreciate your counsel.'

Sarah Proctor put aside a hand from her shawl and patted his shoulder. 'You have well learned these past months. That is a shrewd employment for one so young. I'll do as asked, if you do the same in keeping me apprised of developments that might threaten my position, in the short time that remains before your departure.'

Seagulls feeding on scraps marked the edge of the settlement before the incline that led to Nob Hill. The dog set after the birds and they hovered above and spoke roughly to him and waited skyborne until he'd passed. The track rose into the fog that settled in quicksilver dewdrops on the coastal heath. Between the dun-coloured and vivid-green shrubs, Sam noticed the footprints of the native grey fox, and the dog set off on the spoor and Sam let it go. Sarah was panting and lifting her skirt, and her arms were blotted red as she climbed before him in single file. After twenty minutes they reached the street, and Sarah turned and took in what was visible of the town and embayment, and wiped her brow of sweat and fog-water. Sam led her along the terrace-street and they didn't speak because Sarah was so puffing and had begun to wheeze. She stood in the street with her hands on her hips and her belly thrust forward and looked at the cottages like they were the cottages of her dreams. Among them stood Mr Walker's residence as the most prominent of all.

The Pacific man at the gate was shrouded monk-like in a blanket and looked miserable but his face broke open at the sight of Sarah Proctor. He looked to her hands for luggage but there was none. Instead he bowed and doffed his hat, and Sarah smiled and lifted her skirt over the first step, and he put out a hand and raised her thus.

Inside the parlour, Sarah stared at the walls and the floors and the scrimshaw carvings on the table by the stairs. Down came Sam's mother, wearing a face prepared and eager in its hospitality. She surprised Sam by embracing Sarah and then stood back and looked at her.

'I've prepared a hot bath and will scrub your back myself. It's ready in my chambers. We have much to talk about. Samuel, say goodbye to this lady, whose name I do not know but who I suspect will ken everything about me before the day is out. So eager am I for company.' His mother turned to Sarah and waved her toward the stairs. 'Quickly, lass. I'll speak with my son, but will be with you presently.'

They watched her climb the stairs, looking back every few steps as though in disbelief. 'She seems a friendly sort. Overawed, of course, as I was myself.

She put her mouth to his ear. Held his forearm. 'Is the girl, or any other Sydney-town citizen privy to our plan? Tell me the truth now. Since I last enquired, you didn't tell the Coves about this, did you?'

'No, she isn't. I didn't,' Sam lied.

'Good. I've set her a bath and laid a good feed, because she will not reside here long. Our time is nigh. My husband has confided in me that the paddleboat from Sacramento arrived last night. And that the gold he delivered has been replaced with banknotes sufficient to our needs. Tonight is when you must act. There is a ship at harbour that will take us to Valparaiso in three days. So you must conceal the theft by taking only a portion of the currency, or we'll be discovered. Come to the rear window at midnight, and I'll pass you the key. That will give you ample time. My dear son. Soon we will be free.'

She held him and looked at him and held him again. The smell of rosewater on her skin. 'Be careful, my son. Walker is a dangerous man. Go.'

She kissed his cheek and turned him toward the door.

The cutthroat Anderson Dempsey would have subscribed to certain blood rituals, bowdlerised from the Old Country, before attempting such a task. But the more practical-minded Keane had Sam jumping from rooftop to rooftop and practising the levering of redwood shingles from the roof with a prying-tool borrowed from the farrier. Also from the farrier was a small brick of the softest white clay, to take a mould of the key.

Sam crouched in the dark scrub above his mother's house. In that alien place at that hour he longed for the company of the dog, who was safely with Clement. He'd held the animal against his chest and cooed to it in the expectation that he might never return. Clement was a good man, and didn't need to be asked.

On his way to the hill Sam passed through the Chinese quarter hoping for a glimpse of Ai, where even a shadow on a window would have sufficed. But Chen's establishment was barred and dark and gave off a hostile mood like the man himself when he wasn't pretending. Sam held to the remembrance of her hand in his own, and the smell of the jasmine oil that she combed through her hair. The bright mischief in her eyes. That rare smile and those pretty teeth. The warmth of her body when she sat beside him. Her delicate phrasing of the British tongue.

He was frightened, laid out on his belly in the bushland in the dark. Like the bushland along the Swan River, he could see why the natives, according to Clement, also importuned the night spirits with shamanistic flattery and respectful dances, and otherwise huddled together in temporary domelike structures of bark around a warming fire and were always ready to move camp if the auguries were wrong. Clement told him that the measles and the smallpox had wiped out most of the Ohlone Indians who, like the Swan River blacks, tended the land with firestick and song. It was their absence, in that cold night, that made for Sam a powerful presence, and with the fog on his shoulders and the muffling of sound, the calls of the owl and fox were startling in their proximity.

So he was grateful when the candlelight appeared in the laundry window, which was the sign. Up until that moment his fear at the coming trial was contained in the idea that his next actions weren't quite real. He scampered down the hill, and climbed the stave-fence, and his nerves were restrained by the series of simple actions that were urgent and stealthy in the light of pressing time. His mother's pale hand held the key on a silver chain. It was the first time he had seen her skin, and he looked closely at it because her face didn't reveal itself. He took the key and returned to the bush, and from there made his way down the track and into the lamplit streets of the better part of town.

Walker's storehouse, like each of the major buildings on the plaza square, was gabled lengthwise to the street. There were guards stationed three on the front porch and one at the side entrances and two in the yard at the rear. They sat before braziers, and smoked and muttered, and he listened as he climbed the stairs at the rear of the emporium that was stationed beside the government commissary, and beside that Walker's storehouse. Each of the buildings was three-storeys high, and made out of mudstone block, stuccoed with limewash and mortar.

Sam hoisted himself onto the shingled roof of the Emporium and measured with his eye the pattern of the nailed shingles and the location of the joists. He had been warned by Keane that the constant quaking of the ground loosened the shingles and broke the fixing nails, and that although his instincts would draw him to the roof-peak, he would better avoid that transport because then he'd be visible from the square. So he crawled over the shingles, and many of them were loose, and he felt with his hands the way before him. His nerves were settled, and his way was slow with the required concentration to avoid spilling to his death. He reached the edge of the building and peered below, and saw no guards.

Firming the farrier's tool in its sling over his shoulder, and the knife at his belt, he leapt catlike onto the commissary and settled onto his belly. As advised, he lay there for a goodly time and let the stars turn above him before beginning his traverse toward the next roof. This roof was recently fixed, and his hands met with the buckled and snapped nails from before the latest quake.

He made good time, and peered over the edge at the guard beneath him, and measured his leap and the possibility of his moonlit shadow passing over the guard. But the guard's head was on his chest. He'd made himself comfortable with a Mexican shawl, and his boots were turned out like a man asleep. Sam knelt and fixed his fingers on the rough shingles. He leapt, then lay there for the sound to hide itself in the darkness, waiting for his breathing to settle. But his heart was beating faster and his palms were clammy; his belly began its twitching dance.

Sam returned to action before the nerves overcame him and froze him to the spot. The rough diagram of the internal layout of the establishment carried in his mind. The awareness that guards might be stationed inside.

He sat above the edge of the roofline where the drop inside would be lowest, and began to work loose the shingles with the farrier's tool as he had practised. The roof hadn't been lately fixed and the iron nails groaned as they came loose. He lay the shingles in a neat formation and removed enough to let him inside. He braced himself with his hands and peered into the dark. It was as his mother described. The top floor given over to storage. He saw the bulky shapes of tea-chests piled one above the other, and bales of softer material that smelt of lanolin, and now that his eyes were adjusted the giant hardwood beams, joists and uprights that supported the roof. Very quietly he let himself inside the roofline and felt with his boots the nearest tea-chest and then he was inside. Ears and eyes and all his senses attuned to the sound of boots on the stairs. No smell of torch or pitch or brazier-coke. The great black pipe of the internal heating that rose through the floors gone cold in the shadows.

He could see surprisingly well, and made for the stairs, and each step down through the building he paused and listened and looked around. On the ground floor he made for the corner office. He knelt before the great plate-iron strong-box and ran his hands over its face.

As described, the iron-box was big enough to lock a man inside, fronted by a hinged cast-iron door adopted from a safe. Sam's fingers traced its dimensions and felt the welds and returned to the lock. He placed the key inside the lock and turned his head to regard the windows and worked the key with his ears. It required no great force. He heard the tumblers snip and drop into place. He worked his fingers to the edge of the door and pulled it slowly open. Keane would have kept the hinges unoiled but the heavy door made no sound. He opened it enough for him to slip inside, and pulled it behind him. Lit a match whose brightness burned his eyes and made him look away. Saw the bounty all pressed into shelves and so deep that the match-flame didn't illuminate but only hinted at the gold stored there. Walker's wealth impossible to measure. A shelf given to banknotes in neat array. A shelf given to notables and promissory declarations and bonds and titles to gold-claims and town buildings. A shelf of gold dust and flake placed in leather bags of different weights. A box of nuggets and a sack on the floor of dust and flake, too heavy to lift. A wooden crate of rifles and cartons of ammunition.

Sam regarded everything and returned to the banknotes and as instructed reached into the middle of every pile and extracted notes to the depth of his thumb. There were a hundred or so piles, and he stuffed the notes into his shoulder sling and straightened the piles and made sure that everything appeared as before. The smell of match-head sulphur in the confined space was strong, however, and he admired his mother who had thought of this eventuality and suggested that before departing he wait with the safe-door open for a good while. He stood by the open door until he'd counted to three-score and then knelt and worked the door shut. The door locked easily, and he replaced the key on its chain under his shirt, and with his sleeves wiped away any dirt-smudges from his fingers. He arose through the building and onto the roof as though in a dream. The shingles could not be hammered into place so he sat and listened while he bent the prised nails free of the four shingles and slipped them back under their cousins to form a seal against the rain. The night air was cold against his skin and he felt giddy, and understood that he needed to breathe deeply for a spell. He listened to the muttering of the guards and began to crawl toward the patch of low sky against which was silhouetted the gable peak. He reached the peak and looked down at the sleeping guard and cast his eyes around the scene of the sleeping town shrouded in wood smoke and fog. He pressed his fingers to the leaden gable-cap, took a deep breath and leapt into the air.

20

But where he'd hoped for happiness and relief, his mother's face showed only disappointment. She sat at the porphyry table beside her bed with the banknotes arrayed in piles and measured him with her stare.

'You sure nothin fell lost on your way here? This ain't enough.'

She was speaking her real language, and gone was the disappointment. Her eyes were angry beyond anything he'd seen of her.

'I risked my neck, and this ain't enough. Not to set-up on another shore. Not for more than a few months.'

Sam had delivered the blue canvas bag of money on its rawhide sling in the hour before dawn, as instructed. His Ma sitting in the laundry darkness waiting for him. Didn't speak, just put her hand into the coldness and hooked the bag and the keychain and pulled the curtain shut. He'd returned three hours later when Mr Walker was gone from the house. Could have sworn on his life that he'd stole more money than that. The bag had been fairly bulging.

Now she had her head in her hands. 'It ain't enough, and he suspects. Come here, boy.'

Sam sat beside her on the bed. She slung a sisterly arm around his shoulder, drew him in. 'You was brave, my son. But now we got to take steps. I saw his face, this morning. He took up the key off that there dresser and his face smudged with suspicion. He places it just so. Sets it with angles in mind according to some mathematic of his. So he'll know if it's been moved. I *did* put it back just so, I'm sure. But maybe got it wrong, by an inch.'

Sam squeezed his mother's hand draped around his neck. 'Ma, you got worry. Might be readin—'

Her laugh was a convulsion of ridicule and anger. 'Don't hazard to tell me, boy, what I got right or wrong. I know the bastard. He suspects, and where he suspects, he acts. He don't account for no margin of error. He just goes ahead and exacts his retribution and if he's wrong he don't lose any sleep. So we are likely doomed. The key wasn't right and he knows I moved it. Was there in his voice. What he said.'

'What did he say Ma?'

'Said, slow and clear, what he always says when he intends to punish me. That he'll have *words* when he gets home. And it was then I reckoned his next course of action. The certainty of his next port of call. That fast as his gelding can carry him, he'll be in his strongbox counting his money and matching the accounting against his records. So by now he'll know exactly how much we stole. And then he'll kill me, son, this time he will, you wait and see.'

'I won't let that happen, Ma. I *won't*.'

'I know, son, I know. You're a good, brave boy. But I bought us some time, and I got to apologise about that.'

He looked to her, but she wouldn't meet his eyes. In the midday light her skin was sallow and her hair was haloed by particulates of dust. Her mouth was grim, her lips bloodless.

'Son, I told him what you told me. A mortal secret between us, I know. I had to buy us some time. But I kept your name out of it, I promise. Told him that the whore told me, let it slip. The location of the Coves' strongbox, as you described. All their gold. Their unofficial bank and treasure chest. And that's why we got to act now. The ship I told you about, that's Chile-bound. She leaves at dawn tomorrow morning. We got to be on it, or I'm dead.'

Without knowing, Sam stood away from her. Couldn't believe what he was hearing. 'Where's Mr Walker now, if he ain't countin his money?'

She looked at him without guilt or shame, her chin raised. 'He's gone to the Presidio, with his cutthroats. He means to make the major there an offer. He told me as much. If the major will lead his company of Indun-killers tonight against Sydney-town, acting on Mr Walker's instructions as to the location of their bank, the military may take whatever they desire. All the money and gold they can carry. So long as they burn Sydney-town to the ground...'

She saw his move to the door, even before he thought it, and stood to block him. Held his forearm in a fierce grip. Washerwoman hands beneath the doeskin gloves. 'Son, I know you're bone-weary, as am I. But we got to think straight and act fast. I risked my neck and yours to steal from my husband. That is a betrayal justified by me but, in this lawless place, not by any other. I'll hang for it, as will you. If you love me as your mother, and if you value your skin, you'll do as I say. You must plunder the Coves' strongbox before the army arrives. In the melee that follows their warfare, nobody will notice your crime. We can make the ship tomorrow morning and flee with our lives, and our livelihoods guaranteed against every future hardship. Son, don't struggle...'

For Sam was wrenching this way and that. Tears in his eyes. She began to shake him and he let himself be shook. 'I showed my loyalty to you by stealin from my husband. Now it's your turn. You have loyalty for them that took you in, but you reckon they feel the same? Love you like your mother does? They have given you employment in their devices and their schemes but that is demonstration that they have only used you, an innocent boy, and will continue until you're all used. You're still a wee lad but you got to act manly here. For me. Your lovin Ma.'

It was just a glance but the tears in her eyes were pulsing onto her face. Her lips trembling and her voice shaken by a depth of emotion that she hadn't yet shown. Pleading with him, holding her to him. His own tears soaking the shoulder of her satin bodice.

'Ma, tell me you sent Sarah Proctor down off this hill to the shore. Tell me that.'

'I did, son. I did. I took no joy in abusin her name, but I got to keep you clear of this. Till we are clear and free ourselves. Go now. Steal as much as you can. Meet me on the docks tomorrow morning before daybreak. Keep free of the night's bloodshed. Let the men who've imprisoned us and used us fall upon each other. The ship's name is the *Mary Jane* and we are set on the cabin manifest as Mrs Bellamy and Son. The way it used to be.'

The dog fell in behind. It had blood on its mouth from eating rabbits whole. Sam kept to the track, which had dried somewhat in the hour of sunshine the skies allotted before the clouds closed in again. The ocean was a clotted green colour, and there were flocks of gulls and terns diving into a circle where the water bounced like stones in a sieve about five hundred yards from shore. Three or four great pelicans dove into the spitting wash and scooped a bladderful of whatever it was crowded to the surface. Sam paid the rim of his hat through his fingers in little rips like he had seen others do with rosaries. He didn't feel any better or clearer in his mind.

He had told his mother the truth about the Coves' iron-cage lock-up on the same floor as the armoury and medics' room but that didn't mean he ever reckoned on stealing from it. A boy his age is assumed a natural thief, and he'd been careful to avoid the room and never linger outside the door. He heard the iron door hinges groan when all the bawdy-houses and card games had tallied their takings and delivered them in person every morning. Usually it was Barr who sat at his wooden bench with his sleeves rolled up and drank coffee and counted the money and weighed the gold dust and made a tally in his ledger.

There was an unofficial payday of sorts every Friday when all of the Coves drank together and Keane passed out calico bags to each member according to their cut. A measure of their mutual trust, Sam never once saw a man open his packet in front of the others. Sam was paid his own salary directly from Keane's waistcoat pocket, in accordance with their agreement, dependent upon the men he'd lured to the Cove, and how much they'd lost at table or were otherwise parted with their money by way of ruse or diversion. His own savings amounted to twenty-two gold eagles and near a pound of gold dust. That was more than he would earn in twenty years back in Van Diemen's Land once his ticket came through. It was enough for him to buy land and a house, but in the meantime he'd set his mind on buying Ai's freedom from the Chinaman, something he hadn't told her. But that too would have to wait. There was the matter at hand.

Back at The Stuck Pig, Sam needed a clear head, and lacking Borden's sweetwater ordered ale instead of porter or rum. The old man in the tricorne passed the wooden mug and answered Sam's question. He didn't know where Keane was, but Mannix was said to be with Casey, the Democrat, who was hiding out in Sydney-town. His henchman Charlie Duane was that morning put on the steamer to Panama, and the plan was to exile Casey in the same manner. Clement was asleep somewhere, having waited all night for Sam's return. The Ancient ruffled Sam's hair with a claw that smelt of dishwater and tobacco juice, lifted a plate of roast corn from near the floor and passed it over. Sam took his bench and ate and drank, while the old man fed the dog from a plate of cold stew.

Sam didn't finish the ale or the stick of corn but got up and paced the boards. His guts were a mess. The thought of stealing from Keane and Clement made the walls crowd closer. He needed sea air, and called the dog and took to the streets. If he was going to steal from the Coves' strongroom then now was the perfect time, but he couldn't banish the unease he felt every time he thought on it. The idea of betraying Clement did not abide with any kind of picture of himself that didn't stink of shame. And yet his mother's fear for her life was real. She would understand, if Sam wasn't caught.

The dog got there before Sam. The farrier was hammering at a pony shoe direct from the fire. The room smelt of coal-dust and the goblin-leather of the billows that in repose looked fearful to the dog. The man put aside his hammer and tongs and removed his leather gloves and wiped sweat on his leather jerkin. Sam didn't have to ask him. The man went to the wall where there was arrayed a nail-board lined with keys. He selected the key and held it up to the dim firelight and spat on it and took a small file from a leather satchel and worked its edges and spat on it again and wiped it of filings. He looked satisfied and passed Sam the key, which to the naked eye matched the original in every detail.

'The best I could do. A copy from an impression ain't never perfect. If it don't open, listen with your fingers to where the obstruction is, and bring it back. I always gets it right.'

'Thank you, sir.'

Clement still wasn't in the bar and wasn't asleep in his cot either. Because of the opium resin, when Clement slept it was deep and long and he slept in many places along the street. Keane wasn't upstairs either, and Sam deliberately avoided looking at the strongroom door as though some force might overcome his mind and turn his hand to his mother's bidding. In Keane's office, Sam leaned over the desk. Now that he'd made up his mind, he felt calm. He took up feather and quill and wrote the message in precise little scratches. He held up the parchment and blew on it and watched the ink settle into the fibres and stain where he'd been heavy with the quill.

Sam passed the note to the old man behind the bar. The Ancient didn't have letters, so Sam made sure to tell of the urgency of the matter. The man tilted back his tricorne hat and mock saluted and put the message under a tankard. He called the dog and knelt and scratched its ears, held its head as it watched Sam leave.

Ai looked for the dog in the alley behind Sam, and so he told her. That he would be leaving. Paid particular attention to her response, which was to twist her nose, look away down the alley.

'I got no choice in the matter. Though I ain't goin far. Just south of the equator. They call it Chile. The town is Valparaiso. And I got to ask you. Can you write a letter?'

Ai thought about it, or perhaps about something else. She looked sad.

'I could write to you,' Sam added. 'Come visit you one day.'

But she didn't respond. Scratched one bare toe with the toes of her other foot. Looked from his sheathed knife to the pocket deringer in its sling across his chest. His muddy boots and hat kneaded in his fingers, pushing the brim and waiting for her.

He leaned closer. Bold enough to take her hand. She was still taller than him and he looked up into her eyes. His own eyes bleary and sore from sleeplessness. Hoped he didn't make a bad impression, like some drunk.

'Listen. I got to ask. I know he ain't your father. I know he owns you, like I own my dog. I been in that situation myself, but I got myself extricated. I can help you do that. I got some money coming to me, if money's what it'll take.'

He had hurt her. She made to pull away, but he held to her hands. 'Please. I don't want nothing from you. But I can help.'

She looked at him, shook her head. 'Samuel...'

The word, so beautiful on her lips. But her eyes were distant. The sadness gone. A clarity, come from bitter experience, perhaps, but it aged her voice, made her smile painful to see. 'It's not money. It's a different kind of ... debt. I will never be free of it. You wouldn't understand.'

He winced at the certainty in those eyes. Had to look away, like a fool, down at his hat.

'Those stories of China that I told you, I took them all from picture books. There are no cobbled highways near my village, or curious animals. In my village there was only famine. Every family had to give many sons and daughters. The debt isn't mine alone.'

'Your sister. She's dead, isn't she?'

Ai made no expression. 'Yes, she's dead. Of the typhus.'

Sam nodded. 'You see, you're alone, and I'm alone. And our people. We aren't so different. Everywhere my people go, your people go too. I'm sayin I can try to understand.'

Her gentle smile. 'But I will write to you, Samuel. Once you arrive, and write to me.'

He felt the pressure behind his eyes. Couldn't speak any more. Lifted her hand to his lips, and kissed. Turned and walked down the alley. Felt her eyes on his back, until he rounded the corner, and let himself fall alongside a bullock-team and a sulky with iron wheels and four Russian sealers in pelts and woollen caps singing a low and mournful song up at the empty sky.

There was no going in the roof. The town was built right past the square now, and the hills that rose around were crowded with shacks and canvas tents, and the twack-thwack chorus of hammers on nail. He would be visible from the street and from every side, and there was likely labourers in the goods-floor working the block-and-tackle from the loading bay. Sam straightened his waistcoat and collar and went in the back door. There were bullock-teams direct from the inland sawmills, and from the port, bearing barrels of whale-oil and bolts of cloth and canvas. Flour-sacks and sacks of barley and oats and barrels of salt-pork direct from Australia. Sam nodded at some of the stevedores and bullockies who he knew by name. In the loading bay there were crates stamped from all the world, and bales of spun cotton and pallets of canned goods and open caskets with iron-goods ready for the miner's hand. Wagon wheels and windmill blades and millstones. Shirtless men lugging hessian sacks of flour piled on the loading bay floor. Sam wended his way between them, holding out the message he'd scratched for Mr Walker's eyes only. If he was asked.

But there was nobody guarding the stairwell, just as there'd been no cutthroats stationed outside. As his mother had described, Walker's men were over at the Presidio, prevailing on the major to gather his Indian-killers in a raiding party against Sydney-town. Sam went downstairs, appearing not to hurry. He cast his eyes into the gloom and made out some clerks at their desks in an office made of plank-wood with no ceiling. The babble of salesmen and drunks and the pedalled grindstone of the knife sharpener working at a blade. A hawker of smoked fish calling out his wares.

Sam got to the bottom of the stairs and fell to his knees and began to crawl. There was the old iron safe against the corner and open to view from above shelf-height. He held the gun against his chest and crawled in the dust and got splinters in his palms because he was listening over his back. He got to the strongbox and took out the key from his waistcoat pocket and spat on it like the farrier had told him and rubbed it wet all over. He took out the pistol and laid it on the floor beside him. Put the key in the lock, and closed his eyes, and held his breath as though that might help. Heard the lock snip and the tumblers knock and turn. Took the safe door at the base and pulled it open enough to get inside. Picked up the gun and looked back at the empty floor and went inside the safe. Pulled it shut with the welded handle and finally breathed. Put his hands on his knees and wiped the tears of relief from his eyes. Felt like laying down on the floor and balling himself up small as possible. But there was the darkness and the confinement and the sickness of fear in his belly. He checked that the door was shut and lit a match and reached for the shelves and began to stow away the banknotes. And it was then that he saw the bag. Blue canvas with a rawhide strap. The one he'd given his mother. Tossed onto the piles of money. He opened the neck and looked inside. More than his mother had showed him, as he'd suspected. The same amount that he'd stolen. Didn't know what that meant except the murder of his mother, and then the bolt of anger burst behind his eyes and made it all red. He felt his hands stowing the banknotes but he couldn't see for the red haze of wildfire blood and when the bag was full he didn't see his hands reach for the matchbox and strike a flame and throw the match among the shelved papers; the notables and deeds and claims on men and property. The bonds and the promissory notes and the remaining banknotes. The records of everything Walker owned, including people. But Sam should have been out of the safe by now. Smelt the choking fumes and heard the crackle of paper afire. Felt the heat on his face and the noxious broil against his hands. And suddenly his vision cleared and he saw what he'd done and reached for the door. The door was yanked open, and he fell and was pulled. Held down with a boot on his throat. Looked up at the face of the bearded cutthroat and watched Walker enter the safe and heard his terrible cry. The boot pressed down on Sam's throat and he looked into the man's face but there was no mercy in those eyes or in the set of his mouth. There was fire at the doorsill and Walker emerged with his sleeves aflame and his face blackened and that was the last thing Sam saw.

21

Sam woke up at the drenching. The bucket of water frozen in time. His mouth open and his dripping head. Wet hair in his mouth. Somehow missed the part where the water hit, until he came round again. Lashed to a chair on the top floor of Walker's establishment. Sarah Proctor was tied to a chair beside. Black-eyed and bloody mouthed where her teeth had gone through her lip. She was unconscious, but a bucket was coming for her. He watched Walker's man take the bucket off the block-and-tackle hoist and walk to Sarah and douse her and she awoke with a scream. She had been badly abused. Her pinafore was bloodied and hoisted to her baby-swollen belly. Sam heard the heavy footsteps and knew them for Walker. The angry Southlander hove into view and his face was wet where he'd washed the cinders of his fortune clean. His hair was combed and his black beard glistened. His dark eyes fringed with red. Either the smoke or he'd wept over his loss, it didn't matter now. He stared down at Sam and began to cough and a sooty spittle rained on Sam's face.

'What is it?'

The man in the black suit who'd waited in the sunlight by the loading bay clothed in pale road-dust was by Walker's side. Bearer of bad tidings, his whole aspect said.

'They ain't comin'. Tonight or any other time. I come soon as I was told.'

Walker grabbed the man's throat. Got his face eye to eye. Hoisted him a little. 'Why not? He took my gold.'

The smaller man closed his eyes and let himself be hung but

in the meantime waved to a leather saddlebag by the bay. Walker thrust him away. 'He give a reason?'

'Nothin but what he said to you. Half his company is out on the road, searchin for untame Induns. Didn't fancy takin it up to some white men. But I saw a Vandemonian there, come out of the major's office. Recognised him by his gait and possum-skins. Unsaddled but on a rein, tied to the hitchin post outside the major's door, was the finest damn thoroughbred horse I ever seen, an' the only one I ever seen on this damn coast. Tall and proud and glistenin black. I reckon you can draw your own conclusions there, sir.'

'Course I bloody can. Well, it don't matter. We got the making of a mob outside in the square. Come to watch a hangin'. Get to it.'

Walker waved at two ropes coiled in the sunlight. Sam understood. His letter to Keane warning him about Walker's plan to use the army to burn out Sydney-town had been read and acted upon. Sam closed his eyes again and felt his chair lifted and the sunlight on his face. His feet in the drop. The sound of the crowd and their disapproval at the sight of a boy and a pregnant woman. Hand around his neck, from the back. He opened his eyes and looked over the gathered faces and there were many that he knew and many he didn't. Russians and Germans and Chinese. Mormons in their black suits and hats. Miners with red sashes at their waists and necks and wrists glittering with gold chain. A rough hand pressed Sam's head and Walker stepped out onto the gantry and stood there with his hands on his hips and riding boots shining in the thin sunlight.

Sam looked across at Sarah Proctor, who was looking at him.

'I'm sorry, Sarah. My Ma told me she was sendin you away.'

Sarah spat blood into the wind. 'She was never sendin me away. I was there just for this. She was always goin to frame me up for stealin.'

There were two men in the crowd distributing silver coin to each of the gathered, and Walker nodded approvingly to another at its fringes, who had a bucket of pitch and some kindling torches.

'My Ma, she's alive?'

'No, she ain't. *He* done for her, even after she blamed me. I didn't see it, but I heard it.' Sarah Proctor spat again, licked blood off her lips. 'There's no use blowin on a dead coal, Samuel Bellamy. I was aimin to tell you. I'm sorry for your Ma, but that woman was broken and bent every way. Not an ounce of human feelin left. And I truly am sorry for that. You got to her too late. I seen the like, as described, and was probably headed there myself. Though I ain't now, neither me or my babe.'

Sam's tears blurred his vision and when he blinked them away he saw Clement at the edge of the crowd, slouch hat pulled low, but that familiar set of the shoulders and scraggy beard. Saw him lift his head and take aim at Walker with a revolver and the faces of those around him and the crack of the ball on the iron gantry and the gunsmoke clothing his head as the crowd fell upon him. Pulled him this way and that. Stomped and wrenched him until three of Walker's men got inside the circle and clamped him with their great arms.

Walker turned on the iron beam and smiled at Sam. 'One more for the hangin'. Evidence of his malfeasance for all to see. I expect more and have prepared a welcoming.'

On the rooftops and balconies around the square the hard men of Walker's company arose at his waved command. Some twenty or so. Armed with rifles that glinted in the sun.

There was cursing and kicking behind them as Clement was drug up the stairs.

'You got to be brave now, boy,' said Walker. 'You got to reckon-up with your maker.'

Sam's throat was choked. 'You murderin bastard, you'll pay in Hell. My Ma—'

That made Walker smile. 'Stupid boy. She ain't your Ma. Nothin of the sort. She come out of Moreton Bay convict establishment, where I took her from. That story about her family and the blacks was just a story for these fools. And for you as it happens. When you came to her, I assume she humoured you along. Got you to steal for her. Which is why you're hangin—for the theft and her murder.'

Sam made to speak but Walker struck him on the face.

'God damnation. Hurry him along.'

At the pointed finger of one of his minions, Walker turned and regarded the flagpole in the square. There was no flag on it but the ropeline had begun to clank against the cleats that fastened it. The sun was high, and the drifting fog off the ocean had stilled. Sam felt the first breeze off the eastern land on his face. The smell of brine and seaweed and wood smoke from Sydney-town.

Sam looked to his right and Clement was standing there bound in hemp. His face was bloodied and his mouth was gagged but he nodded in kindness at Sam. Then a noose went over each of their necks and for the first time Sam looked down at the drop. The weeds in the banked dirt. The stains of spat tobacco. The prints of boots and bare feet in the wheel-churned muck. A panic came over him, and he glimpsed his dog in his mind, and closed his eyes and apologised to the dog and to his mother that he'd never know. A gag was thrust into his mouth, and he couldn't breathe, and with every beat of his heart the fear got worse, and the terrible weight came over him even as he floated above himself.

He saw the black snake then, watching him, and he apologised to it as well. The snake stared long and hard in reply, and then it did what no snake had ever done—it blinked, and closed its lidless eyes.

Sam came round when Walker shouted, paraded to the edge of the beam as he'd done before, and threw up his hands to the gathered crowd.

'Good people of this town. Lately the most terrible kind of

betrayal has been visited upon me by the condemned stationed behind. A calculated and evil scheme hatched in the parlours of Sydney-town by those noted cutthroats who have plagued us too long. My beloved's life was taken after the worst kind of deception—perpetrated by a boy masquerading as her long-lost son, but I stand before you today as evidence of the prevailing force of justice. Those torches being distributed and the knives and guns at our disposal will be our means and a true measure of this manifest force. As we carry the flame down to the stinking shoreline, we carry among ourselves the divine—'

The first shot broke over the square and rang in its empty spaces and bent the heads of the gathered men. A hard volley followed that made even Walker flinch, and reach for his revolver, and take aim at the horse-charges that broke into the square from the northern and eastern streets led by Keane on one flank and Mannix on the other, followed by Southlanders on foot bearing muskets and bayonets and flaming torches, shouting fiercely to break the spirits of the gathered mob. In this they were successful, and Walker swore, and began firing, as did the men behind Sam.

Walker shouted to one of them to turn Clement off, but the man refused because he was using Clement as a shield, as Sam was used. The Southlanders tossed the flaming torches onto the porches of the establishments and turned to their guns and some of them were shot and some of them brought down the rooftop men and the snipers on the balconies who fell and were still.

Walker crouched and emptied his revolver in the direction of Keane but the gunsmoke blew into the loading bay and made it hard to see. Walker holstered his emptied pistol and clambered through the smoke, pushing Sam toward the edge but something held him fast. He looked to Clement, who was on his toes twisting in the wind while the cutthroat in black fired from behind. Sarah Proctor was making herself small, and twisting her head to get away from the terrible noise of the pistol at her ear. Sam felt his hands come free at the back, and his chair get dragged away from the edge. He was lifted and laid down, and pulled by his lifeless arms out of the line of fire. He recognised the rescuing party as the steersman on the whaler who he'd rescued in turn, cut free of the wheel and seen go over the edge. The steersman didn't say anything, just gave over his newly charged pistol to Sam and ran for the stairs.

The gunman behind Sarah Proctor looked in his powder-bag to recharge his rifle but the bag was empty and he saw the gun that Sam trained on him and backed away and fled down the stairs as well.

The man in black behind Clement levered another charge into his pistol and took aim but the blood was back in Sam's legs and he crawled to his feet and took a step, Clement watching him come. The fear made Sam's steps heavy like he was wading in mud, but the man was turned away, and that made it easier. Sam didn't fire because his finger wouldn't allow it, but he nevertheless got a leg raised and kicked the man behind the knee, and when he buckled, pushed him again and over he went.

Sam laid down the revolver and untied the knot at Clement's ankles and unwound the length that finished at the old man's wrists. Clement grunted, and took off the noose and did the same for Sarah Proctor, and they didn't speak because the sound was deafening, and the flames were growing bigger as the pine-board shopfront and shingled rooftops caught fire in great sheets. Sam took up the pistol again and looked down into the melee and saw the great redheaded Mannix drive his horse up to Keane and in the midst of the confusion and the other man's firing, Mannix lifted his pistol and fired into the back of Keane's head. Turned his horse and called his men and bolted into the nearest street. Sam's body went limp and he stared until he felt Clement by his side and when the old man saw the fallen Keane dragged about by his stirrups he cried out a terrible sad cry.

There was a tugging on Sam's sleeve, and he looked to his feet as a sheet of flame closed the loading bay. Sarah Proctor was pulling him toward the stairs. The second storey was on fire too, and the flames danced about in pretty whirlpools in the sawdust and the bales of cotton roared into life and leapt one upon the other. On the ground floor the plank-wood partitions were aflame, enticing the fire through the building one room at a time. Sam saw the strongroom door open and a handcart with a wooden wheel taking weight, and he led Clement through the smoke and raised the pistol and opened the soot-blackened safe door and there was Walker, bag of gold dust in each hand, ready to toss onto the handcart. The shelves where his paper money and notables had burned now charred and wet. Walker saw that Clement was blinded by smoke and blood and looked at the gun in Sam's hand and laughed. For he had taken his measure of the boy already. Didn't even look at the shaking hand or the frozen finger or the knees that were trembling. Dropped the gold dust and reached out from the scorched insides of the safe to disarm Sam but the pistol fired and opened Walker's side and spun him into the shelving. There was no more shot or ball for the pistol. Sam fell to the nearest bag of gold and hefted it above his head and brought it down on the great dome and the man grunted and crumpled and immediately started to raise himself. Sam raised the bag one more time but heard a warlike shriek and saw Sarah Proctor charge into the room with a pitchfork that she thrust bayonet-like into Walker's ribs who so impaled fell sideways into the ashes of the earlier fire. The great fork trembled as he thrashed and was still.

'Pass it.'

Sarah Proctor's hand beseeching, claiming the bag of dust in the leather sack. Some twenty or thirty more of the same. Beams were falling onto the storey above them and Sam bent to his labours and the handcart was too heavy and Sarah Proctor disappeared and returned with another. Clement righted the last one and transferred its weight across. The box of nuggets and the singed bag of banknotes Sam had delivered to his mother. The unloaded revolver in Walker's holster.

The two handcarts were taken one each by Sam and Sarah Proctor to the great bolted rear loading-bay door where looters were clamouring for entry. Sam and Clement clothed their hoard with blanket and miners' sieves and Clement unlocked the door and the looters flooded into the flaming building. The same people out in the square they were. Numbered at five score or more, Russians mostly and a few Americans in canvas trousers and red shirts and oilskin coats and armed with knives. The party ran to the stairs and Clement kicked over a cart-board, and the handcarts were walked carefully down the plank and onto the heated dirt.

The fire was all around them and they watched it spread across the hill into the squatters' camps and up Russian Hill to settle in a great swathe of red-green flame at the base of Nob Hill while behind them it burned in a strangely precise angle up the side of Goat Hill. They wove the carts through the square until they came to the fallen Keane. Nothing of his face remained, and Clement groaned pitifully and fell to him and wept and took up Keane's great revolver and hefted it and made the face of war. They weren't in a position to carry the tall man and all the horses were bolted, and Clement shook the revolver on his thin arms in a way that defied natural strength, and suggested the inhuman capacity of the enraged man for final acts of revenge. He shook the revolver until his arms finally weakened, and then he lay the gun on the handcart and turned from the body.

The buildings around were already guttering while others burned in tall columns that hissed and roared. The way to Sydney-town opened up to the east with the groan and collapse of buildings there burnt out and they huddled together and Clement lifted the revolver and pointed it at anyone who looked close. For the lags of Sydney-town had followed the flames down from their camps on the hill and up from the shore and they entered the square with bags and picks and drawn knives ready to loot and plunder. They were many of them drunk, and cheering as establishments fell inwards and windows burst and beams cracked and thumped the ground. All the way down the hill Sam watched the carrion-birds from the Southland picking over the charred remains with picks and poles.

The air quietened as they left the flame-front behind. The looters amongst the ashes and cinders who were spread across the hellish flanks of the old town took on the postures of seashore fossickers, picking over the fallen beams and charred boards.

'They look for the yeller, or the strongbox, in the melt and the burn.'

Clement was struggling, a hand on Sam's shoulder, limping along. The barrow was heavy and the road was sandy with ruts and puddles. The old man took to muttering and shaking his head. They paused in the street to rest and saw horsemen bearing torches led by Mannix enter the Chinese quarter and begin to shoot and burn.

'It was Mannix that shot Keane,' Sam said. 'I saw him take his chance in the gunfight.'

Clement squeezed Sam's shoulder. 'It's good that you told me. For now you must never speak of it again. The world of Sydney-town, the world I knew and favoured, has gone.'

They looked down the hill to the Cove and despite the fact that because of the north-easterly wind there was no fire burning in that quarter, alone among the whole town, the truth of Clement's statement was manifest in the vision of Mannix, his blood up and revolver spearing fire into the unarmed Chinese, raising a clay-jar of whisky to his lips in a toast to his deeds.

Sam left the handcart handles and took up the pistol, but Clement stayed his hand.

'I warned Ai, you know. I told Chen this morning the likely turn of events. Like many of his kind, he will have taken to the sand dunes to watch and wring his hands but live another day. Don't concern yourself with Mannix. His kind aren't easily killed. That is the nature of devils.'

Sarah Proctor coughed and spat black into the dirt. 'I want to thank you, old man. I know you favour this boy, as do I, who I think of as a little brother. Because you surely fired at Walker from the square, so as to get yourself a noose alongside us. For to bring your friends to our aid.'

Clement smiled. 'Which is not to credit that I didn't aim true.'

'Thank you, Clement. And I'm sorry about Keane.'

The old man nodded. 'He was like a son to me—that is true. A remembrance of myself at that age. And now he is gone, although the truth is strange and melancholy. It was a matter of time, as he would have said. For he longed to depart this world, and he wore that longing in a cloth of courageous action and ready alarm. I'll miss him, Samuel, but you must not be like him. For I see myself in you also, at your age, in your capacity for fellow-feeling. There are too many who bear the human form but there is a part of them dead. Mannix is such a man.'

Clement took the pistol from Sam's hand, and placed it on the handcart. 'You see, we stand in the street and discourse on fate and goodness, and it transports us from the task at hand. Woman, I don't know your name, but I see no reason why the contents of that handcart mightn't be yours to cleverly hide, and in hiding, bear you good fortune for the rest of your days.'

'I hadn't thought to ask your blessings, old man, but I reckon a place, sure enough.'

Sarah Proctor embraced Sam and kissed the top of his head, and took up the handcart. Sam and Clement followed at a quiet distance, within pistol-range, to protect her if needed from the leering fools still leaving the Cove to loot in the hills above. But she looked so bloodied and the contents of the handcart so wretched that she wasn't molested, and they watched her trundle along the shoreline street, up toward the bawdy-house where she was quartered, the lemony sunlight reflected off the bay catching in her matted hair and the strong muscles of her shoulders as the cart rolled forward.

'My wager's that she'll sink the load in the privy forthwith, clever woman that she is. Where nobody'll think to look.'

Sam looked to Clement, even as he saw the dog bowl out of The Stuck Pig and down the steps and roll its hindquarters in the dusty street before straightening into a run, its tongue lolling and its ropey legs building speed as its joyful eyes trained on Sam and nobody else.

'And us, Clement, the same?'

The old man laughed. 'No, I have a secure pit for my hoardings, beneath the fettler's yard. Let's go directly, and not look back.'

The dog leapt and the concussion in Sam's legs nearly took him over. He held the dog by its red scruff and buried his face into its neck.

Clement sat upon their trunks like no man would shift him, smoking his pipe and taking his measure of the clipper's captain, supervising the loading into the hold. Beside him stood Sarah Proctor, wearing a new velvet dress but otherwise cautious of displaying her wealth, her belongings contained in a single leather bag. Joseph Borden's more substantial property was presently being loaded: tea-boxes and trunks filled with mining supplies for his Victorian expeditions. He and Sarah had struck up a friendship the night before, and it was clear when he looked at her the direction things were headed.

The wind off the bay was right for departure, and the rest of the clipper's crew returned in drunken groups of two or three from Sydney-town. Several of them purged their stomachs over the docks in preparation for a rough voyage. The clipper was bound for Hawaii and then New Zealand, and finally Melbourne-town, where Sam and Clement would disembark. It was a long journey but they were well provisioned. They wore their regular kits so as not to arouse suspicion, and had gone about their regular business these past weeks. Mannix was proving a predictably rough leader, and the men drawn to him would not be tempered or controlled.

Mayor Bannon and the newspapers railed at the outrage that saw Walker murdered and the city burned down, excepting the Australian quarter, but even Bannon quieted after a period, because it was clear that all the merchants were busy with the rebuilding of San Francisco that had begun almost immediately. The inland mills delivered timbers the very next day, and soon rough-hewn shacks and huts numbered among the earliest dwellings. The stone commissary on the town square that'd been plundered acted once again as the offices of government, and the three-storey frames on the land-blocks about the square were already well advanced. There was work enough for every hand in the rebuilding, and the ships from all over the world kept coming. New gold finds were reported daily but many stayed to work in the old trades. They were paid in gold dust and spent their wages in the grog and bawdy houses of Sydney-town and the favoured brothels of French-town, and the gambling saloons clustered round the plaza square. The Chinese quarter was near rebuilt, and it echoed with the sound of hammer and nail, and sawing and shouted commands as the longhaired Chinese labourers and tradesmen worked the timber into shape.

Sam clucked at the dog and it came to heel, followed him with nose down through the streets lined with sawdust and plaster and offcuts piled for the fire. Sam had visited Ai every day this past week, and she knew that he was leaving. They usually sat in the yard, their faces turned to the sunshine, although on one occasion Sam was allowed to chaperone her amid the Chinese quarter to a herbal doctor for Chen's medicine. Ai no longer disguised herself as a boy, and Sam took the opportunity to treat her to a cordial-flavoured soda-water in a nearby saloon. The two of them seated at a table attracted attention, and they didn't speak much; Ai so distracted by looking at the world outside the Chinese quarter, but when their eyes met, Sam liked what he saw.

Sam now entered the alley beside Chen's tailor shop and opened the gate and helloed to the piglets that ran around and sneezed and grunted. Their mother was looted in the riot, but the drunken Southlanders hadn't caught the piglets and they gathered around the dog that stared at Sam, who shook his head. The dog looked disappointed, but sat and waited.

The back door cracked open and Sam smiled and tilted his hat. Ai shyly repeated the gesture with an invisible hat and smiled and climbed down the steps. Sam felt sad at the thought of not seeing her again, but there was no way around it. He pressed a letter into her hand, addressed to the post office in Melbourne-town.

'One day soon they'll find gold in Australia, I'm sure of it. I'll look for you there. In the meantime, there's this.'

He took the bag of gold dust from his jacket, heavy in his hand. 'Hide this and call upon it when needed. It's for your family's debt.'

Ai looked at the bag and she smiled and her eyes softened and there were tears there, even if they didn't fall.

'That won't be necessary,' she said.

Sam didn't understand, and Ai put her arms around him in an embrace that just as soon was over. 'Your friend Mr Clement came here five nights ago. He told Mr Chen what Mr Borden had told him, about Victoria. Many from Chen's clan have now been told. Many have brothers or uncles from their clans already in Australia, and have sold everything to buy passage there. Mr Chen has sold this house too. He is tired and, I can tell, scared of this place. We are leaving on the same ship as you. Are you going to take my arm?'

Sam took Ai's arm. He didn't believe it until they left the alley and rounded into the street. There was Chen, supervising two men loading a cart with trunks and hessian-wrapped bolts of cloth, sheets of leather and barrels of brined beef, baskets of fruit and bags of ricc. Chen saw them but turned instead to the bullock-driver and nodded.

The clipper's brass bell rang through the port streets. The dog trotted beside them, down the hill toward the bay, its tail raised and its nose in the wind.

Author's note

Walking the downtown San Franciscan neighbourhood today bordered by Montgomery and Stockton streets at the base of Telegraph Hill, there's no trace of the area that was once known as Sydney Valley, or Sydney-town. Nor would you be able to tell that in 1852 it was estimated that one quarter of San Francisco's population was Australian. Some of these Australians were honest migrants attracted to the 1849 gold rush, but many of them were what the local media dubbed 'hard citizens', 'Sydney Coves' or the pejorative 'Sydney Ducks': a community of criminals that operated unchecked for many years and was blamed for burning San Francisco to the ground no less than five times between 1849 and 1855 (though Sydney-town itself was never burned). The reaction, when it came, was severe. 'Judge Lynch' was applied by vigilante groups and many Australians were hung, exiled, or fled back to Australia where a new gold rush was taking place. San Francisco got on with the job of becoming one of the world's great cities. While the reputation of the Australian criminals was such that any visible reference to Sydney-town's Australian roots has disappeared, the area's notoriety lives on in the storied reputation of the neighbourhood subsequently called The Barbary Coast, a nineteenth and twentieth century media catchword for licentiousness, depravity and criminality.

This novel is based on real events and historical figures. While I have used some real names and historical situations in the telling of this story, I have also changed dates and amalgamated characters for dramatic purposes and to better suit the truth of fiction.

Acknowledgements

I owe a deal of thanks to the helpful and knowledgeable librarians at the San Francisco Public Library's History Centre. To say that I was greeted with courtesy and enthusiasm is an understatement. Thanks also to gun crime writer Tom Pitts, who showed me the streets and dive bars of his city—it all filtered through. I'd also like to thank the staff at the City Lights Bookstore, located in once Sydney-town, for their advice and historical acumen. Thanks too to the staff at the Chinese Historical Society of America Museum.

I'd like to acknowledge the generosity of *The Coves*' first readers, who gave it the once over when it was a very rough draft—Brooke Davis, Sean Gorman, Deborah Robertson, Ian Reid and Paul Daley, along with my brother, sister and mother—Peter, Kerri and Rosemary. Thanks to historians Keir Reeves, Ben Mountford and Tim Causer for their advice and sharing. Thanks to Loretta Martella at Artsource for keeping my writing studio going—others might see a bare room but to me it's a sanctuary. A special thanks to the team at Fremantle Press, and especially my terrific publisher and editor, Georgia Richter, for her imagining what the early draft might become, and her patience and labour that brought it there.

Finally, thanks to my wife, Bella, for everything. If I'm remotely near the straight and narrow, it's because of you. This novel started when my eight-year-old son came to me and asked me to write a story about him. When I said that I couldn't do that, he countered slyly with 'Then can you write a book about a boy *like me*?' This book is that, Luka Fergus, and I hope I've done the precious subject justice.

AVAILABLE FROM FREMANTLEPRESS.COM.AU

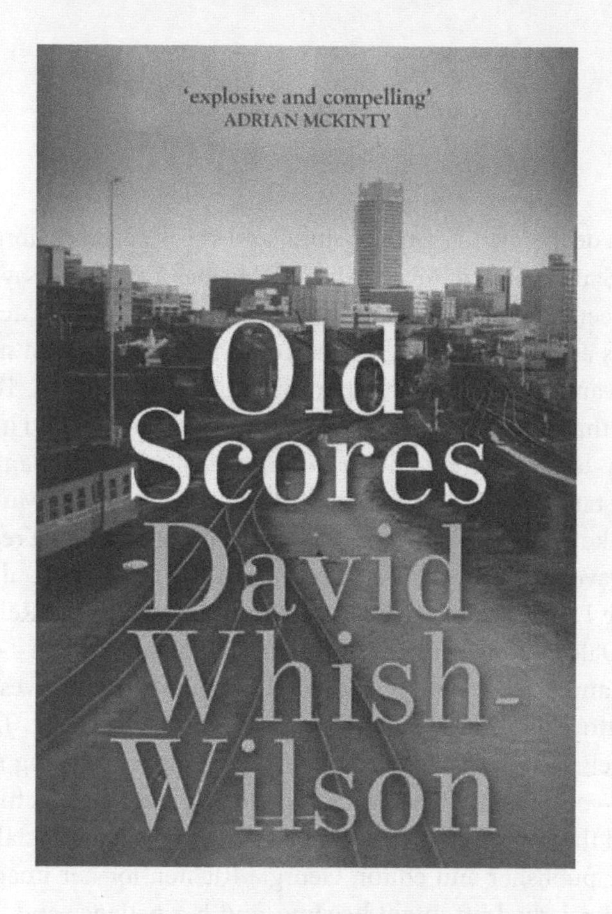

It's the early 1980s: the heady days of excess, dirty secrets and personal favours. Former detective Frank Swann is still in disgrace, working as a low-rent PI. But when he's offered a security job by the premier's fixer, it soon becomes clear that someone is bugging the premier's phone—and it may cost Swann more than his job to find out why.

'a remote wild-west mirage' *Australian Book Review*
'fast-paced and entertaining' *The Weekend Australian*

AND AT ALL GOOD BOOKSTORES

Wiremu Heke of Aramoana joins a sealing boat on a quest to avenge the destruction of his village. He finds himself a part of a violent and lawless world inhabited by men from many nations—men who plunder seal colonies and steal women and children from the indigenous communities living on the islands and shorelines of Australia's south.

'beautifully drawn' *Sydney Morning Herald*
'gripping and eye-opening' *NZ Listener*

First published 2018 by
FREMANTLE PRESS
25 Quarry Street, Fremantle WA 6160
(PO Box 158, North Fremantle WA 6159)
www.fremantlepress.com.au

Copyright © David Whish-Wilson, 2018

The moral rights of the author have been asserted.

This book is copyright. Apart from any fair dealing for the purpose of private study, research, criticism or review, as permitted under the Copyright Act, no part may be reproduced by any process without written permission. Enquiries should be made to the publisher.

Cover photograph Paris Pierce / Alamy Stock Photo
Printed by McPherson's Printing, Victoria, Australia

A catalogue record for this book is available from the National Library of Australia

The Coves
9781925591279 (paperback)

Department of
Local Government, Sport and Cultural Industries

Fremantle Press is supported by the State Government through the Department of Local Government, Sport and Cultural Industries.

Australia Council for the Arts

Publication of this title was assisted by the Commonwealth Government through the Australia Council, its arts funding and advisory body.